Pipetown Sandy

By JOHN PHILIP SOUSA

AUTHOR OF
"The Fifth String"

I0563592

ILLUSTRATED BY
CHARLES LOUIS HINTON

Fredonia Books
Amsterdam, The Netherlands

Pipetown Sandy

by
John Philip Sousa

ISBN: 1-58963-305-9

Reprinted from the 1905 edition

Fredonia Books
Amsterdam, the Netherlands
http://www.fredoniabooks.com

In order to make original editions of historical works available to scholars at an economical price, this facsimile of the original edition of 1905 is reproduced from the best available copy and has been digitally enhanced to improve legibility, but the text remains unaltered to retain historical authenticity.

CONTENTS

PIPETOWN SANDY

PIPETOWN SANDY

CHAPTER I

IT'S ALL IN THE FINGERS

Miss Latham rapped sharply with her ruler.

"Class in arithmetic, attention, please!"

The boys recovered from their lounging positions and sat upright, awaiting further instructions from the speaker.

"Sponge your slates and sharpen your pencils."

The class at once became surprisingly active. The buzzing sound of the children's whisperings and the clatter of slates and pencils grew louder and louder.

"Less noise, please," the teacher admonished.

After quiet had been somewhat restored, Miss Latham cast her eyes carefully over the class. All the pupils, save one, were ready for the lesson. This delinquent sat with a hang-dog expression on his face and a snake-like gleam in his eyes. The sneer on his lips and his air of indifference were very annoying to the school-mistress.

"Thomas, we are waiting!"

"I don't want to do no sums," was the reply.

"Where is your slate, Thomas?"

"In my desk," growled the boy.

"Get it immediately, and prepare to take down the figures I call off."

Shuffling his feet and moving about sullenly, the boy took his slate from the desk and let it fall with a crash.

"Thomas, how many times must I tell you not to bang your slate?"

"I didn't bang it; it banged itself!" he snapped back.

"Quiet, I say; do not talk so loudly!"

"I ain't talkin' loudly. If yer think it's loudly yer 'd better stick a bale er cotton in yer ears," —and Thomas looked around for some sign of approval.

"You must behave yourself and not be impertinent," insisted the teacher, with an effort to be patient.

" 'Tain't impertinent. I don't want to do no sums, an' what's more, I ain't goin' to do no sums!"—and he buried himself in his seat, with legs extended under the desk and hands thrust into his trousers pockets.

"Come here," called Miss Latham, in a manner more severe than is generally accredited to a pretty young woman of twenty-four, with a melodic voice and a sympathetic heart.

"I'll see yer scorchin' in the fi'ry furnace fust," cried the boy.

"Thomas Foley, do you hear? Obey at once!"

"I'll swing afore I do," came the swift retort.

"Then you must remain after school every day for a week, and I shall see that you do not sneak away as you did last Monday. Your mother thought you were here, when you were on the river skating. You shall not deceive her again, if I can help it. Bring me your skates, and I will keep them until you promise better behavior."

"If yer wants 'em, come an' git 'em,"—and squarely, he placed his elbows on the desk, as if to protect the skates within.

Miss Latham quietly walked toward the refractory pupil, then firmly removing his arms from the desk, raised the lid and took out the skates. The boy made a grab for them, and in the scuffle struck her a stinging blow in the face with his open hand. Grasping his coat collar, the teacher shoved him back into the seat.

"You're a mean, contemptible coward; take your books, you are dismissed!"

She returned to her desk, where she nervously wrote a note and sealed it. "Give that to your mother; it will explain why you have been sent home."

"Who cares?" he said, as he came forward to take the note, and then shambled toward the door.

With this incidental excitement over, the class once more settled to work, and slates and pencils were brought into requisition. Miss Latham rapped for attention.

"Write on your slates, for addition, the following: 4-3-6-11-8-13-9,"—and the musical voice of the pretty teacher intoned the figures clearly and roundly.

"As soon as any one sums them, let me know."

She had scarcely completed the sentence when a little hand, thin and almost transparent, was raised.

"Please, Miss Maisie!"

"What is it, Gilbert?" asked the schoolmistress.

"I have the answer." The boy was very pale,

frail and slender, with lustrous black hair and brown eyes, and apparently not over twelve in years.

"Bring your slate here, Gilbert, and let me see it." The lad walked quickly to the desk and handed it to her.

"Correct, and very neatly written," — and Miss Latham patted the little fellow's head approvingly.

Within a few minutes all the boys but one had mastered the example. He sat with his head resting on his left hand, his tongue projecting from the corner of his mouth, the perspiration dotting his forehead in great beads, and his eyes glued on the problem before him. His lips moved as he wrote, and figure after figure appeared on his slate only to be rubbed out. Long-drawn sighs were heard at intervals, and despair seemed pictured on his face.

"Sandy, we are waiting; all the pupils have the answer but you."

Sandy looked up with an apologetic air, and drawled: "It's mighty tough on ev'rybody havin' ter wait on me, Miss Maisie, but I ain't quite got the hang of it yet,"—slowly shaking his head and heaving another hopeless sigh.

Gilbert looked across the aisle and observed the other boy. It was Gilbert's first day at school, and he had been so engrossed with his studies and the exciting incident of the day, that he had paid little attention to his companions, save in the most desultory way. Sandy, the boy who was struggling with the problem, was fairly tall, raw-boned, much freckled, with a little stubby nose, and hair that was very red.

"Homely as a hedge fence," was the general description of him, but with all his plainness there was a look of sincerity in his face, and through the merry twinkle of the bluest of blue eyes shone a soul fearless and brave. Gilbert was attracted to him immediately.

Sandy, still intent on his task, sighed again, then raised his hand slowly, and said: "Mebbe I've got the right answer, Miss Maisie." He arose, half reluctantly, and tiptoed toward the teacher.

Miss Latham glanced at the slate, and, with a slight touch of asperity, said: "Sandy! Sandy! will you ever learn? Your answer is all wrong." Her foot tapped impatiently on the floor, and then looking in the direction of Gilbert, she said: "Take your slate and sit down by the little fellow.

Perhaps Gilbert can explain to you how easy this sum in addition really is."

Sandy slowly retraced his steps down the aisle, and, crossing over, sat down by the side of Gilbert, who took the older boy's slate to see how the example was written out.

With a good-humored smile at the odd twisting of the figures, Gilbert turned, and, placing his hand on the other's arm, with assurance and sympathy, began:

"My father says there have been some awfully smart people high up in the world, who were not worth shucks in doing sums in arithmetic."

"When did yer father say that?" doubtingly asked Sandy.

"Oh, lots of times. He says one of the great Roman generals had to have some one around to count up for him, and you know great Roman generals were away up, and no mistake," said little Gilbert impressively.

"Yes, I seen one in the theater onct, actin', but he didn't git 'way up, 'cause he couldn't do no sums,"—and the older boy dubiously shook his head.

Without apparent notice of the interruption, Gilbert continued with a mighty, philosophic air:

"The Roman general wasn't half so much interested in sums as he was in war; if he had been, he would have learned them all right!"

"I ain't a-sayin' nuthin' 'bout what a Roman gen'ral would or wouldn't 'a' done, but I know my pore old mother would be mighty glad if somebody squirted some book-l'arnin' into my noddle. Folks all tells her I won't never amount to nuthin' in school, an' I'm beginnin' to believe it myself, fer I'm fifteen years old."

Gilbert, looking at the dejected boy, carefully sponged out Sandy's incorrect work and put the figures of his example across the top of the slate —4-3-6-11-8-13-9.

"Now, let's take the figure 4 for a starter, and then add 3. We do that by taking three of your fingers and adding them to the four; four, five, six, seven," counting on Sandy's upraised and outstretched hand, and turning down each finger until seven was reached.

"That's right," said Sandy. "Lemme try it alone." Slowly he told off three of his fingers. "Yes, that comes out two times runnin', an' I see jest how it's done."

The boy's face seemed illumined by a new light.

"We take the next figure, 6," said Gilbert, his manner a laborious copy of his teacher's. "We already have seven, and now we add the six, by counting all the fingers on one hand, and one on the other; thus—seven, eight, nine, ten, eleven, twelve, thirteen. Now you try it." After some hesitation on Sandy's part he succeeded in the addition.

"Then we will add the next, eleven."

"'Leven's a whopper!" exclaimed the older boy.

"Hold up both hands," said Gilbert. "Eleven uses up all your fingers and thumbs, and one of mine. That makes thirteen, fourteen, fifteen, sixteen, seventeen, eighteen, nineteen, twenty, twenty-one, twenty-two, twenty-three, and my finger, twenty-four. Take eight more fingers," counting them off, "that makes thirty-two; the thirteen, all yours and three of mine, summing up forty-five, to which we add nine fingers, making a total of fifty-four, which is the answer. Now, you try it from the beginning; you can do it all right," said the smaller boy, carefully concealing his pride in his superior knowledge.

Slowly, but with confidence, and occasionally prompted by his little preceptor, Sandy successfully and triumphantly did the example. A great happiness crept into his heart, as, for the first time in his life, he added figures with certainty. He gazed on Gilbert with unmistakable admiration.

The little fellow had led him out of the maze of puzzling addition. At last he knew why 11 and 4 were 15, and not 51, when placed underneath each other. He laid his hand lightly on the shoulder of his new-found friend and said:

"Hope-I-may-die, but ye're the cutiest little codger I ever seen."

He held up his left hand and slowly counted. "Yes, he's right; it's all in the fingers. An' to think I never had 'nough gumption to see it afore this little codger showed me." Then he took the slate to Miss Latham, who praised him for accomplishing the task.

"It's dead easy; I never knowed afore, 'cause yer never told me nuthin' 'bout fingers; 'deed yer didn't, Miss Maisie. Yer said a lot 'bout numerals, an' sich like, but nuthin' 'bout fingers."

"It's all in the fingers," soliloquized Sandy, as he returned to his seat. "It's all in the fingers, an' I never knowed it afore."

The recess bell rang and the boys filed out. No

sooner had Sandy passed through the door than a complete metamorphosis took place. With a long-drawn Indian war-whoop, ending in a "dare yer to foller," he executed a series of cartwheels and handsprings, winding up by standing on his head, and then turning a number of somersaults.

It was a transformation indeed, from the slow-going pupil of the school-room to the quick active boy outside, all life and spirits. In truth, there was no one in Pipetown to approach Sandy as an all-around athlete.

Gilbert had spent much of his life in the sick-room, and like most frail boys had always been fascinated with sports that demand skill and muscle. In Sandy he saw the embodiment of the youthful hero. Sandy was coming on with a hop-skip-and-jump, and, turning at least ten successive handsprings around his new-found admirer, he said:

"Say, little feller, don't yer know how to do these 'ere things?" and he turned another hand-spring.

"I never was allowed to try," said Gilbert, and then, apologetically: "You see, I have been sick nearly all the time since I was five."

"Gosh, that's tough!" said the older gravely.

"But if yer wants to try one, I'll show yer the hang of it. They're as easy as dirt when yer git useter 'em,"—and by way of illustration he executed a dozen backward and forward.

"Golly, that's great!" gasped the little fellow.

"Jest try it onct, I won't let yer hurt yerself."

"I'll try it, but I'm sure I can't do it," said the younger boy, although anxious to follow Sandy's instructions.

"Git down on all fours; now put yer hands flat on the ground like a monkey. Give me yer feet; that's all right; I'll hold yer up by the legs an' rock yer, while yer git useter the rush o' blood in yer noddle."

After Sandy had swayed Gilbert for a minute, he exclaimed, "How's that?"

"All right, I guess," pantingly replied the little one, the exertion proving almost too much for him. Sandy, realizing this, helped him to his feet.

"That's bully good. Yer've got sand in yer craw, an' as soon as yer gits a little muscle, yer'll do 'em as slick as yer please."

Before the recess was over, Gilbert had almost succeeded in accomplishing a handspring, with but slight assistance from his athletic companion.

Then, as Sandy and he walked into the school-room together, the older boy patted him on the back and remarked: "Yer've got lots 'er sand and ye're all right."

"Do you think you can teach me?" queried the younger.

" 'Tain't no teachin' in it 't all, it's jest sand an' gittin' the hang of it, that's all. Why, if I don't have yer doin' cartwheels in a week, yer can call me a liar, an' my name ain't Sandy Coggles."

The little fellow's eyes sparkled with a sudden joy. Was it a dream, he thought, or would he really do a cartwheel in a week?

"O Sandy, you don't mean it!" he exclaimed.

"In course I do," said Sandy with absolute assurance. "Yer see, everythin' is everythin' in this 'ere world. If yer ain't got it yer might as well cave in. In handsprings an' sich, sand is everythin'. In 'rithmetic an' numerals, it's fingers. All yer have to have, is to have it, an' there ye are! Yer'll be doin' cartwheels in a week, hope-I-may-die if yer don't."

The boys went back into the school-room and resumed their seats.

The class in geography was called, and the members stood in the aisles next to the wall. The first boy was about to name the states forming the northern part of the Union, when a sharp knock was heard at the door, and almost immediately Tom Foley's mother rushed in, holding her unruly son by the collar, and literally dragging him after her. The woman was so angry that she did not notice how at every stride she ran the boy against some obstruction. First it was the door, then the hat-rack, and finally the chairs loosely placed about the teacher's platform. Each separate bump brought a cry from the boy, but the excited woman grasped his collar more tightly, and shouted: "I'll teach you to bring disgrace on your hard-working mother!"

"I ain't doin' nuthin'," came with the yells from her son.

"Please do contain yourself, Mrs. Foley," implored the teacher.

The irate woman, in appearance almost too young to have a son of fourteen, her handsome face flushed with excitement, her eyes flashing with anger, brought up suddenly in front of the desk. Plumping the terrified boy firmly on his feet, with her hand still on his collar, she addressed the schoolmistress.

"Maisie Latham, this is the third time this

brat has been sent home this month. Do I pay
you to suspend him, or to eddicate him? Answer
me that! You get fifty cents a month in advance
for teachin' him, and I'm not a-payin' for nothin'.
I've brought that paper-backed book you sent me
before this boy came to your school, to remind
you what I'm payin' for."

She took from her pocket a small pamphlet,
and read slowly and emphatically: " 'The object
of Miss Maisie Latham's school for boys, is:
First: To arouse the mentality of the pupil and to
awaken his power to think. Second: To foster
a sturdy moral nature and develop the scholar's
individuality. Third: To perfect the student in
those general studies that lead to a preparatory
course.'

"Now, that's the object of your school, as you
say right here in black and white. 'Tain't nothin'
'bout suspensions, and bein' incorrigible, as I can
decipher,"—and triumphantly she closed the book
and waited for the teacher's reply.

"Mrs. Foley," said the young schoolmistress,
"I feel that your anger is justified. My own patience with Thomas is exhausted, for I have tried
over and over to make him see the error of his
ways."

"See the error of his ways!" said the mother, accentuating her words by shaking the boy. "See the error of his ways!" she shouted still louder; "'tain't no good tryin' to make him see the error of his ways; make him feel 'em. Ouch!" she cried, as the boy suddenly grasped her arm and bit until the blood came.

"You imp of darkness, I'll whip you within an inch of your life for that." In an instant she had seated herself in a chair, and, pulling him over her lap, she gave him a thrashing that remained in the memory of every boy present as the most thorough dressing-down he had ever beheld.

When Mrs. Foley, breathing heavily, had finished punishing her son, she stood him on his feet until his lamentations changed from ear-piercing shrieks to subdued sniffling. Then she said, almost coaxingly:

"Now, Maisie, take him back, if it's only to keep him out of the street. He won't do a blessed stroke of work about the house, and if he don't go to school, he'll go to the dogs sooner than he would anyway."

"All right, Mrs. Foley," said the teacher, "I'll take Thomas back, and I trust he will be a good boy in the future, and give us no further trouble."

"Thank you, Maisie, I do hope you'll excuse me. That boy cuts me up so I lose myself, and jest bile over." Turning to her son: "Go back to your seat and behave yourself. If you're sent home again, I'll skin you alive. Your daddy was a loafer, and I'll kill you afore I'll let you foller in his steps."

She shook hands cordially with Miss Latham, and walked toward the door with the parting shot: "If you're sent home again, I'll bury you so deep the Lord won't find you!" And she was gone.

Tom walked sullenly to his seat, ever and anon rubbing his nose with his sleeve. Dink Dabney, who was next to Curley Harris, whispered:

"If I knows what I'm talkin' about, I spec' Tom would be powerful more comf'table if he wuz standin'." Whereat Curley laughed, and the teacher rapped to start anew the interrupted lesson.

Gilbert, being the newest scholar, was placed at the foot of the class. The system permitting the pupil correctly answering a missed question to "move up one," or two or more, according to the number of failures, was in vogue at Miss Latham's school.

Before the lesson was over, Gilbert, by leaps of fives, and tens, and twelves, was at the head of the class. Sandy, who had been solidly intrenched at the foot since the opening day of school, became once more a fixture there.

"Sandy, name one of the Northern States," said Miss Latham.

"Did yer say one of the Northern States, Miss Maisie?" echoed Sandy, sparring for time, and scratching his head.

"Yes, that is my question."

"Lemme see,"—drawling this slowly, stroking his forehead, and looking perplexed.

"Hurry, Sandy, we can not wait all day," said the teacher a little impatiently.

"I'm awful sorry, Miss Maisie," replied Sandy, "but jest now I disremember whether Lou'siana will do fer an answer; but if it don't how would Georgy fit?"

"Sandy, Sandy, will you ever comprehend? When the class go to their seats, you sit down by Gilbert Franklin and let him teach you the names of the Northern States. He might be able to get them through your head; I despair of doing so."

"Yes, I'll go right off," responded Sandy, delighted, while the little fellow was overjoyed at the prospective pleasure of having Sandy next to him.

The older boy came, and opening his geography at the page containing a map of the Northern States, he whispered: "There they are, all bunched together, an' they look harder'n a puzzle."

Smilingly Gilbert commenced. "My father says absent-minded people forget things, because they do not consider them of sufficient importance. Perhaps that's what you think about the Northern States?"

"No, I ain't absent-minded," said Sandy slowly. "We had a man down our way, whose folks called him absent-minded. But one day, when the snow wuz a foot thick, he came out in the street with no more shoes on than a crow, an' the bug-doctor grabbed him an' clapped him into the 'sylum. The bug-doctor said he wuz luny. That ain't my trouble. I've got all my buttons. I simply ain't got no noddle fer l'arnin'."

From the moment these two boys had come together, until the last one of their school-days, Gilbert impressed upon Sandy that he was not the only one deficient in the things he was trying to learn. Then, too, he saw, even though vaguely, with a child's imperfect comprehension, that Sandy's chief need was a stimulus to his interest. We have already noticed in the simple addition, how the mist was swept from Sandy's brain by using the fingers for counting, and, as the studies progressed, Gilbert, with true pedagogic instinct, employed the game of base-ball, the names of streets, the number of houses in a block, the different species of birds, and almost any concrete thing for purposes of intellectual aid. Before the school was dismissed on this first day of their meeting, Sandy had learned to name every Northern State, from Maine to Delaware.

As the two boys filed out after the second session, they walked slowly down the street, and at a little store on the corner a block from the school, Sandy stopped and said:

"Jest wait a minit, Gil, while I go into Jebb's. I've got ter git some darnin' yarn fer mother, an' I'll be out in a jiffy."

While Sandy went inside, Gilbert stood on the corner swinging his books, and feeling very, very happy. The distinguished consideration on the part of the boy who was teaching him to do handsprings, and now asked him to wait, was most gratifying.

Tom Foley and Dink Dabney, about a hundred yards off, were coming toward him, and by their gestures it was clear that Gilbert was the subject of their conversation.

"I'll allow he knows his lessons better'n the rest of the gang, but I'd rather never know nuthin' than be a mama's-boy," said Tom.

"He don't look like no mama's-boy. In course, he ain't strong and healthy like us, but he don't look like no mama's-boy," ventured Dink.

"I betcher he is, an' what's more, I'd betcher ten potterskills, if I had 'em, I'd scare him outer a year's growth by jest sayin' Boo!"

"Well, I ain't got no ten potterskills to betcher, but if I had, I'd betcher he ain't no mama's-boy, an' he won't scare worth a cent," retorted Dink warmly.

"Watch me," said young Foley. By this time they were within a few yards of Gilbert, who was gazing through the window into the store. As the boys came nearer he turned, and, with that smile which one boy always gives another when he wishes to get on particularly friendly terms, he looked inquiringly at Dink and Tom.

"Eh, mama's-boy, I wants to talk to yer," sneeringly called the latter.

Gilbert drew himself up quickly, and a slight flush suffused his face.

Foley came closer, leaned forward with half-clenched fists, and snarled: "I hears yer laughed when my old she-cat mother wore herself out whackin' me to-day."

Gilbert looked the other boy squarely in the face, and answered: "Well, you didn't hear right; I was sorry for you."

"I don't want none of yer sorrer!" hissed the other. "D'yer hear me? I don't want none of yer sorrer, an' I gives yer to understand, she didn't hurt me, nuther."

"I thought she did," said Gilbert, looking into the sneaking eyes of the bully. "She must have, for you cried like a yellow dog."

"What d'yer mean by callin' me a yaller dog?" shouted Foley, drawing back his left as if to strike.

Gilbert surveyed the larger boy from head to foot with a look of smiling curiosity, and said gravely, "I did not say you were a yellow dog; I said you cried like a yellow dog."

"Well, it's mighty lucky fer yer that yer took'd it back, fer if yer hadn't, I'd a-punched yer head in a minit."

Sandy came out of the store at this moment, and in three strides was between the boys. He looked at Tom and said:

"Punch nuthin'! Why, Snarley Foley, yer wouldn't punch a cabbage-head, 'less it wuzn't lookin'. What yer pickin' on the little feller fer?"

"He said I hollered like a yaller dog when the old woman whacked me, an' I'm going to take it out er his hide, see if I don't." But he made no effort to carry his threat into execution.

"You won't take nuthin' out er nobody's hide. Put that in yer pipe an' smoke it."

Sandy turned, and, looking at Gilbert as if he were mentally weighing the outcome between the two boys if they should clash, he said: "If I sez the word, the little feller 'ud fight yer at the drop of er hat, but I ain't goin' to let him sile his hands on yer; leastwise, not jest yet,"—and he gently backed the smaller boy away. Young Foley made a step toward Gilbert.

"Oh, I see," said Sandy, "yer sp'ilin' for a scrap. Well, if yer wants to fight, here's Dink; he's yer size, an' what I say, Dink'll say, won't yer, Dink?"

"In course I will," said Dink, proud of the mighty Sandy's patronage.

Sandy, pointing the forefinger of his left hand at Tom, spoke slowly:

"I sez, Snarley Foley, that yer hollered like a yaller dog when yer mother whacked yer."

"An' I repeats it," said Dink in a louder tone. "Yer hollered like a yaller dog, so yer did."

"An' I sez, furthermore," continued Sandy contemptuously, "yer squealed like a stuck pig."

"An' squealed like a stuck pig," repeated the imitative Dink, getting closer to the scared bully, who now began to back away.

"An'," added Sandy, doubly pleased with the addition of this invective, "yer bellered like a sick calf."

Dink, with his fists doubled, eyes glistening, and a look that boded no good for the frightened coward, fairly howled at Tom, "An' yer bellered like a sick calf."

With a look of fear, Snarley turned tail, and ran as fast as his legs could carry him.

The three boys laughed loudly and derisively at the fleeing figure, and shouted after him in unison: "Go bag your head; boo-oo-oo! boo-oo-oo!"

Then they picked up their school books, and at the next corner, where Dink parted from Sandy and Gilbert, he confided to them that "If Snarley

Foley had er sed beans, I'd banged him anyway."

Dink assured Gilbert, with many protestations of eternal friendship: "If that Snarley Foley ever interferes with yer, jest tell him to call on me, an' I'll polish him off."

"I knowed he'd run like a scared dog when I sick'd Dink on him," said Sandy, and he and Gilbert disappeared down the street.

CHAPTER II

Had it not been for the family physician's mandate that Gilbert should be allowed to go out and mix with the other children of his age, and not be for ever confined within the four walls of his home, the boy probably would never have been enrolled as a scholar in Miss Latham's school. In all likelihood, by another year he would have been goose-greased, mutton-tallowed, red-flanneled, and quinined into an untimely grave.

Luckily for the happiness of Gilbert's family, the old physician's patience at last became exhausted. One night, on being sent for because the little fellow was "wheezy," he said sternly: "If you want to raise that boy you had better let him out to get all the fresh air of heaven he can in his lungs."

"But, Doctor!" exclaimed the grandmother apprehensively, "suppose he gets into a draught?"

"Or if his feet get wet?" added the mother nervously.

"And diphtheria is so prevalent," protested his sister Edith alarmingly.

"Or," lisped little six-year-old Lillian in a croaking voice, "wake up with a croup, like me."

And the four alarmists appealed to the doctor not to bring such dire calamities upon Gilbert.

"Do not let us borrow trouble," protested the old practitioner wearily. "Let us hope, rather, that the boy's mind will have a rest from incessant study, and that his nervous condition will disappear when he is playing outside. Should his feet get wet and cold, he will run about until they are dry and warm again, and the change from the over-heated temperature of this house to the life-giving air that blows without, no doubt will discourage all sorts of disease germs. I tell you now, I will not be responsible for consequences, if you fail to follow my advice." He arose, and drew on his driving-gloves and departed.

There is no edict so imperious, so inimical to further opposition or argument, so all-compelling in its scope as the family doctor's "I will not be responsible for the consequences."

From Grandmother Franklin down to little Lillian, the decree was accepted, and Gilbert was spending his first day at school.

The family expected him home at a few minutes after three. It was now nearly four. No watchers for the return of a loved one from afar, after years of absence, could have shown more restlessness than did the Franklin family when the hour at which they had looked for the boy had passed and he had not yet appeared.

"I wonder what keeps him," nervously asked the grandmother, going to the front porch and with shaded eyes looking up the street in the direction of the school. Returning to her chair in the parlor beside the window, she watched intently for his coming, ever and anon repeating her quest and her question.

"I hope and pray no accident has happened to him," said the mother, showing grave concern.

"Sho', Mis' Nanny," broke in the colored cook, Delia, addressing Mrs. Franklin; "nuthin' ain't goin' ter happen ter ma little honey boy. It's only fo'h by the kitchen clock, an' mebbe he's a-restin' of hisself afore comin' home. I spec's yo'll be seein' him mos' enny minit."

"I think I had better go and find him. I'll never forgive myself if anything has happened to him. One of us should have remained with him on this, his first day at school, and the only time he has

ever been away from us. I'm going to find him,"
—and the foolish parent, nervous and worried,
went to her room for her bonnet and shawl.

This useless anxiety on the part of the women
of the Franklin household had pursued Gilbert
since he was a mere child, their attitude at all
times being one of fear that something dreadful
was about to happen, and that, if it did not, the
escape was providential.

Once more the grandmother jumped up, laid
her knitting down, and with an expression of relief and happiness walked to the front door. Gilbert was in sight a block away, and was just bid-
ding good-by to a taller boy, who turned down a
side street.

Calling to the mother, the old lady shouted:
"Nanny, Nanny, hurry down! Here he comes,
and I do declare, he is a hop-skip-and-a-jumping
as if he had never been sick in his life." The
mother came quickly, and went out on the porch
with the older one to greet the little fellow as he
bounded up the steps.

Gilbert was almost breathless, his cheeks were
flushed and his eyes sparkled with excitement.
He kissed them both lovingly, and taking each by
the hand, exclaimed:

"Oh, grandma, mama! you should see me do a handspring! Oh, it's great! Sandy says I've got the sand, and you can always do handsprings if you've got the sand and get the hang of them. Come on, let's go in, and I'll show you how I do them."

"Handsprings!" exclaimed the puzzled but happy mother, and the three generations, hand in hand, marched proudly into the house.

"Now, watch me!" said Gilbert; "you see they are done this way. I get down on all fours and spread out my hands just like a monkey. Now, grandma, you take hold of my right foot,"—and he raised that particular pedal extremity, while she obediently followed his instructions. "Now, ma, you take hold of the other foot; there, that's right. Hold me up straight, and you'll see I am standing on my hands."

"But, Lord alive, child, you'll have a rush of blood to the head!" The two ladies showed alarm.

"That's nothing!" said Gilbert with absolute nonchalance. "Sandy says that's nothing; all you have to do is to rock the body to and fro, and get used to it. I am already used to it. Just try me." And together they swayed the little fellow.

"Now, let go," he quickly called. Then he balanced himself on his hands for a moment, and scrambled to his feet all breathless, but proud of his achievement.

"Of course, I can't do them well, but if you want to see how beautiful handsprings really are, you should see Sandy do them." Then, with a sudden burst of enthusiasm: "Sandy says he will have me doing cartwheels in a week. Won't that be great?"

Mother and grandmother in turn pressed the little fellow to their hearts and kissed him tenderly. The older lady led him over to her chair, and putting her arms around him, asked:

"Who is this Sandy you are telling us of? I hope he is a good boy."

"Sandy is wonderful, grandma, though he says himself he never had any opportunities. Up to this year, he has had to do chores and be generally handy, just to keep the pot boiling, but now he is going to school regularly. He told me all about his family when we were coming home from school this afternoon."

"Who is his father?" asked the grandmother.

"His father was Mr. Dan Coggles, Private Dan Coggles. He was a soldier and went to the war. Abe Lincoln called for volunteers, and Sandy's father went right up and said he'd go. Sandy's mother didn't want him to, but as he had promised, she said it would not be right for him to back out. So he went, and she took in plain sewing. Sandy said his father wasn't afraid of anybody that toted, I mean carried, a gun, and they marched off with the bands playing, and Sandy's mother crying as if her heart would break.

"The regiment hung around here and there, skirmishing and scouting, and getting used to being shot at, besides, and doing all sorts of desperate things for the honor of the flag. After a while they got right on the battle-field before they knew it, and the firing began, bang-bang! ping-ping! The regiment was facing grape and canister and chain shot, and Heaven only knows what else, and besides were outnumbered ten to one. And lo, and behold!"—continued the little fellow, his eyes blazing as he strode up and down excitedly,—"everybody was shot down and cut to pieces, except Sandy's father and the general. The general rode down the line, waving his sword and shouting, 'Mr. Coggles, all is lost; if you want to get out alive, you'd better run like hell.' "

"What!" exclaimed his grandmother, aghast.

"That's what the general said," insisted Gilbert with an air of conviction; "I'm sure of it, for Sandy said so, and Sandy wouldn't tell a lie—I mean a falsehood—for anything. Sandy's father yelled to the general, 'The Coggleses never run,' and he started toward the enemy. The entire enemy shot at him, all at once, and off went his leg,"—and here Gilbert struck an attitude. "Of course, the enemy saw that it was not fair to shoot at a man with one leg, so they requested him to surrender. He wouldn't have done it, but he had run out of ammunition, and, besides, he hadn't got used to hopping around on one foot; so he gave up, came home, and received eight dollars a month pension, besides a cork leg every two years, 'which was mighty little,' says Sandy, 'when everything was so high.' "

The little fellow mentally reviewed his recital of Sandy's story, to note if he had forgotten anything of importance. Putting his arms about his grandmother's neck, and stroking her silvery hair, he continued confidently, "I'm sure you'll think Sandy splendid, when you meet him."

"I earnestly trust all of us will find Sandy as splendid as you do,"—and the grandmother went

out to greet Gilbert's father, who was just returning from his office.

After supper the little fellow gave an exhibition of his newly-acquired accomplishments in
athletics for every member of the household in
turn and then, tired and sleepy, he went to bed.

His grandmother came, snugly tucked the cov-
erlets about the tired boy, and bent over to kiss
him a fond good night. He closed his eyes, and
drowsily murmured: "Grandma, don't you wish
you could do handsprings? If you want to
learn, I'll have Sandy come—I'll have Sandy—
Sandy—" and he was fast asleep.

At the home of Mrs. Coggles there was much
surprise and delight, when the supper things were
cleared away, to see Sandy take out his arithmetic
and geography, and sit down to study. It was
the first time he had been known to apply himself to his books, or even to bring them home.
When his mother would ask where they were, his
usual answer was: "I kind er disremember jest
this minit where I left 'em. I wuz a-playin' ball,
an' Dink Dabney, or Curley Harris, or mebbe
somebody else, is lookin' out for 'em. They'll
turn up all hunkey to-morrer."

"MUM, WE'VE GOT THE CUTEST LITTLE CODGER A-COMIN' TO
MISS MAISIE'S YER EVER DID SEE"   Page 35

It is not difficult to imagine the joy of Mrs. Coggles when she actually saw her son prepare for study.

Five minutes passed in absolute silence. The mother arose, went to the stove, raked the ashes from underneath the grate, returned, and sat down to her sewing. Another five minutes, and the only sound was the ticking of the mantel-clock. Sandy looked up and said: "Mum, we've got the cutiest little codger a-comin' to Miss Maisie's yer ever did see."

"Law sakes, Sandy, what makes yer think so?" asked the mother with genuine interest, for he was a most reticent boy, and it was "like pullin' teeth," she had often remarked, "to git anythin' out er him 'bout anybody or anythin'."

"'Cause I know," replied Sandy, in a voice that carried absolute conviction.

"Who does he belong to?" said Mrs. Coggles.

"He's Mr. Franklin's boy, as lives up on G Street, in that 'ere three-story house with the bay-winders an' the big front yard, all filled with trees," answered the son.

"I knows the place well," nodded Mrs. Coggles, "it's where Sukey Bell used to cook an' do general housework an' washin'. Sukey says they're orful nice folks, got lots of money, an' ain't stuck up a bit about it. Sukey says, too, that they has double parlors on each side of the hall, with communicatin' doors that jest open an' shet like an accordeon. Sukey onct told me, in her opinion, it was the mos' scrumptious house in Pipetown, an' she orter know, for sence she's been out in service, which is nigh on to ten years, she's worked for every family about here. What wuz yer goin' to tell me about their little boy?"

"Well, the little codger come to school to-day for the fust time in his life, an' he beats anything holler I ever seen. Why, he's a walkin' diction- ary," said Sandy with enthusiasm, bringing his hand down on the open book before him.

"Do tell—a walkin' dictionary!" and the mother put special accent on "walking."

"That's what I sez—a regular walkin' diction- ary. Now, I'll jest show yer. Ask me how much six, seven, an' eight is. Go ahead quick; jest ask me,"—and Sandy leaned forward, expectant of the question.

The old lady, not knowing just what a walk- ing dictionary had to do with the question, said, almost mechanically: "How much is six, seven an' eight, Sandy?"

"Now, watch me," said the boy. "We start with six, then we add seven, that's all the fingers on one hand an' two on this 'ere one. That makes six, seven, eight, nine, ten, eleven, twelve, thirteen; now we add eight; that's five fingers on one hand an' three on t'other. That makes thirteen, fourteen, fifteen, sixteen, seventeen, eighteen, nineteen, twenty, twenty-one, an' that's correct, an' yer can't fool me. Yer kin count thousands an' thousands without ever gittin' left; all yer got to have is fingers enough."

"Oh, Sandy, how did yer learn it? It's the fust time I ever know'd yer to sum up,"—and proudly the woman walked over to her son and kissed him.

"It's all in the fingers, mum; the little codger show'd me, an' I never know'd it afore."

"Now, take g'ography," continued Sandy, warming up. "It's jest the same 'cept g'ography is base-ball, an' 'rithmetic is fingers. Fer ninstence, take the Northern States; Maine is right field, New Hampshire is center field, Vermont is left field, New York is third base, Connecticut is short-stop, Massachusetts is second base, Rhode Island is fust base, New Jersey is pitcher, Delaware is ketcher, an' Pennsylvania is at the bat. Now ask me what third base is; New York, in course. Yer can't fool me, an' I never know'd it till the little feller told me."

The interested boy took a piece of paper, and drawing the plan of a base-ball field, wrote the names of the states in the positions with which Gilbert had associated them, then handed it to his mother and said, "I dare yer to try to fool me."

To all her questions, his answers were invariably correct, and mother and son were proud and happy. It was getting late, and Sandy put out the milk-can, closed the shutters, locked the door, and waited for his mother to retire. After she had gone he blew out the light, and softly mounted the steps leading to his little garret room. As he crept under the patchwork quilt on his bed, he softly soliloquized, "He's the cutiest little codger I ever seen, an' he ain't brash 'bout it. nuther."

CHAPTER III

ZORAH DABNEY

Early on the next morning unusual noises reverberated throughout the Franklin residence. It was evident that something of an athletic character was going on in Gilbert's room. At seven the little fellow appeared at breakfast, with glowing color in his face and appetite keen and hearty.

"I have been trying handsprings for more than an hour," he exclaimed, proudly exhibiting a variety of bumps and bruises as mute witnesses of his efforts.

"Get the arnica, Delia," called the grandmother apprehensively.

"Please, grandma, don't treat me as if I were a baby," pleaded Gilbert.

"But, dear, it will soothe the aching and the misery," said she sympathetically.

"Please don't bother," persisted the lad, "these bumps don't amount to much, anyway; besides, Sandy says when you have sand in your craw and can stand the gaff you don't need any pain-killer, and before you know it you are as hard as nails. So please let me have my way."

"Certainly, dear, if you insist, but promise me not to be too reckless in your play."

"Of course, I'll promise that, grandma. Sandy doesn't believe in being reckless. He told me so himself. He says everybody knows that any boy who wouldn't take a dare isn't worth powder and shot to blow him to Kingdom-come, but he doesn't think a boy should be reckless."

"I'm afraid that's a distinction without a difference," observed Mrs. Franklin.

"I am going to help Delia put up my lunch," said the little fellow, going into the kitchen, where he found the colored woman carefully selecting an apple from a barrel.

"Ain't dat a beauty?" said the cook, holding in view a Newtown pippin.

"Yes, indeed, but you had better put four like it in my basket, Delia," suggested Gilbert.

"Lor' honey, yo' couldn't eat mor'n one of dem yer in a day, if yo' tried."

"I know it, Delia, but Sandy just loves pippins and russets all the time, and says he does not believe he could ever get enough of them."

"All right, honey, but if yo're goin' in fer to feed all creation, yo'll eat yo' daddy out o' house an' home, an' sen' us all to the porehouse." Then to show that she took no stock in her words, the good-natured Delia put four of the largest apples in the basket.

"I don't believe you have sliced enough bread and tongue," continued Gilbert, scrutinizing the pile of appetizing sandwiches she was preparing.

"Bress ma soul, dere's enuff yere for a small-sized reg'ment,"—and she held up a heaped tray.

"Yes, perhaps generally," said the little fellow slowly, "but Sandy and Dink just dote on sandwiches. Dink told me yesterday, he wouldn't care if he were cast away on a desert island for the rest of his life, if he were supplied with tongue sandwiches. He says, when they are cut thin, with butter on both pieces of bread, they beat canvasback duck all to pieces. So please have plenty of them!"

" 'Deed chile, ef yo' wants to have mo', I'll have to give yo' de market basket to put 'em in, an' mebbe Matt better bring de horse an' wagon roun' for to tote yo' pervisions to school,"—and Delia sat down, shaking with laughter at the idea.

After closing the lunch basket, the cook looked

at the clock, and finding that the boy need not leave for some moments, she sat down by the fire. Beckoning Gilbert toward her, she almost whispered, "Honey, I wants to ax yo' sumthin' that's bin on ma tongue ever so many times."

"Go ahead, Delia, I am all ears,"—and Gilbert seated himself, waiting for her question. She began slowly and impressively.

"Las' night, me an' ma brudder Matt went roun' to de Odd Fellows Hall to see a panoramy what wuz called *Bunyan's Pilgrim's Progress.* We had awful good seats up in Buzzard's Roost, an' enj'y'd ev'ry minit we wuz dere. Dere wuz a man what told us all about de picters an' what dey meant. Dere wuz picters of angels, an' angels, an' angels, a-movin' along. Dere wuz pink-faced angels wid long flowin' white robes, an' den would come white-faced angels wid long flowin' pink robes, an' dey kept on comin', an' I watched, an' watched, an' watched, but nary a black angel came, wid no kinds of robes on 'tall. An' it set me thinkin' powerful hard. I sez to Matt, who wuz tryin' to git through his wool what de panoramy wuz all 'bout, an' not makin' much headway, I sez, 'Matt, do yo' 'member ever havin' seen a black angel?' An' he sed, laughin', looney-like, 'Go 'long, Delia, an' stop yer foolishness.'

"An' I didn't say nuthin' to him no mo', but when de entertertainment wuz over, I waited fo' de minister, who wuz dere wid all his folks, an' I ups and sez, 'Axin' yer pardon, Mister Cunningham, but is der sich a thing as a black angel?'

"He coughed mighty hollow-like, three or fo' times, an' hurryin' past, said, 'Delia, yo' jest run 'long an' don't ax no silly questions.' I stood dere five minutes, tryin' to make out why ma question wuz foolish, an' I didn't come to no concludin' p'int, which wuz mighty unsatisfyin' to me, cos I wuz jest whar I started from.

"I walked home a-thinkin' an' a-thinkin', an' I sez to myse'f, ef dere ain't no black angels, what's de use of ma puttin' quarters in de contribution-box ev'ry Sunday. Ef I'se payin' in advance for lodgin's in de manshuns of de blest, I wants ter know if dey is gwine to gimme a room when I dies, or jest let me set out on de curbstone, 'cause I'm black, an' I jest got wool-gathered a-thinkin'. Honey, what I wants to ax yo', is yo' 'pinion, fo' I knows yo' knows lots an' lots more'n most folks I could name. I wants to know if in yo' 'pinion, hones' an' trufful, does cullud people go to Heaven anyhow when dey dies?"

"Why, of course, Delia. Why shouldn't they? I'm sure your soul is just as white as any one's. The only difference between white people and yourself is the pigment in your skin."

"De pigment in ma skin, honey?"

"Yes, father told me all about it. It's very queer. If you hadn't a pigment peculiar to your race, you would perhaps be as white as anybody."

"Is dat de trouble wid me?" she queried, her face shining with perspiration.

"I can't recall any other reason. But, Delia," he continued ingenuously, "just think what it would mean to us. If you hadn't any pigment in your skin, the chances are you wouldn't cook for us, and then what would we do?"

"Come yere, yo' honey boy," she cried impulsively, pulling the little fellow toward her and pressing him tightly to her ample bosom. "Yo' listen to me. If I hadn't no pigment 'bout me, an' I wuz white as alabaster, I would cook fer yo' until I drapped in ma tracks."

It was now time for Gilbert to go to school, and, picking up his lunch basket and books, he was off with a good-by.

Delia sat musing until her train of thought was interrupted by the entrance of Matt, who had come over for something to eat. He was Mr. Franklin's man-of-all-work. When he was comfortably seated at the table, his sister spoke:

"Matthew, dat honey boy o' mine has made me feel pow'ful better sence I seen yo' las' night."

"How's dat?" exclaimed the hungry brother, taking the second helping of sausage and potatoes.

"He done tol' me all about cullud pussons, an' why you don't see no black angels."

"An' what does he calkerlate am de reasin?" asked Matthew slowly, between swallows of coffee, with his elbows resting on the table, looking expectantly at Delia.

"It's all de pigments; our souls er jes' as white as ennybody's, he sez, but our skins air turned black from de pigments."

"I'se a feelin' yo'," said Matt, "but I can't see yo',"—and dubiously he rubbed his lips.

"De little honey is de most knowledgeable boy I ebber seen, an' he sez it's pigments in de nigger's skin. Derefo' der ain't no black angels, an' I feels it in ma bones dat dat am correct. For sakes 'live, niggers am powerful fond of hog-meat, enny way it comes, an' dat wuz de trouble always.

'Twan't de Lawd Almighty wot made de cullud pussons black, but it wuz dem fool niggers when de world got started, a-eatin', an' a-gorgin', an' a-stuffin' demselves wid pigments an' cracklin's, an' all t'other kinds o' hog-meat."

"Am dat a fac'?" said the brother.

"Dat am it. Dey should 'a' bin mighty keer-ful at de beginnin', an' not 'a' let de pigments black der skin fo' ebber an' ebber, after de Lawd made Heaven an' earth an' all dat derein lies. Amen."

Delia resumed her work with a final thrust. "I nebber did hab no use for dem foolish-goin' nig-gers what don't know nuthin' nohow."

"I don't see why yo're lettin' dat worry yo'," said Matt reproachfully. "Pigments or no pig-ments, a nigger's jest as good as ennybody, as long as he's a nigger; but when he tries to play white man, he ain't as good as a nigger."

Gilbert's second day at school passed without any special interest, as did many weeks that fol-lowed. It was universally admitted, except for the carping remarks of Snarley Foley, that Gilbert was the brightest boy in his class. Miss Latham said he was a wonderful child, and Sandy almost daily reiterated his original opinion.

"Gil is the cutiest little codger I ever seen."

One of the surprises was the rapid advance made by Sandy in arithmetic and geography. He was permanently seated next to Gilbert, whose particular care it was understood he should be.

To the little fellow's sympathetic assistance during these weeks was due Sandy's progress. To the older boy's kind instructions could be credited a knowledge of handsprings and cart-wheels, on the part of Gilbert, besides two fairly successful attempts to walk on his hands, and a projected double-somersault. Thus Gilbert's body and Sandy's brain were running a race, and it was neck and neck.

With the improvement in the younger lad's physical condition, came a love of mischief and a desire to play good-natured pranks. As Sandy was a past master in the art of perpetrating jokes he found in Gilbert a ready accomplice.

Among Miss Latham's scholars, next to ring-ing the bell and keeping the fire up, the bringing of drinking-water was the most important duty, and, as Sandy was the strongest boy, he had thus far always been deputized for that most enjoyable task. He had the privilege of selecting a helper, and, naturally, Gilbert was his choice.

At least five times each day the buckets were refilled. It was Friday, and that was fish-day in Pipetown. Everybody was especially thirsty.

A hand was raised. "Please, teacher," piped the shrill voice of a dry-lipped boy.

"What is it, Edward?" This from Miss Latham, to the boy standing near the buckets.

"'Tain't no water in the pails."

"Sandy, bring some."

"Yes, Miss Maisie," responded Sandy, at the same time jerking his thumb over his left shoulder toward Gilbert, meaning thereby, as plainly as words could say: "Come on, little feller." The younger boy, taking his cap from the rack, picked up one of the buckets and followed.

Once outside, the pair went by a round-about path through the back yard, over the fence, and into an alley in the direction of the pump, a block away. Suddenly Sandy stopped and peered through a hole in the fence, examining closely an object lying just on the other side.

"If that ain't a pot er black paint, I'm a liar," he called out.

"That's what it is," responded Gilbert, also looking closely.

"Findin's keepin's; so jest take it along, Gil,"

said Sandy, handing it to the little fellow, and putting the paint-brush in his pocket. "I spec' some painter left it here fer us to find, an' ain't never comin' back no more to see if we've got it. Findin's keepin's. Come along."

At the pump Sandy filled the two buckets, and then hid them in a doorway near by.

"Now, Gil," said the older boy, taking the pot of paint from his companion, "jest run across the street an' git behind the fence till I come over. I've got er n'idea. Yer can see any proceedin' by jest a-lookin' through a knot-hole."

Gilbert went over and awaited developments.

Sandy scanned the street up and down, and, finding it deserted, quickly dipped the brush into the paint and started to coat the pump-handle. When he had finished, he surveyed his work with a critical eye, and soliloquized: "I don't believe I could git no more on that 'ere handle, if I tried fer an hour."

The handle was, indeed, completely covered.

Again Sandy looked, and saw a boy approaching.

"If that ain't Fatty Beeks a-comin', I'm a liar. I owes him one fer his nobs, an' I guess this is where I pays it."

Young Beeks moved lumberingly, his head was haughtily erect, and he waddled with an air of stupid importance. He was fourteen, and very fat. His hair was a mass of golden ringlets, and he wore low shoes, white stockings, knee-breeches, velvet jacket, with lace-ruffled shirt, and a Tam-o'-Shanter.

Sandy, bowing with theatric mimicry, patted the puffy cheeks of the youth, and said: "What ho, my friend, one moment, I pray thee!" Being an inveterate Saturday night patron of the drama, and having learned "play talk" by the hour, he now tried it on the fat boy.

"Prithee, fair youth with the golden ringlets," he began grandly, "dost thy mother know ye're out?"

"Yes, indeedy," lisped the boy, staring blankly at Sandy.

"'Tis well, beautiful one with the velvet jacket! As thou art a knight an' a gentleman, I prithee guard this precious casket while I proceed hence, an' rescue the beauteous damozel encased in yonder basement deep." And Sandy lifted the pot of paint from the ground, held it aloft dramatically and placed it in the mystified boy's hands. "Guard it with thy life, an' when I return I will give thee gold an' precious jewels, an' a little mountain home."

Then with sh! sh! sh! and one finger warningly placed to his lips, he glided across the street. Going round the corner, he jumped the side fence and joined Gilbert.

The fat boy, holding high the pot of paint, was undecided whether to remain or waddle away.

"Look! look!" whispered Sandy to Gilbert, gluing his eyes to a knot-hole, "here comes Tom Foley's mother, an' if she ain't goin' right to the pump, yer can put me down fer a liar."

This quick-tempered but hard-working woman walked mechanically toward the pump and placed her pail on the nozzle. She grasped the pump-handle firmly, but only for a moment, then with a scream of astonishment and anger, looked at her paint-covered palms and fingers in dismay.

"What imp of darkness has been here and done this?" she cried, at the same time espying the fat boy, holding the paint-pot and giggling at her plight. Fairly yelling, she jumped at him, with, "I'll teach you to play tricks on your betters; take that; and that; and that!"—and over went the paint, covering Fatty's ringlets, running down his back, and smearing him from head to feet.

"I'll skin yer alive, you fat-head, you brat— you—you,"—the last words were lost in a resounding smack, as Fatty slipped and rolled through the pool of paint on the sidewalk.

She stood over him for a minute, in a sort of *sic semper tyrannis* attitude, then filled her water-bucket and hurled its contents at him. Fatty was a sight, and Sandy and Gilbert behind the fence danced for joy.

Turning about frequently, and occasionally shaking her fist, Mrs. Foley slowly disappeared, while the two young culprits came from their hiding-place and returned to the spot where the paint-covered boy was standing.

"Methinks," said Sandy in sepulchral tones, "somebody's bin here ere now sence I've been gone."

Gilbert laughed uproariously, until Sandy, turning to him, said very gravely, in the manner of Cæsar to Brutus: "Silence, friend of me bosom. As I love thee, I beg thee behold this gallant knight." Fatty was crying.

"Ah, ha! I see it all," said Sandy with sudden force, jumping up and cracking his heels together, —"yer wuz attack'd by robbers, pirates, an' sich like, an' they done yer up, fer sure." The victim was still sniffling, and trying to squeeze the paint from his yellow hair.

Sandy struck another tragic attitude. "Go, an' go in peace. Dry thy tears. Away to thy lovin' ma, an' tell her to soak her little darlin' in turpentine. The next time I meet thee on the Rialto, a large red apple shall be thine. Git!" And the fat boy waddled homeward.

"I wouldn't 'a' played th' trick on him if he wuz white," said Sandy. "That fat-head's got the yallerest kind er streak I ever seen in any boy."

"How's that, Sandy?" asked the little fellow.

"I seen him yesterday throw a brick at a little dog an' break his leg. When I hollered at him he kicked the dog as hard as he could an' run away inter the house. An' that's why I'm glad we played it on him."

Thereupon, with a consciousness of duty well done, the boys returned to the thirsty pupils awaiting them.

As Gilbert was going home, he passed Miss Gransey's school for girls. His attention was attracted by the sobs of a child seated on a bench in the play-yard. Fearing some accident had occurred, he hurried to her and said, all sympathy and gentleness:

"What's the matter; can I help you?"

She looked up, and then sobbed afresh.

"Now, come, tell me what is the matter,"—
and Gilbert spoke coaxingly.

"Miss Gransey sent me home," said the child,
amid a fresh outburst.

"Never mind,"—and Gilbert stroked her head.

"Teacher sent me home, and told me to tell my
mother to scrub my hands, and, and,"—after a
great sob,—"she said I was ugly as sin,"—and
another flood of tears came.

"That doesn't make it so," said Gilbert, trying
to soothe her.

"It's no use for mother to scrub my hands. I
scrub an' scrub an' scrub 'em ev'ry day, lots of
times, but I can't make 'em white, an' I want to
die."

"No, you don't,"—and the young lad bent over
her. Tenderly, he took the little one's hand in his
own, and imprinted a hearty kiss on it.

"My hands wouldn't be black if I hadn't been
runnin' wild all the year on Aunt Harriet's farm,"
said the maid with conviction.

"Now dry your eyes," he said reassuringly,
still holding her hand and looking at it admir-
ingly.

"I had to go down to the farm and run wild, 'cause the doctor told my folks to send me, and I'm awful sunburnt."

"That's it, the sun has made your hands olive-tinted."

"Olive-tinted! what's that?" said the little girl, forgetting her troubles temporarily, and opening her eyes with sudden interest.

"Olive-tinted," echoed the youthful cavalier, "olive-tinted is the color that all gipsy queens have; in fact I do not believe any one could be a gipsy queen unless she had olive-tinted hands, and olive-tinted face, and olive-tinted neck, and olive-tinted shoulders."

"Do gipsy queens run wild by the doctor's order?" asked the girl, deeply interested.

"There is no doubt of it. They are in the open air all the time, and of course run wild."

"I ran wild so long that sister Crissie says my shoulders are as black as a nigger's; but they ain't, are they?"

"Of course not," replied Gilbert reassuringly; "they are only olive-tinted."

"When I came back from the country, sister Crissie said, if I was picked up dead, she wouldn't have known me. I was so black."

"But you are not; you are simply olive-tinted," protested Gilbert.

"What else do gipsy queens have, like me?" questioned the little girl intently.

"Well, they have hair as black as a raven's wing."

"Yes, yes; and what else?"

"And eyes that would put to shame the twinkling stars," said Gilbert, quoting readily.

"How nice! And what else?"

"And teeth like pearls." The child's face was wreathed in smiles, and she was struck with wonder and admiration.

"What is your name?"

"Zorah Dabney."

"Are you Dink Dabney's sister?"

"Yes, that's who I am. Dink's my brother," said the now talkative Zorah.

"I know him," said the boy, "he goes to the same school with me. Dink's all right. Sandy says Dink's all right, and Sandy knows."

"Who is Sandy?" asked the little girl.

"Oh, hasn't Dink told you about Sandy? I thought everybody would tell everybody else about Sandy, if they knew him."

"No, you see I've been running wild and just

got home a week ago, and haven't seen much of Dink."

"And Dink hasn't said anything about Sandy?" asked Gilbert with a shade of surprise.

"Nope, he never told me anything about Sandy."

"Well, Sandy is just Sandy, and that's a heap. He can turn cartwheels so fast it will make you dizzy watching him. Oh, say, there's nothing Sandy can't do, and you wouldn't know anything about it, if you waited for him to tell you. You must meet Sandy, and I am sure you will like him. Tell Dink to have him come and see you."

"Yes, I will. Dink's got to shovel our coal to-morrow, and I'll tell him to have Sandy come and help him, and then I'll see him."

"That's a good idea," said Gilbert, as he hurried away to meet Sandy down at Jebb's corner.

CHAPTER IV

"PICKIN' AIGS"

The children of Pipetown took second place to none in their interest and devotion to the various annual holidays. Christmas brought its visions of gifts, mince pies and gaily-trimmed trees; Washington's Birthday, or in the small boy's verbal perversion, "Birthington's Washday," came with its attendance at church, its reading of the first president's Farewell, its pleasures of skating, sledding, football play, or "shinny on your own side;" Fourth of July, carrying with it the cannon and fire-cracker, pistol and torpedo, was made notable by the reading of the Declaration of Independence, and brought to a glorious ending by a fine fireworks display; New Year's was, in reality, but a winding up of the Christmas festivities, while Thanksgiving meant plenty of turkey, nuts and candy. But the most pleasurable time, perhaps, for the Pipetown boys, was the Easter holiday, because it was so long drawn out.

For two weeks before, and during the Easter

58

week, the boys of the town were deep in the game of egg-picking, and "Got er naig to pick?" was the familiar greeting from morning until night.

Then, too, this was the time for the annual concert, at which was usually given a cantata on a biblical subject.

The girls of Miss Gransey's school, together with the boys of Miss Latham's, were assiduously rehearsing the cantata *Rachel* in Odd Fellows Hall under the direction of Professor Faniels.

"It's mighty funny," volunteered Sandy to Gilbert during one of the rehearsals, as he pocketed an egg just won from a boy standing next to him in the chorus, "it's mighty funny 'bout music pieces, 'specially if they ain't got no nigger in 'em."

"Don't follow your drift," said Gilbert.

"It's this 'ere way. I means, if a music piece's got nigger in it, it jest keeps yer foot goin' all the time an' the chune comes to yer jest nacheral like. It's powerful likely yer'll be whistlin' it by the mornin', but this 'ere kind of music pieces we've been practisin', 'tain't no foot that'll go with 'em. I've tried over an' over to keep time, but both my hoofs jest stay planted. The gals they screech, an' screech, an' screech, an' when they stops the boys beller, then we mixes up the screechin' an' the bellerin' till it sounds like the devil afore day."

"But we must wait until the professor has rehearsed enough, and then it will be all right," suggested Gilbert.

"I want yer to understan' one thing, little codger, 'tain't only pieces with nigger in 'em I like. Them soft dreamy kind er chunes, that grow sweeter an' sweeter all the time, then sort er die away, have er powerful influence on me, 'specially when I'm all run down, an' feel like a b'iled owl."

"Oh, if you were educated in music, Sandy, there's lots and lots of it you would love, that you can't understand now."

"I spec' that's right, little codger. Howsomever, I ain't got no use now for any chunes 'cept they have nigger in 'em, or are soft and sleepy, like the woods in summer-time. Mebbe I would, if I wuz eddicated like you are, but I don't know."

"I know you would," spoke Gilbert positively. "Pieces by Bethoven, Mozart and Haydn would be just as pleasant to you as nigger tunes, if you heard them as often."

"I guess you're right, 'specially if they're as pretty as you sez they be."

Rehearsal being over, the boys hurried to the

street, eager to challenge one another, and try con-
clusions with their "busters," otherwise known as
eggs carefully selected from a large number, for
points and butts of exceptional thickness and
strength.

Possession of the fleetest race-horse by a mil-
lionaire sportsman, or of the gamiest fighting
cock by a chicken fancier, could not have been
matter of keener pride to the boys of Pipetown
than the ownership of a champion "buster."

The first boy Sandy met was Curley Harris,
and "Got er naig?" came simultaneously.

"You bet!"

"Want er pick?"

"Mebbe; let's see yer aig."

The eggs were produced from mysterious pockets and reluctantly shown at a safe distance.

"That looks like a ginny keet," said Sandy.

"'Tain't no ginny keet an' yer knows it, that is
if yer knows anythin' 'bout aigs," snapped Curley sarcastically.

"Lemme try yer aig."

"Lemme try your'n."

The eggs were exchanged, then facing each
other the boys made a test of them by tapping
them, points and butts, against their front teeth.

As Sandy returned Curley's egg to its owner and received his in exchange, he asked, "What 'vantage d'yer give?"

"I don't give no 'vantage; points up, butts up an' nuthin' more."

"Go' long, yer've the best aig, gimme a show fer my white alley."

"Well, I'll give yer jest this much an' no more," —and Curley placed the egg in the palm of his hand, then gently closed his fingers over it, displaying a very small portion of the point.

"I won't pick with no feller like you. Show me some fowl, an' I'll pick yer."

"All right, I'll give yer this much fowl an' no more,"—Curley exposed the egg about half an inch from its point, and Sandy, taking his between thumb and finger, rolled the point around that of his opponent and suddenly struck. Curley's egg, being the softer, was cracked. Then ends were reversed, the process was repeated and Curley lost again. Sandy pocketed the cracked egg, and walked off triumphantly.

"No use talkin', Gil, but this has been a mighty good day fer aigs."

"How many do you think you've won?" asked Gilbert.

"I don't know, but I guess I'll stop to count, an' yer can help me carry 'em." Then Sandy fished from his pocket seven eggs, one of them a duck's.

"Where did you win this one?" asked Gilbert, holding up the duck egg.

"I jest picked this little bantam ag'in it, an' she cracked it, but it was a mighty dangerous thing to do. 'Tain't one hen aig in a milyun that can crack a duck, but this little dandy done it,"— and he held up a small brown egg to Gilbert's admiring gaze.

"Wouldn't it have been awful if you had lost that little bantam," said the younger boy sympathetically.

No self-respecting boy in Pipetown would be seen with a duck egg in his possession during picking time, so Sandy felt quite guilty that he had not thrown away the egg after winning it.

"I guess I'll chuck it over in the lot, afore any one sees it," he said.

"No, don't do that; let's wrap it up carefully and lay it on the pavement for some one to kick," suggested the little fellow slyly.

"I don't advise that," said Sandy. "Some lady might kick it, an' ladies never did see no joke like that. Then he added, "I've got it!" and he pointed down the street. Gilbert looked in the direction and saw Fatty Beeks waddling up. Sandy went gleefully through a hurried pantomime.

"D'yer twig?"

"Cert," said the little fellow.

Young Beeks was abreast of them.

"Got an egg?" called Gilbert, holding up the duck egg.

"Nope," said Fatty, "mama won't let me pick eggs. She says it's wicked and leads to gambling when you are a man."

"Mama is right," said Gilbert, in an attitude of Chesterfieldian grace. Then, taking the fat boy aside, he whispered: "I've just made a bet with that big boy there, that I can hide this egg on you and he can't find it."

"I don't want to play with you," young Beeks exclaimed, as an unhappy recollection of paint and pump came to his mind.

"This isn't play," said Gilbert commandingly, "this is betting, and if I win, I'm going to give you the egg; but don't breathe a word."

"All right, I'll do it if I get the egg," said the other boy under his breath.

"You'll get it, don't fear,"—and Gilbert winked slyly. "Turn your head, Sandy, while I hide the egg."

"Now tote fair, Gil, don't put it where nobody couldn't find it."

Gilbert winked again, and then slowly lifting Fatty's Tam-o'-Shanter, placed the egg on the boy's head and carefully covered it with the cap.

Fatty by this time was deeply interested, and when Gilbert said, "Don't give anything away, and we'll fool him," Beeks blinked like an owl in the sunlight.

"All right, Sandy, we're ready," shouted Gilbert.

Sandy turned slowly and came toward the fat boy with an air of absorbed interest.

"I knows ye're awful cute, Gil, but I'm goin' to try an' find that 'ere aig if I bust a button."

The search began, and Sandy felt around Fatty's shoes and stockings, up and down his legs, into his trousers and coat pockets, into the bosom of his blouse, about his ears and then slowly returned down to his ankles.

"It's mighty funny where you could 'a' put it," and Sandy stooped, gently pressing the boy's toes as if the egg might be hidden near them.

"If I don't find it soon I'll have to give it up. I ain't goin' to stay here for ever, jest fer one aig," said Sandy, with an assumption of disgust.

Fatty was holding in his breath and blinking furiously.

"I never knowed er naig ter hide like that afore; it beats all holler where yer could a put it, Gil."

The fat boy dug his nails into the palms of his hands and set his teeth together firmly. Suddenly Sandy rose to his full height, stumbled awkwardly and let his hand fall heavily on the head of the unsuspecting victim. Fatty lifted his cap and felt the smashed egg slowly oozing down his face and neck.

"If I hadn't 'a' stumbled, I'd 'a' found that aig," said Sandy with an injured air. "Don't holler like ye're dead; 'tain't nuthin' but er naig."

"Don't cry," whispered Gilbert. "It's tough, but just think of the poor egg."

"That's it," added Sandy, "stop yer yellin', go home to ma like a darlin' little boy, an' tell her to turn on the garden hose; yer need it." Then Sandy and Gilbert sauntered off.

"That was two for his nobs, an' he won't break no little dog's leg ag'in, I'm a-thinkin'," said the older boy as they parted.

CHAPTER V

OLD MAN JEBB

"The Corner" was the best known and most popular place in Pipetown.

It was a store fashioned after its kind, supplied with a limited assortment of groceries, dry goods, hardware, guns and pistols, and the thousand and one things known under the head of general merchandise.

Titcomb Jebb was the proprietor.

The credit system was very popular. It was often remarked that if a list of all the books in Pipetown were taken, a certain little leather-backed kind, having on its cover the title, "In account with Titcomb Jebb, General Merchandise," would outnumber any other, not even barring the Good Book. What was the reason for this large custom?

The grocer made it a rule never to turn away those who were dilatory in settling, and never even to throw out a hint to the unfortunates who could not pay. Among these two classes he enjoyed a large, if not remunerative trade, and he naturally had their good will besides.

The "good pay" customers spoke well of his fairness—a rare concession, indeed, for that most imperious class. It was known that the inspector of weights and measures came weekly at Jebb's request and tested the scales. Those of the neighborhood who desired to be present during the ceremony were cordially invited. Besides, added to every proof of Jebb's scrupulous honesty toward his patrons at The Corner, seventeen ounces constituted a pound, and a "baker's dozen" and one over stood for twelve.

Of course "cash down" patrons were especially favored. Cash down meant any time within three months, and gave the purchaser an advantage over the "six-monthers" and the "never settles."

To the "cash-downer" came a reduction of ten per cent., also three guesses at the jar of beans; yet with these tremendous advantages, the "cash-downers" never arose to any dignity of numbers, and their names might have been written upon a tiny scroll of fame.

Among the boys and girls of the neighborhood the grocer enjoyed the most enviable reputation. Three or four barrels containing crackers, dried apples, cream nuts and pickles, temptingly placed around the store, and especially behind the various posts, added to his popularity with the youngsters.

Jebb's good nature and sympathetic disposition never deserted him, although he believed he had been miscast in the drama of life. He fondly cherished the delusion that he was a poet, and scarcely a day passed on which he did not add some new verses to his stock of rhymes.

Though Jebb had written much, for a long time he kept the knowledge of his poetic ambition and efforts secret from his neighbors and customers. But this could not last for ever. One day a verse appeared, painted in large letters on a card stuck in a new barrel of sugar. To his patrons it was a new way to advertise, combining poetry with groceries. It ran thus:

> Granulated sugar in the morning,
>   Granulated sugar for your tea;
> If you want to be a winner
> You must have it for your dinner
> And feed it to your fam-i-lee.

These lines were speedily memorized by the children of the customers and soon became public property.

One local critic, waxing enthusiastic, pronounced them "bully good and rhymin' 'cordin' to rule, which is a lot to say 'bout po'try nowadays."

Jebb, after much quizzing, acknowledged authorship, and the ice was broken. Everything he now wrote must needs be read to those among his acquaintance who would listen. Tablet and pencil in hand, he could be seen, when not professionally engaged in dispensing groceries, deep in meditation and jotting down what he was pleased to call his "wayward thoughts."

Once, and only once, he sent some verses to a magazine, but they were returned "respectfully declined." He did not rail or carp at the judgment displayed, but contented himself with saying: "Perhaps 'tis best that these stray waifs of my brain should remain with me, and not suffer from the arrows of adverse criticism."

Although disappointed at the rejection of his manuscript, his manner continued as kindly and as cordial as though he were the most favored of writers.

One morning as the grocer was putting the finishing touches on his latest stanzas, an effusion idealizing the object of his secret admiration, Dink Dabney strolled in.

"Good mornin', Mr. Jebb."

"Good morning, Dink; if you're not in a great hurry, I'll be ready to serve you in five minutes. I'm just polishing up a new piece."

"Don't bust yer b'iler on my 'count, Mr. Jebb; I ain't in no hurry, I kin wait,"—and Dink walked around the store, deeply interested in the contents of several open barrels.

At last Jebb put down the pencil and scanned the paper in his hand, then turning to the waiting customer, said: "Dink, what can I do for you?"

"I want er stick of peppermint candy, Mr. Jebb, but it must be fresh."

"It came in yesterday."

"Well, if that's so, I'll take it. I hates like sin to waste my money on stale candy, but if yer sez it's fresh, Mr. Jebb, I'll take two cents worth of it."

The grocer took the candy jar from the shelf, extracted the fattest stick of peppermint and handed it to the boy.

"That looks all right," said Dink, eying it critically, "so here's yer money."

Jebb dropped the pennies in the drawer.

"Dink, if you're not in a hurry and are fond of poetry, I'd like to read my new verses to you."

"Go right ahead, Mr. Jebb, I'm mighty fond of

po'try, 'specially when I'm chewin' peppermint candy." The boy seated himself on a convenient soap-box.

"'This poem," said the grocer, "is a wayward thought, that I have entitled *Have You Seen the Lady?* It reads as follows:

> "Have I told you the name of a lady?
> Have I told you the name of a dear?
> 'Twas known long ago,
> And ends with an O;
> You don't hear it often round here.
>
> Have I talked of the eyes of a lady?
> Have I talked of the eyes that are bright?
> Their color, you see,
> Is B-L-U-E;
> They're the gin in the cocktail of light.
>
> Have I sung of the hair of a lady?
> Have I sung of the hair of a dove?
> What shade do you say?
> B-L-A-C-K;
> It's the fizz in the champagne of love.
>
> Can you guess it—the name of the lady?
> She is sweet, she is fair, she is coy.
> Your guessing forego,
> It's J-U-N-O;
> She's the mint in the julep of joy."

"What's the answer, Mr. Jebb?" said Dink, greatly puzzled.

"It has no answer, Dink, except in my heart."

"Oh, I thought it wuz one of them—if a herrin' an' a ha'f cost a cent an' a ha'f, how much will twelve herrin's cost," observed the boy.

"No, Dink, it's just a wayward fancy of mine, written within the week."

"Well, it's mighty good, Mr. Jebb; if it gits talk'd 'bout it'll be jest as funny as the farmer with the fox an' the hen an' the bag o' corn, tryin' to cross the stream. But it's mighty good po'try, Mr. Jebb," said Dink, with a look at the jar of candy. "Mighty good an' no mistake,"—this more pointedly.

"Here's another stick of peppermint, Dink, and I'm glad you like the verses," said the delighted grocer, handing the boy the coveted candy.

"I cert'inly do, Mr. Jebb. Whenever yer feel lonesome to read to somebody, jest whistle me up. I don't mind; yer can't feaze me if yer shot yer po'try out of a cannon at me,"—and Dink walked out.

"Fer the sake of sufferin' Moses, why did yer stay in there so long?" exclaimed Curley Harris, who had been impatiently waiting for Dink's return.

"Oh, ol' man Jebb wuz a-readin' me a piece of new po'try an' gimme some candy fer list'nin'."

"You must like him lots to waste yer time hearin' him spout pieces."

"I do like him," answered Dink. "I like ol' man Jebb 'cause he never noses into other folks' bizness. I deals with him 'cause he don't 'spicion nobody."

Whereupon Dink emptied the contents of his pockets into his hat. The net result of his walk among the barrels was shown in an assortment of dried apples, cream nuts, raisins, crackers and lump sugar.

"I bought the candy," Dink explained, with inferential uprightness and grave assurance, "an' jest picked up them other things layin' round loose. That's what I likes 'bout ol' man Jebb; he never 'spicions nobody."

"Mebbe he could if he wanted to," volunteered Curley, sampling the sweets in the hat with great satisfaction.

"Mebbe he could," slowly echoed the other, "but he don't, an' I 'low he's white clean through, fer persons as is white clean through never 'spicions nobody." And the two went away to find a secluded spot to feast on the contents of Dink's hat.

And now a few words by way of introducing

"The Jedge." This sobriquet he had earned years and years before while acting as referee in the many cocking mains, county fairs and racing events held in the vicinity. He was rugged and weather-beaten from the effects of a strenuous life as hunter and fisher, extending over a period of more than forty years. Rheumatism had begun to claim him as its victim, and now at sixty he was eking out a modest existence by breeding hunting dogs and rigging fishing tackle.

With an abundance of time on his hands and a strongly-developed love for companionship, he was a constant visitor at The Corner.

Carlyle says somewhere, that "habit is our fundamental law! Habit and imitation; there is nothing more perennial in us than these two." It therefore seemed the most natural thing in the world for the Jedge, as soon as he had eaten his supper, to fill his pipe, light it with a hot coal from the kitchen, and proceed to Jebb's for a chat with the grocer and "the boys."

The boys were the duck-hunters and those interested in sports, afield and afloat. Nightly, in a little room in the rear of the store, these worthies congregated and discussed guns, dogs, birds and game generally, with that unflagging interest felt only in a community where quail and pheasant, woodcock and waterfowl are plentiful and much sought.

The Jedge was a central figure in this circle and every subject of argument and dispute was unhesitatingly referred to him. Whether a pointer was better than a setter, a breech-loader better than a muzzle-loader, a choke-bore better than a spatter-dab, a partridge quicker than a blue-wing, binocular surer than single sight, and, in fact any question affecting gunning, hunting and fishing in their varied ramifications, was left to him for adjustment.

It was a blustering evening in the late winter months, and the Jedge had entered the little room where the coterie of faithfuls assembled. With hearty salutations exchanged, he seated himself in his accustomed chair in line with a rat-hole at the side, that served him as a convenient cuspidor.

"Enny ducks flyin', Buck?"—this addressed to a tall, unshaven young man who lived by hunting on the river.

"Plenty of ducks flyin' this mornin', Jedge, but I never seen 'em so knowin'."

"Ducks does get awful knowin' sometimes," interposed the Jedge.

"When me an' Codfish Richards," continued Buck, "got out on the P'int this mornin' an' set our decoys, Codfish up an' sez, sez he, while he was a-blowin' his fingers warm—it wuz as cold as sin—'It 'pears to me we're goin' to have some shootin',' an' I didn't see no reason fer to conterdict him, so I didn't say nuthin' an' I jest got inter the blind. Whitebacks come 'long mighty soon an' ev'ry time they'd git near the decoys, they'd go way up in the air as if they wuz scrapin' their backs ag'in the clouds, an' then fly on. Me and Codfish stayed thare until we wuz froze stiff. Then we picked up the decoys an' went 'shore an' lit a fire to thaw out. An' I hope I may die, if a gang of canvasbacks didn't sail by us high up, a-puttin' up their feet 'gainst their bills, jest like yer seen boys do behind yer back, and we never got a feather. 'Tain't no use talkin', ducks is gettin' mighty knowin' these days."

"Them actions," said the Jedge to the interested listeners, "is what scientific men call ornithological sagacity,"—and all present held their cheeks suggestive of the jaw-breaking quality of the remark.

"I spec' I never tol' yer 'bout poor Ned Doogey an' his duck."

"No, Jedge; never told it to me as fur as I kin think," said big Bill Dabney.

"Or to me," came from half a dozen voices simultaneously.

"I kalkerlate ye're right, fer I entirely disre-member the time that I told it to a soul, if I ever did," ventured the Jedge.

"Go ahead, now, Jedge; we wants to hear it, an' we'll hump ourselves a-list'nin'," exclaimed Buck Wesley, drawing his chair closer to the old man.

The latter emptied the ashes from his pipe, slowly refilled the bowl with kinnikinick, then dexterously taking a lighted coal from the grate, lit the tobacco, and for a full minute puffed in silence.

"Takin' it by an' large, I should say, Ned Doo-gey wuz the quietest mortal I ever seen. Ther' wuz nobody as I ever laid my eyes on, as could beat him list'nin', an' he wuz that perlite he wouldn't a-crowded the mourners at his own funeril; an' gals, gals scared him most to death when they'd look at him, an' that wuz mighty of'en, fer Ned wuz cert'nly a scrumptious-lookin' feller. He got to shyin' at the gals so, we talked of puttin' blinders on him.

"Me an' him wuz mighty chummy, an' in cahoots fer lots o' years, until ther' comes a change in Ned's career. Long 'bout this time, a man an' his wife an' a raft of children from 'way up ther' somewher' comes an' rents a house next door to Ned. It wuz one of them awful nosey families what tries ter smell what yer have fer dinner, an' peeks over an' counts yer wash when it's hangin' on the line.

"Ther' wuz 'n old maid in the gang who probably turn'd sour first time she heard thunder. She wuz tagged Simphronia, an' she looked it. Simphronia wuz a screamer, an' no apology to nobody. She could outcackle a hen convention, an' fer nacherel beauty, she had a potato trap like a poor man's rent, from year to year. As fer flesh, she wuz jest 'bout as thin as the last run o' shad.

"Well, to make a long story short, she hypnotized, or mesmerized, or galvanized, or some other 'ized' poor Ned, an' afore yer know it, he wuz steady comp'ny an' wuz callin' ev'ry evenin' from eight to ten, punctual. 'Twan't more'n four or five years afore she nailed him an' he wuz a goner.

"The first I know'd of it wuz when Ned meets

me, an' sez, 'Jedge, I wants yer to stan' up with me.'

" 'Stan' up with yer,' I sez, fearin' the worst.

" 'That's it, stan' up with me,' he sez, lookin' aroun' like a scar'd dog.

" 'Who's the lady?' I says, pretendin'.

" 'Simphronia,' he sez.

" 'Simphronia,' I sez; 'great Scott, how did it happen?'

" 'I ax'd her,' he sez, gettin' red all over, 'cause he never could tell a whopper an' not show it.

"Well, sir, in a month Ned wuz hitched to Simphronia, an' then his troubles begun, sure 'nough. If ther' ever lived a torment on this 'ere mundane sphere, as scientific men would say, Simphronia was her cognomen.

"Afore the honeymoon wuz over, she begun to clapper-claw an' tongue-lash poor Ned from daybreak to dark.

"A bunch of fire-crackers explodin' in a flour barrel wuz the stillness o' death compared to her goin's-on when she got warmed up. When he come home from work she'd make him go round to the back door an' brush hisself till she concluded to let him in, an' then she'd keep him tied to her apron strings, jest as if he wuz a baby. He couldn't go two hoots an' a holler, without gittin' bullyragged by her, an' takin' it all in all, his marriage wuz a failure, but he sed nuthin' to nobody.

"After a while she gits it into her head that she wuz ailin', an' she'd groan an' roll her eyes like a dyin' calf, from sun-up to bed-time. Ther' wuz no new-fangled disease that got talked about, but what she'd have it right on time.

"I'm a-callin' to mind Ned tellin' me that poor Simphronia wuz full of misery an' aches, an' I sez, 'What is troublin' her?'

"'It's insomny,' he sez, 'insomny, an' she sleeps through it so hard, I has to run aroun' the room a-shoutin' "House afire!" and "Mad dog!" at the top o' my voice afore she wakes up.'

"As I wuz sayin', I never found nobody as could beat Ned a-list'nin', but hones' to goodness, if she didn't wear him out at that. One day he comes to me a-lookin' as thin as a shadder, an' mighty peaked, too, an' he sez, 'Jedge, the doctor sez I must have a change, an' I don't know jest what to do.'

"'If I wuz you, Ned,' I sez, 'I'd take a half-day off, an' go out on the river an' amuse myself.'

"'I don't believe Simphronia would like it,' he sez, a-coughin' fer a whole minute.

" "'Tain't necessary fer her to know nuthin' 'bout it,' I whispered coaxingly.

" 'But how kin I do it without her knowin' it?' he sez, scared like.

" 'Easy as rollin' off a log,' sez I. 'Jest take my skiff an' gun an' I'll give yer a horn o' powder and a shot pouch, an' you paddle down to Pencote a-huntin' fer ducks. Mebbe you'll find some, an' mebbe yer won't. But that won't interfere with the huntin', jest the same.' He agrees to my advice an' takes the afternoon off, the first Saterday comin'. When he gits down to the P'int jest t'other side o' Pencote, he sees a solitary duck a-cavortin' round in the cove. He creeps up cautious, an' lets fly. Down dives Mr. Duck, an' after a while comes up 'bout fifty yards further off, with nary a shot in him. Ned loads again, picks up his paddle, an' creeps up. When he's near, bang! bang! he goes, an' down dives the duck onct more.

"Well, sir, he chases that duck all round Pencote, an' in the course of the afternoon he runs short o' powder an' shot, an' he never as much as teches a feather. Then he goes home."

"What kind er duck wuz he, Jedge?" interrupted Bill Dabney.

"He wuz what scientific men call a grebe, but known round here as a 'water witch.'"

"An' if yer enjoys spicy language, 'hell diver' suits him mighty well," added Buck.

"They b'longs to the loon fam'ly, an' 'tain't no trick fer 'em to dive when yer click yer trigger, an' when the smoke clears away, up they bobs, sassy as a monkey on a stick."

"Fer a cute duck, I puts my money on a grebe ev'ry time," concluded Buck.

"Next Saterday Ned takes the gun an' paddles down ag'in. When he gits to Pencote, what does he see but that 'ere same duck a-movin' round. He crawls up an' shoots an' shoots, an' when it wuz nigh unto dark, Ned had run out er ammernition, an' that duck wuz still swimmin' round as lively as yer please.

"When Ned gits home that night, Simphronia wuz havin' the hypo, an' she jest wore her jaw out a-lashin' him, but, oh Lor', he didn't mind, he wuz a-thinkin' of that 'ere water witch. He got anxious fer next Saterday ter come, an' when it did, down the river he steals ag'in. I'm a liar if there wuzn't that same duck, an' he begun shootin' at him an' missin' him as usual. Ned sed 'bout the thirty-fourth shot he tho't he hit

him, but while he wuz watchin', up bobs the
diver, an' shook his head, as if he was laughin'
an' sayin'—'That wuz a mighty close call, stranger'—an' then dove round, jest playful like. Ned
sed the duck seemed to take awful chances that
afternoon to sort er encourage him, 'cause he
could see Ned wuz kind er down in the mouth.

"Well, sir, that 'ere water witch got so used to
Ned comin' ev'ry Saterday, he'd swim out in the
channel an' welcome him. Ned sed he b'lieved
that 'ere duck wuz full of sportin' blood an' enjoyed the pleasures of shootin', jest as if he carried a gun hisself.

"'Long toward spring, he seemed to know
when Ned's powder wuz used up, an' would foller
the poor feller up the river as far as his boat
landin'. Ned sed it wuz mighty entertainin' to
watch him circle round the skiff, an' after a while
he got so familiar he'd wait at the wharf, and fly
clean to Ned's home an' then skedaddle fer Pencote.

"Bimeby, poor Ned takes to his bed sick, an'
mighty sick at that, an' when Saterday comes he
couldn't go a-shootin'. And when the next three
Saterdays come, he couldn't go a-shootin'. He
had what scientific men calls tuberculosis, but

what I calls nothin' else but gallopin' consumption.

"'Long 'bout the fifth Saterday, poor Ned sez to me, while I wuz sittin' by his bed, 'If I could only see my duck ag'in I'd die happy,' an' lo an' behold, I heard a tappin' at the window, an' if ther' wuzn't that water witch a-lookin' in! I raised Ned up, an' I hope I may die if the duck didn't nod his head as familiar as possible. Ned wuz satisfied, an' right there an' then he gave up.

"We buried him out in the cemetery, down close to the river, an' when the first Sunday comes, I goes out with a rosebush to put over Ned's head, an' when I gets ther' I sees somethin' strange a-lyin' on his grave. It wuz Ned's duck, stark an' stiff in death. An' I sed then, an' I sez now, it wuz a clear case o' suicide, or I'm a liar."

"What did yer do with him, Jedge?" asked big Bill Dabney.

"I buried him right next to Ned, an' put up a shingle with these 'ere words carved on it:

" 'He loved not wisely but too well.' "

After a thorough discussion of the peculiarities of ducks generally, and of Ned Doogey's in particular, the coterie started to go. Buttoning coats and turning up collars, for it was unusually cold, they filed out with a friendly good night to the grocer.

The Jedge alone remained. His Llewellyn setter dog, Rover, which, until this moment, had been stretched lazily before the stove, raised himself slowly, stood up, yawned and stretched his forelegs to their full length. He blinked his beautiful eyes, shook himself, and going over to the Jedge, placed his head softly and lovingly on his master's knee and looked into the old man's face quizzically. The Jedge stroked the setter tenderly, saying, "Think it's time to go, do yer, Rover?"

The dog wagged his tail joyously, and he and his master walked out of the back room into the store. Jebb was sitting back of the counter engaged in writing. He looked up and said: "Jedge, if you're not in a great hurry, won't you stop and have a night-cap with me?"

"Titcomb, yer knows my weakness. A night-cap is a powerful argerment,"—and the Jedge seated himself on a barrel.

Jebb drew from under the counter a bottle of rum and a pitcher of molasses, together with two tumblers.

"Titcomb, don't make it too strong. Yer kind

er put in too much licker las' night. If yer don't
mind my suggestin', I like about three parts rum
to one o' molasses. But bear in mind, it's only
my suggestion."

The grocer handed a tumbler to the Jedge who
lifted the glass and said, "Well, here's what
killed dad." He drank the contents with evident
relish, after which he wiped his mouth on his
sleeve and continued: "Titcomb, do yer realize
that we're enjoyin' blessin's denied to less favored
mortals?"

"In what way?" asked the grocer.

"I was a-readin' in the *Philadelphy Inquiry,*
that Jamaicy rum and molasses went up five cents
a gallon yesterday, an' if we're not careful nobody but millionaires can drink it, which is
mighty hard on those poor miserable sinners who
can't buy it by the year, like me an' you." Thereupon the Jedge reached for a second glass of the
same mixture.

"Jedge, have you traveled much?" queried Titcomb.

"Oh, well, I should say considerable. I've
been all the way to Philadelphy twice, an' I have
flucterated roun' other p'ints of the compass between times."

"I asked you this question, Jedge, because I know you are an experienced man of the world. I must confide in some one. I'm in love."

"I'm a-list'nin'," said the old man, taking a long sip from the tumbler.

"And what I want to ask you," said Titcomb, "is this. Is it proper for me to love a lady without communicating the fact to her?"

"That's er enigmy, as scientific men would say, but my opinion offhan' is that yer had better tell her, an' not remain er access'ry before the fact."

"Jedge, day and night, sleeping and waking, I have thought to tell her, but I've always been afraid. Her image never leaves me, and if I should die, I believe that like that Queen of England who said that *Calais* would be engraved on her heart, you would find *Mary* engraved on mine."

"Yer've got it bad, Titcomb. 'Tain't no funeril of mine, but I don't think it would be right to keep the lady in the dark."

"Yes, but what shall I do? I am afraid to tell her."

"What are yer afeard of? Don't act like a poor boy at a huskin'; speak out like a man."

"You don't understand, Jedge; she is not a

single girl, let me tell you, but the mother of a
half-grown boy."

The Jedge jumped up quickly, and, grabbing
his tumbler, burst out:

"Titcomb Jebb, what's this shenanigen yer
givin' me?"

"Sit down, Jedge, you don't understand."

"I'm ashamed of yer, Titcomb, a-comin' an'
askin' me to tell yer how to carry on a flirtation
with a married woman. Shame on yer!"

"You don't understand, Jedge. She was married once."

"Married once; well, an' what is she now?"

"She's the Widow Foley."

"The Widder Foley?" and the Jedge laughed
uproariously. "An' to think I was putterin' 'bout
an' raisin' Cain 'cause I thought yer wuz tryin'
to gallivant round forbidden fruit! But I sees
it now. Bully for the widder!"

After the Jedge had dried his eyes, which were
wet from laughter, and had taken a fresh chew of
tobacco, he said:

"Titcomb, she's a fine-lookin' woman. She's as
pretty a piece o' calico as yer'll find in this 'ere
place; but oh, Lord, she's got a temper."

"She has much to worry her."

"I dunno whether yer can get her workin' in double harness ag'in or not. She had a ornery mate, I've bin tol', when she trotted with Dennis Foley, but mebbe she can be coaxed into the traces onct more."

"And that's why I want to talk to you. I don't want to break it to her too suddenly."

"'Tain't necessary fer yer to do that, Titcomb; jest start in by a-readin' yer po'try to her. Women are powerful fond of nater and sich like things, an' when ye've kind er got her in the runnin', yer can spring the question on her, after her soul has b'en swayed by breezes and treeses, an' doves an' loves, an' if she don't drop like a ripe persimmon, yer can call me the little end of nuthin'."

"I'll try your plan, Jedge; it can't do any harm, anyway."

"'Tain't no woman kin fly in the face of sich po'try as you write, Titcomb, an' I kin already see the lady a-writin' her name, Mrs. Titcomb Jebb," said the old philosopher slowly and impressively.

"Mrs. Titcomb Jebb," echoed the grocer, happy in the newness of the sound. But he shook his head dubiously. "Jedge, it seems like an impossibility."

"Titcomb," said the old man, rising and going

toward the door, "I've blown out the candle more times than you have, therefore I sez I kin see the lady a-writin' her name Mrs.—Titcomb—Jebb." And the Jedge and his Llewellyn were homeward bound.

CHAPTER VI

WHEN THE LORD MADE THE RIVER

Egg-picking was long past; Easter had come and gone; the frost had vanished before the warm breath of spring and the verdure of nature was again on the earth. June in all her splendor was here. Miss Latham's school term was nearing its end. Examinations were over, and little remained but to pick up the odds and ends of the scholastic year and prepare for the closing exercises.

The day was almost sultry and the morning sun was streaming through the windows of the school-room. That restlessness so common among children, when the days of study have past and the pleasures of summer are calling, was particularly observable, and, in flagrant cases, called forth the teacher's mild censure.

One boy alone was quiet. It was Sandy. With elbows resting on the desk, his hands supporting his head, he was gazing half dreamily and wistfully out and beyond the open window near him.

The soft breeze came from the south, lazily rustling the leaves of the open book before him, and then, as if tired of the exertion, died away.

Turning from his reverie, Sandy sighed, then closing the book, looked at Gilbert sitting next to him, and said: "Don't yer think the Lord wuz pleased when He made the river?"

Gilbert raised his head and gazed smilingly at the other boy: "You remember what the Bible says, Sandy, *And God saw everything that He had made and, behold, it was very good.*"

"Yes, I heerd that afore. I disremember jest this minit who said it. It might 'a' been the minister, or mebbe Mr. Parker in Sunday-school, but I heerd it somewhere. An' I knows it's true, 'cause it's in the Bible. But is ther' anythin' in the Bible specially 'bout our river?"

"Hardly," answered the little fellow. "The Bible, of course, does speak of rivers, particularly in Revelation; but, why should it mention just our river, Sandy?"

"I don't know nuthin' 'bout t'other people's rivers, but I does know our'n backwards, upside down, from the Pencote clear to an' beyond Oyster Shell Landin', an' that's mostly all of it. An' it's great! An' that's why I thought mebbe the

Lord wuz specially pleased with the makin' of it, an' said so in the Bible."

"No, Sandy," answered Gilbert, "I've read the Bible from Genesis to the end, and I'm sure there's nothing about our river."

"Now yer look a-here, little codger,"—a sudden animation taking possession of the older boy, as with forefinger moving up and down, he began: "Let's take the river from year in to year out, from January to January. When New Year comes it gits too cold fer to sail a boat or hunt ducks; the river freezes up so yer kin skate, an' play shinny, an' cut yer name on the ice. An' it stays frozen, off an' on, till March. Then the thaw comes an' yer go fishin'. An' the river gits itself full of 'em. Yer put out yer seine an' yer haul in shad an' herrin', an' yer drap yer lines overboard an' yank in rock, an' perch, an' catties, an' so on.

"Then the river sez, 'spec' yer want a change,' an' it's gittin' roun' spring. The jack-snipes are dartin' an' turnin' like cork-screws, an' the yaller-shanks an' killdees are hoppin' 'long the shore, an' ye're havin' a time with 'em. Then yer goes Mayin' an' watches the swallows skimmin', jest gittin' yer second wind like. But the river don't rest; it sez to yer, it's mos' time to go swimmin'. An' the water gits warm an' yer tumble in ev'ry day jest as much as yer like, an' about the time the air gits chilly, and ye're tired of swimmin', the ortolan an' reed-birds commences to fly, an' then when they git scarce the ducks are swoopin' down on yer decoys, an' afore yer know it, it's January ag'in."

Sandy once more looked out of the window in the direction of his beloved river, and drew a long sigh. To him it meant a world of beautiful dreams.

As a little child he had gathered shells and pebbles along its shore. When the tide was low he had splashed and waded in its pools. Down by the Old Burnt Bridge he had learned to swim, and from Pencote to Bladensburg he had paddled and sailed, and shot and fished since earliest boyhood.

And the river! Is it as beautiful as Sandy dreams?

Its sinuous channel now winds in and out of the tangle of wild rice marshes; now silently sweeps abreast the banks of green beyond the dotted beds of wankapins and lily-pads; now circles past great emerald hills whose bases are edged with ivoried sand, and shadowed by the drooping limbs of weeping willows and gray-hued boughs of mighty oaks.

Again, straightened and stately, it courses on 'twixt lines of latticed reeds, and now, spreading over amber-colored shoals, deep-chested coves and beds of matted grass, it flows with rhythmic grace to meet the waters of the greater stream beyond.

Sandy's enthusiasm over the river was quickly absorbed by Gilbert. The impatience of the scholars, generally, was brought to an end by the ringing of the bell and the dismissal of the pupils for the day. When the two boys were outside the building, Sandy said:

"Gil, if yer don't mind, please take my books home with you, an' I'll come fer 'em after supper. I wants to see somebody 'bout somethin' orful partic'lar, an' I'm in er all-fired hurry."

"I'll go with you, if you want," volunteered Gilbert.

"I'd ruther not have yer, Gil, an' don't ask me no questions an' I won't tell yer no lies. Mebbe to-night, if I sees yer, I'll tell yer why."

And Sandy was off like the wind. He stopped in front of a little frame house, the Jedge's humble abode, and found that worthy seated in a

SANDY FOUND THE JEDGE SEATED ON THE PORCH   *Page 97*

large chair on the pleasant porch, back of the kitchen.

The old man was busily engaged in whittling smooth the knots in a long thin hickory pole intended, clearly, for a fishing-rod, as evidenced by the cords, hooks and sinkers lying about.

As Sandy drew near, the Jedge exclaimed: "Hello, Sandy, yer seem to be in er hurry."

"Yes, Jedge, I want er have a talk with yer 'bout a boat, an' I wants to git it off my mind as soon as possible."

"Sail right in, my boy, I'm a-list'nin'."

"Jedge, I was out on the river yesterday lookin' at that boat yer give me two years ago, an' I finds it's done for."

"I spec' the worms must have nearly chawed it up afore this, Sandy, for it's a powerful old boat."

"But it's done fer now, Jedge. When I tried to haul her out o' the shed to float her, she jest drapped to pieces, she was so rottin. She's petered out, sure 'nuff."

"She wuz a good one, Sandy, an' no mistake. I built her nigh on ter twenty-five years ago. I don't think boats nowadays are put up like they wuz in my time."

"I spec' that's so, Jedge, an' that's why I come

to see yer. D'yer think I kin build one as good as her?"

"Are yer askin' me first hand, Sandy?"

"I haven't breathed it to a soul, Jedge."

After a long pause: "D'yer inten' buildin' a keel, or a flat-bottom?"

"A flat-bottom jumper, Jedge."

Another long pause, during which the Jedge kept on smoothing the knots in the fishing-rod.

"Sandy, I've watched yer caref'ly these many years, an' I've seen all along that ye're a biddable boy, an' I haven't failed to tell other folks that ye're a most biddable boy. But I must say, if I don't want to monkey with the truth, to build a boat like that 'ere one I gave yer takes a powerful intellect, to say nothin' of hereditary propensities, as scientific men observe when they mean ye're born a-knowin' how."

Sandy's face wore a look of bitter disappointment.

"To put up a boat what won't spring no leak, an' will float an' don't turn over if yer forgit to part yer hair in the middle, is a mighty big job," continued the old man.

"Well, Jedge, don't yer think I might try?"

"That's jest what I wuz gittin' to, Sandy. I

wants yer to do the trick right here in my back yard, under my instructions, which I will give free-gratis-fer-nuthin', without pay, an' if we don't put up the best jumper in this 'ere neck o' the woods, we needn't say so."

"Thank yer kindly, Jedge. How much will it cost fer the stuff to build 'er?" and Sandy waited eagerly, while the Jedge made a mental calculation.

"Lemme see; we want two seven-eighths planks o' dressed cedar fer the sides, 'bout four oak knees, one midship mold, a cedar bottom, oak transom, seats an' rudder, bow piece, nails, screws, rivets, oar-locks, stuff to caulk her, sails an' a few other things, besides. I should think we could build her fer eight dollars."

"D'yer think she could be built fer that much, Jedge?" asked Sandy anxiously.

"Mebbe, a quarter or fifty cents more, if yer wants to put on luggs; but I spec' that will be 'nough to put up a good boat. How much has yer salted away as a starter, Sandy?"

"I've got thirteen cents now, an' I'm goin' to git fifteen cents more fer carryin' in the minister's coal when I leave here. An' that ain't very much, is it, Jedge?"

"No, that ain't very much, Sandy. If I wuzn't jest a bit strapped fer money, I'd lend yer the balance. But what's in yer mind to git it?"

"I thought mebbe I could go out afore light a-fishin' an' peddle what I ketched, an' that wouldn't be hurtin' nobody."

"That's all right, Sandy, an' I'll speak to Titcomb Jebb to-night, an' mebbe he'll take some of yer ketchin' fer the store, an' that would help amazin'. I'll see him afore bedtime, an' you see him fust thing in the mornin', an' find what he'll take of yer ketchin's."

"I'll do it," said Sandy, "an' mebbe, afore I knows it, I'll have the spondulix, and we kin commence on her. I hope the fish 'll bite, at least eight dollars' worth, mighty soon."

The boy went straight to the minister's house, and shoveled and stored coal for three hours, for which he received the fifteen cents already mentioned as part of his assets. Then he hurried home, and after eating his simple meal he went to Gilbert's for his books.

In the months that these boys had become friends, Gilbert had often invited Sandy to his home, but a certain diffidence had caused the older boy always to offer some excuse for staying away.

The size of the house, and the general air of material superiority on the part of Gilbert's family, were largely responsible for this shyness.

Sandy had hoped, as he approached Colonel Franklin's residence, that Gilbert would be under the trees in the yard, or out in the front, but he was disappointed. He stood hesitating for some time, and watched the dwelling until he saw the lights shining brightly through the parlor windows.

Finally he concluded to go around by the kitchen, hoping to meet a servant, who would get his books and allow him to leave unnoticed. He walked slowly up the path that was hidden in the shadow of tall trees. As he neared the house, his attention was arrested by the sounds of music from within. Piano and violin were in duet, and as he leaned against a tree, the clear soft tones of the violin sang out Schumann's exquisite *Träumerei.*

"That sounds jest like Heaven," he murmured, and, creeping toward the window, he made an effort to see who the players were.

It was too far from the ground to peer in, so softly he retraced his steps toward the trees. Then, as if by inspiration, he climbed a maple directly in front of the parlor, and, sitting astride one of its boughs, full fifteen feet above the ground, he leaned against the trunk, and looked into the window below.

"Well, I'll be darned! The little codger never told me he could play the fiddle!" he exclaimed, as he saw Gilbert with a violin, playing for the pleasure of his family.

The Spring Song, followed by *Consolation* from Mendelssohn's *Songs Without Words*, floated out into the velvety June night and held Sandy fascinated and silent under the spell of melody.

When Gilbert had laid aside his instrument, he came out on the porch with his father. They seated themselves in a large chair, the boy nestling close, pressing his cheek against the parent's.

"I don't know what was the matter with Sandy to-day; he just flew away after school," said the son, as if the older boy were a subject of paramount interest to every one at all times.

"Perhaps he had some errand for his mother," suggested the father tritely.

"No, I don't think it was that. He was talking about the river, and I believe that had something to do with it."

"Maybe it had; who can tell?" said the father, with commonplace attention.

"He told me though, if I didn't ask him any questions he would tell me no lies, and maybe he might tell me to-night, but I'm awfully afraid he won't come."

"Yes, he will, little codger, fer he's here now," came a voice from above, much to the surprise of the Franklins, father and son.

"Why, Sandy, is that you up there?" asked Gilbert joyously.

"I've been up here a-list'nin' to yer playin' the fiddle, an' yer come out afore I could sneak down. So don't think I wuz eavesdroppin'."

Sandy lowered himself from the tree, and Gilbert took his hand and pulled the bashful boy toward the porch.

Colonel Franklin gave Sandy a cordial invitation to sit down and feel fully at home. After much demurring, the boy took a place on the top step of the porch where he was joined at once by Gilbert, the father in the meantime enjoying his evening smoke.

"'Twuzn't no great secret I had on my mind this afternoon, Gil, but I don't like ter say I'm going ter do a thing unless I am sure I kin do it."

"What can't you do, Sandy?"

"That's jest it. I wuz afeard I might not be able to build a jumper, an' I didn't know exactly what 'twould cost, so afore I would tell you anythin' about it, I asked the Jedge fust."

"And what did the Jedge say?" asked Gilbert, greatly interested.

"It can be done fust-rate fer eight dollars, an he's goin' to help me." Then Sandy unfolded his plans. Gilbert offered to pay half the cost, but Sandy would not agree.

"I wants to own ev'ry nail in her, from top-mas' to keel, from stem to gudjin. I wants to enj'y myself invitin' yer to sail in her, Gil, an' I can't if ye're half-boss."

"I'll lend you the money," persisted the younger.

"Not muchee, little codger. I'm a-goin' to git it by the sweat o' my brow, ketchin' fish."

"But it will take some time to catch and sell eight dollars' worth."

"I knows, but the Jedge is goin' to ask Mr. Jebb to buy what I ketch, an' that'll help along."

"Fish is mighty good food," said Gilbert, his face brightening with a sudden idea, "and I believe people should eat more of it than they do.

Everybody should eat fish, at least twice a day; don't you think so, father?" asked the little fellow.

"Medical men say much in favor of the beneficial effects of a fish diet. No doubt there is truth in this," spoke the father.

"I'm sure there is, and I'm going to study up on it right away," added the young son.

While the two boys sat talking of the boat, Gilbert's little sister came out to bid father and brother good night. Gilbert, calling her over, said:

"Lily, this is Sandy Coggles, my Sandy."

"Yes, I know Sandy," she exclaimed joyfully. "Gil told me all about you, lots and lots of times. You aren't afraid of anything, ghosts, or pirates, or demons, or burglars, or anybody else, even if you've got one hand tied behind you."

Sandy remained bashfully dumb.

"I must go to bed now, so I'll say good night," —and lovingly she put her arms around his neck and pressed her childish lips to his forehead. "That's one 'cause Gil loves you,"—then turning his left cheek toward her,—"that's another 'cause I love Gil,"—and again turning his head so as to present his right cheek,—"and that's one for good measure, and 'cause I love anybody Gil loves. Good night."

It was the first time in Sandy's life that he had been kissed, save by his mother, and even his freckles grew browner.

The child and father went into the house leaving the boys alone outside. There was a long silence, while they both lay back-down upon the steps, and Sandy finally spoke.

"Yer never told me yer could play the fiddle, little codger, an' I never know'd there wuz so much music in one till I heard yer play."

"Oh, pshaw!" said Gilbert carelessly. "I've played the violin since I was six. You know I was in the house so much, it seemed just the thing to do."

"Yes, an' it wuz the thing to do, an' I'm glad yer done it. My! when I wuz a-settin' up there list'nin' I jest saw Heaven. I never knew afore jest what Heaven looked like. But I kind er saw it plain, 'specially when yer played that 'ere third piece. What der yer name it?"

"That was a piece by Mendelssohn, called *Consolation*."

"Was yer teach'd it?" asked the other earnestly.

"Oh, not exactly; I had teachers when I studied, but not for that particular piece."

"Well, I felt it in my bones. I ain't heerd nuthin' like that in a 'coon's age, no, not even afore that. It sounded too good to be teach'd."

"That's a funny idea," said the younger, smiling at Sandy's enthusiasm, "perhaps you never heard as fine a violin as mine."

"Mebbe not," said Sandy, "but yer fiddle didn't play by itself."

"No, that is so, but my violin is a very rare make, and I love to play on it," earnestly responded Gilbert.

"Is it better than any other fiddle?" questioned Sandy, still doubting the power of the instrument without the player's skill.

"My father says," answered the younger, "violins are like women. The one you love is the best in the world; so I think mine is."

"I'm a-takin' that all in, little codger, but I sticks to my p'int to the close; fiddle er no fiddle, if the angels didn't have no hand in the playin' o' that 'ere piece, then I sez I've got no license to go to bed in the dark."

He walked slowly down the path, stopped a few times and looked back. Gilbert was still sitting on the porch, his eyes following the retreating figure of his friend.

Suddenly Sandy stopped and retraced his steps.

"I came near forgittin' what I was goin' to say, Gil. I told yer I wuz a-goin' to build a boat, an' how I was a-goin' to git the money by sellin' fish, but I didn't tell yer I was goin' to call her the *Lillian,* jest like yer little sister."

And he was off.

CHAPTER VII

MR. JEBB'S WOOING

"It beats all how that boy hates to get up,"—and Mrs. Foley called for the tenth time. "Are you up, up there? I do believe boys are like those other reptiles and would sleep six months runnin', if you'd let 'em." She stood with broom raised in the air, about to descend on the cupboard, then with a stroke of it against the door she called again:

"Thomas, are you up, up there?"

A mumbling sound from above and all was still again.

"You imp of darkness! I have to drive you to bed every night, and I have to drive you out of bed in the mornin', and it's nothing but drive, drive, drive. Here it's nearly six o'clock, there's not a drop of water in the rain-barrel, and I've got three washin's to do, to say nothin' of Sukey Bell a-comin' here to-morrer to help iron. Get up; do you hear me?"

Another mumbling was heard from above.

"Thomas Foley," called his mother again, "do you hear me callin', or shall I come up and make you hear?"

"What's the matter, d'yer want ter wake the dead?" snarled a voice from up stairs. "I heerd yer callin' an' answered yer."

"Why didn't you answer louder, and not let me wear myself out a-hollerin' at you?" shouted the mother.

" 'Tain't no fault o' mine if yer can't hear; better git er ear-trumpet."

"Are—you—up, Thomas?" called back the irate Mrs. Foley.

"Old Nick hisself couldn't sleep when you're round bellerin' like all out-doors from mornin' to night down there," answered the boy, sitting up in bed and shaking the shuck mattresses vigorously.

"Hurry up down. I want you to fill the rainbarrel, it's getting after six." Then in softer, and more entreating tones, "Hurry up down, that's a good boy."

"I'll be down directly, mother dear," came in perfect imitation of the inflections of his parent's voice, and the young rascal dropped again on the bed, and, turning so carefully that not the faintest rustle was heard, curled up snugly and closed his eyes. His brain dozed and his body rested, but his ear was on the alert.

"She's cleanin' up the kitchen," said the ear, "an' sweepin' the dirt inter the gutter. She's list'nin' to Nellie Pendleton's mocking-bird whistlin' fer the doctor's dog that's runnin' up and down the street lookin' fer his master."

The auricular picket reported the mother's return to the house and her determined strides as she approached the stairs leading to the bedroom.

"Tom Foley, I'll give you jest two minits to get down stairs, or I'll skin you alive."

The boy jumped from the bed, made a dash for his clothes in the corner of the room, and hastily dressed. Then calling, "Don't fash yerself, I'm puttin' on my duds as fast as I kin," he shortly appeared at the landing. "Fooled yer that time, didn't I? Spec' yer thought I wuz in bed a-snoozin', when I was makin' my twilight an' jest dyin' to see yer."

"Now do hurry, Tom, and fetch the water," requested Mrs. Foley coaxingly, making at the same time a vain effort to smooth the rumpled collar on her son's shirt.

"Yer ain't goin' to make me work like a nigger

afore I've had my grub, are yer?" whimpered the boy.

"Jest run and get me a pail of water, and I'll have your breakfast ready when you get back," soothingly said the mother, preparing a place at the table for Tom.

"I won't get no water till I'm fed. My stomach feels like my throat's cut. I want er eat fust."

"I never did starve you, Tom, and if I give you both molasses and butter for your bread, some honey, fried eggs, cold meat and hot coffee, will you promise to carry the water and won't run away like you did yesterday?"

"Gimme my grub fust, I ain't goin' to promise nuthin' while I'm starvin'."

The mother placed the food before her boy and he ate voraciously. After he had devoured everything on the table, he got up and walked to the door leading to the street. When he was well without, he called to his mother: "Eh, old woman, carry yer own water; over the river, ta-ta!" and away he went as fast as his miserable legs could carry him.

Mrs. Foley, standing in the doorway, heard his parting shot, and stood motionless in a stare as he scampered away.

"What will become of him? 'Tain't no use tryin' kindness, he's too ornery to appreciate it. It's the sins of the father visitin' the child, and God knows, he's gettin' more and more like Dennis Foley every day." Sadly, and with just the suspicion of a tear, she picked up the water-buckets and started for the pump.

Sandy and Titcomb were in earnest conversation as Mrs. Foley drew near. The grocer left the other and walked toward the widow.

"A very beautiful morning, Mrs. Foley," he began.

"I hope it is to the rest of the world, Mr. Jebb; it's anything but beautiful to me."

"I sincerely trust your health is good,"—this with great solicitude.

"'Tain't no bodily ailment, Mr. Jebb; it's that boy of mine. He no sooner stuffs himself than he lights out, and lets me fetch water and work like a heathen Turk."

"Allow me to fill the buckets for you,"—offering to take them from her.

"Oh, law, no indeed, Mr. Jebb! If it was jest one pailful I wouldn't mind, but I can't let you work for me." She moved toward the pump.

Titcomb gently took the pails, saying, "Mrs.

Foley, if you'll watch the store Sandy and I will fill the barrels for you."

When the man and boy were beyond earshot, Jebb said: "Sandy, I've promised to buy all the fish you catch, at five cents a dozen."

"That's what I understan'," answered the youth.

"Now, Sandy, if you will fill Mrs. Foley's rain-barrels every day I'll give you ten cents a dozen for all you bring me. Is it a bargain?"

"Jest watch me an' see if it ain't a bargain," Sandy quickly replied.

"Remember though, on your honor, not a word to the widow, except that you are anxious to carry the water."

"I'll 'tend to that, Mr. Jebb, don't fear,"—and Sandy winked knowingly.

When they returned with the water, Mrs. Foley had seated herself in a chair fashioned from an old flour-barrel. The boy, still holding the buckets, said:

"Mrs. Foley, I've jest been itchin' to carry water for anybody as would let me. Yer see, down at my house, the landlord, he built an artesian well by the kitchen an' the pump nozzle comes right in the door, an' I don't git no more exercise, 'cause the water runs by itself. If yer don't really mind, I'll be much obliged if yer'll let me fill yer rain-barrels every day."

"Oh, Sandy," said Mrs. Foley, "I don't know whether I ought to let you, when I have a good-for-nothing boy that ought to do it for me."

"Mebbe Tom's got the spring fever, an' it's struck in. I jest escaped it by the skin o' my teeth, a-sweatin' it off choppin' kindlin's an' that. Why, I'm jest itchin' to fill yer rain-barrels."

"Well, as you want to so badly, I'll let you, and thank you for your kindness."

"Yer jest set down an' talk to Mr. Jebb, an' watch me enj'y myself." Off went Sandy, swinging the buckets in circles about his head.

"What a blessing a boy like Sandy is!" said the grocer, pointing in the direction of the pump.

"Just one in a million; no monkey-shines; 'tends to business strictly. Sandy is a prize package in a pile of blanks," replied Mrs. Foley.

"I believe he will make a fine man," added the grocer.

"Mebbe, if he don't get sp'iled in the makin'."

"But why should he?" asked Titcomb.

"Mr. Jebb, boys grow into very foxy men sometimes. There was my man, Dennis Foley.

It seemed as though butter wouldn't melt in his mouth when he was courtin' me."

"Those must have been happy days," half-whispered the grocer sentimentally.

"I thought so, then," wearily spoke the other. "Dennis chased and chased and chased me for months, afore I married him, and then,—I had to do the chasin'."

"All men are not so changeable, Mrs. Foley."

"Mebbe not all, but they're a mighty foxy crowd, as a rule, and I have no confidence in 'em."

"Oh, well, perhaps some day your views will change."

"I ain't seein' how they will," mechanically replied the widow.

"How do you know but, sometime, somebody will come knocking at your door?"

"And you bet I'll be out," laughingly said Mrs. Foley.

"Do you like poetry?" tenderly inquired Titcomb, remembering the Jedge's injunction.

"Po'try? Po'try? That was Dennis' strong suit. Afore we were married he used to write on every piece of paper he came across, 'If you love me as I love you, no knife can cut our love in two;' but after we settled down, he was shoutin',

'We won't go home till mornin',' and he never did, unless he was carried. Thank you, but no po'try in mine."

"Ah, yes, but life is hopeless without poetry," earnestly remonstrated the grocer.

"Fiddlesticks, Mr. Jebb! po'try don't go with a hard day's washin'. Poor folks like me don't have time for such foolishness,"—and she snapped her fingers scornfully.

"You should find time."

"When?" she asked.

"Now—any time. Every minute counts in this world. Sandy is bringing water; you can't do your washing until the barrels are full; what better could you do than hear a few lines of my poetry?"

"Your po'try?" exclaimed the widow in amazement. "That's a horse of another color, Mr. Jebb. I was afraid you meant the 'no-knife-can-cut-our-love-in-two' kind, but *your* po'try, that's all right. The one about granulated sugar is mighty good; Sukey Bell sings it to a nice chune when she sprinkles the clothes."

"What I'm about to read to you is a poem entitled *Juno*. It is a secret avowal—as it were—so to speak—I might say—of a lonely heart to a fair lady." Clearing his throat, Titcomb read:

> "When the jacksnipe leaves the marsh,
>   And the robin seeks its nest,
>   When the nightingale
>   Spreads out his tail,
>   And scoots for the Golden West;
>   My love, I will come to thee,
>   'Way down by the trysting tree.
>
> My love, I will come to thee,
>   Wherever you may be,
>   In trouble dire,
>   Or house on fire,
>   My love, I will come to thee."

"I do declare, Mr. Jebb, that just makes me feel goose-fleshy all over." Then watching Sandy: "I really b'lieve that boy will run that pump dry afore he fills the barrels. Excuse me interruptin', I ain't used to po'try like that."

Mr. Jebb went on:

> "When the tomtit tunes his pipe,
>   And the clock strikes half-past eight,
>   Oh, why; oh, why,
>   Do I sadly sigh,
>   And say, though it's getting late,
>   My love, I will come to thee,
>   'Way down by the trysting tree?
>
> My love, I will come to thee,
>   Wherever you may be,
>   Though it may be wet,
>   You need not fret,
>   My love, I will come to thee."

"That's mighty spunky, and I like spunky people," said the listener. " 'Tain't every fellow would do that, leastwise, if he didn't have an umbrella and gums,"—and she again looked toward the pump. "I do believe Sandy will wear himself out fillin' that barrel. Pardon my lack of parlor manners and a-continually interruptin' you, Mr. Jebb. Please go on with the story; it's awfully interestin'."

"This is the last verse with the refrain,"—and Titcomb stood up.

"When the turtle-dovelets coo,
This vow I humbly make;
Noon or night,
Dark or light,
Tired, hungry, asleep, awake,
My love, I will come to thee,
'Way down by the trysting tree.

My love, I will come to thee,
Though you live beyond the sea,
And the whale may wail,
And the hail may hail,
But, my love, I will come to thee."

"It's beautiful," said Mrs. Foley, "it's all so nacherel; you can see him all the time. And what did you say was the lady's name?"

"Juno," he replied.

"Well, Juno ought to feel as happy as a clam

at high tide," said Mrs. Foley. "I would if I was Juno."

"Would you?" said Jebb quickly and with unreserved enthusiasm.

"Yes, I would, if I hadn't no encumbrance, and —Sandy—Sandy, law, boy, how much water have you took to the house? It ain't no steamboat."

Sandy came, stood beside the widow, and spoke: "I've filled the barrils, an' set the b'iler on the stove. Yer bluin' tank is full, chock-a-block, an' yer scrubbin' tub's runnin' over, an' I thank yer, Mrs. Foley, cordial fer lettin' me carry the water."

The widow looked at the two fully half a minute. Man and boy stared into vacancy and moved with a suggestion of fidgets.

"It beats me," she said slowly.

Titcomb and Sandy watched her as she walked to her house.

And thus ended the first chapter of Jebb's wooing.

CHAPTER VIII

THE SCHOOL EXERCISES

"Boys!" Miss Latham stood behind the desk and cast a benign look over her pupils. Books were closed, whispering ceased, and the school awaited the teacher's further remarks.

"I desire to state that the scholastic year closes on Friday next. It has been a year fraught with interest, and I trust its manifold opportunities have not been lost on any one of you. I am about to prepare the program for our final exercises on Monday, and I wish to ask what scholars are prepared to volunteer numbers for the occasion."

A long silence ensued, and then Sandy raised his hand.

"What is it, Sandy?"

"Miss Maisie, I wish yer would ask the little feller to bring his fiddle an' play. He jest beats anythin' yer ever heerd playin'."

"What do you say, Gilbert?"

"Why, Miss Maisie, if you would really like it, I'll bring my violin with pleasure."

"It will be delightful, and I thank you; also Sandy for the suggestion." Up went Sandy's hand again.

"Mebbe the little codger'll speak that piece, *The Charge of the Light Brigade*. I heerd him say it an' it sounded like it really happened. Me an' Dink an' Curley heerd him say it."

"Gilbert, may we presume on your good nature?"

"Of course, Miss Maisie, if you care to have me to do both."

Sandy patted Gilbert on the shoulder approvingly, for his cheerful willingness.

Dink next attracted the attention of Miss Latham: "Well, Elijah, what is it?"

"Please ma'am," said Elijah, alias Dink, "Mr. Jebb read me a piece of po'try an' gimme a stick of peppermint fer list'nin' t'other day, an' I spec' he'll do it ag'in if yer ask him."

"A good suggestion, Elijah; I will see him about it personally."

"Lemme go an' tell him," volunteered Dink, as visions of more candy loomed up large before him.

"No," observed the teacher thoughtfully, "I think perhaps it would be better for me to write a note and invite him to take part in our exercises."

"That's all right, ma'am, if he brings 'nough knickknacks fer list'nin'. I'm powerful fond o' Mr. Jebb's po'try, when the knickknacks is thrown in, an' that's why I'd like to go on the errand to him."

"I'll allow you to deliver the note to Mr. Jebb."

"That'll do most as good as if I tol' him to his face," said Dink with evident satisfaction.

"Now, let me see," said the teacher, drumming a pencil against her teeth. "First, we'll have a prayer by the Reverend Nathaniel Mosher, then a song by the class, *Oh, How I Love the Merry, Merry Sunshine;* next a recitation, *The Charge of the Light Brigade;* address to the school by Mr. W. B. Parker; violin solo by Gilbert Franklin; and possibly a poem by Mr. Jebb, followed by presentation of the medal and premium books, and closing with the benediction. Just before the distribution of prizes I shall make a few remarks, and that will be sufficient for the occasion. Remember, you may invite your relatives and friends; the hour will be eleven A. M."

Monday came, and with it enough visitors to crowd the little school-room. The Franklins.

Mrs. Dabney and Zorah, Mrs. Foley, Mrs. Coggles and Titcomb Jebb were prominent in the gathering. Near the door stood the Jedge, making himself useful by directing the visitors to their seats, and, with kindly comments, spreading a spirit of good humor.

"These 'ere occasions," he was saying to Doctor Mosher, "are chock full of interest to them folks that feels the need of eddication. Eddication an' book-l'arnin' are all right when yer can't nacherly git the heft o' things. I seen a pig in a circus onct, an' he could play cards an' drink whisky. He wuz jest eddicated to it. Eddication's great. I believe in the young idea l'arnin' to shoot, even if it don't hit nuthin'."

The exercises opened with prayer. Gilbert's recitation was a great success, and his violin solo met with storms of applause. As it died away, Mr. Jebb walked to the platform, took out a roll of manuscript, and looked over the assembled gathering with a kindly eye and cordial air. He spoke:

"Miss Latham, ladies and gentlemen, boys and girls, and all others: You will perceive on perusing the order of exercises for this most important day, that my name is down for an original poem, written expressly for the occasion. This wayward thought I have entitled, *The Feast of the Monkeys.*"

Jebb read slowly and distinctly:

THE FEAST OF THE MONKEYS

In days of old,
So I've been told,
The monkeys gave a feast.
They sent out cards,
With kind regards,
To every bird and beast.
The guests came dressed,
In fashion's best,
Unmindful of expense;
Except the whale,
Whose swallowtail,
Was " soaked " for fifty cents.

The guests checked wraps,
Canes, hats and caps;
And when that task was done,
The footman he
With dignitee,
Announced them one by one.
In Monkey Hall,
The host met all,
And hoped they'd feel at ease,
"I scarcely can,"
Said the Black and Tan,
"I'm busy hunting fleas."

"While waiting for
A score or more
Of guests," the hostess said,

"We'll have the Poodle
  Sing *Yankee Doodle*,
  A-standing on his head.
  And when this through,
  Good Parrot, you,
  Please show them how you swear
"Oh, dear; don't cuss,"
  Cried the Octopus,
  And he walked off on his ear.

The Orang-Outang
A sea-song sang,
About a Chimpanzee
Who went abroad,
In a drinking gourd,
To the coast of Barberee.
Where he heard one night,
When the moon shone bright,
A school of mermaids pick
Chromatic scales
From off their tails,
And did it mighty slick.

"All guests are here,
  To eat the cheer,
  And dinner's served, my Lord."
The butler bowed;
And then the crowd
Rushed in with one accord.
The fiddler-crab
Came in a cab,
And played a piece in C;
While on his horn,
The Unicorn
Blew. *You'll Remember Me.*

To give a touch
Of early Dutch
To this great feast of feasts,
I'll drink ten drops
Of Holland's schnapps,"
Spoke out the King of Beasts.
That must taste fine,"
Said the Porcupine,
Did you see him smack his lip?"
I'd smack mine, too,"
Cried the Kangaroo,
If I didn't have the pip."

The Lion stood,
And said: "Be good
Enough to look this way;
Court Etiquette
Do not forget,
And mark well what I say:
My royal wish
Is ev'ry dish
Be tasted first by me."
Here's where I smile,"
Said the Crocodile,
And he climbed an axle-tree.

The soup was brought,
And quick as thought,
The Lion ate it all.
You can't beat that,"
Exclaimed the Cat,
For monumental gall."
The soup," all cried.
Gone," Leo replied,
'Twas just a bit too thick."
When we get through,"
Remarked the Gnu,
I'll hit him with a brick."

The Tiger stepped,
Or, rather, crept,
Up where the Lion sat.
"O, mighty boss
I'm at a loss
To know where I am at.
I came to-night
With appetite
To drink and also eat;
As a Tiger grand,
I now demand,
I get there with both feet."

The Lion got
All-fired hot
And in a passion flew.
"Get out," he cried,
"And save your hide,
You most offensive *You*."
"I'm not afraid,"
The Tiger said,
"I know what I'm about."
But the Lion's paw
Reached the Tiger's jaw,
And he was good and out.

The salt-sea smell
Of Mackerel,
Upon the air arose;
Each hungry guest
Great joy expressed,
And "sniff!" went every nose
With glutton look
The Lion took
The spiced and sav'ry dish.
Without a pause
He worked his jaws,
And gobbled all the fish.

Then ate the roast,
The quail on toast,
The pork, both fat and lean;
The jam and lamb,
The potted ham,
And drank the kerosene.
He raised his voice:
"Come, all rejoice,
You've seen your monarch dine."
"Never again,"
Clucked the Hen,
And all sang *Old Lang Syne*.

Jebb rolled his manuscript carefully, and put it back into his pocket.

"I desire to state, boys, that the Jedge will hand each of you a package of knickknacks, as you file out after the exercises."

"I know'd he brung some," whispered Dink; "there ain't no po'try that fits in with knickknacks like Mr. Jebb's, an' I wuz anxious all the time he wuz readin' fer fear he had fergotten 'em. Jimmineddy, I wish the show wuz over now!"

The grocer's announcement met with vociferous applause. As conclusion, Miss Latham called the names of those pupils fortunate enough to receive prizes.

The gold medal went to Gilbert for general excellence in scholarship and deportment.

"In English grammar and history," read Miss

Latham from the list, "Master James Bray." A large-headed, undersized boy came forward to claim his book.

"For reading and Constitution of the United States, Master Sidney Robinson." A nervous lad, with puffy eyes, walked to the desk and accepted eagerly his volume, returning hastily to his seat.

"For penmanship and spelling, Master Edward Grimes." As the aforesaid youngster sought his place, he scanned with eager eyes the title of the book that had been handed him.

At this point, Miss Latham stepped forward, and spoke while every member of the class listened with breathless attention.

"Before bestowing the last premium, a few words will perhaps not be amiss. I have in my class one whose life has not been rich in the opportunities vouchsafed most boys. His father fought in the war, and was sacrificed on the altar of patriotism. Up to within a year this lad has helped to support his mother by selling papers, and turning a hand to any other honest endeavor. I take extreme pleasure in announcing that the prize for arithmetic and geography is awarded to Master Alexander Coggles."

Gilbert was on his feet in an instant and jumped for sheer joy.

"Hurrah for Sandy!" he cried; "come on, boys, three cheers for Sandy Coggles!"

During the outburst of shouts and applause, the fortunate pupil went forward, with face red and perspiring, and received his prize from the minister.

"Yer could 'a' knocked me down with a feather, I wuz so flabbergasted," explained Sandy, as he described his sensations, "an' I'd never have got it, little codger, if you hadn't fust show'd me."

The benediction was spoken and the audience slowly dispersed.

Sandy good-naturedly took Gilbert's violin case out of his hand, and, insisting on carrying it, walked ahead.

Dark-eyed Zorah, finding her way through the crowd, intercepted Gilbert and asked demurely, "Do you remember me?"

"Don't I, though?" answered the little fellow gallantly.

"Teacher hasn't sent me home once since I saw you," volunteered Zorah.

"And I trust she never will again," added the other.

"I've been thinking lots about you,"—this very archly.

"Oh, say now"—began Gilbert, but her earnestness kept back the banter that was on his lips.

"I remember what you said about gipsy queens, about their hair, their eyes and their skin. Is there anything else lovely about them that you can think of?"

"Oh, lots, and I'll tell you volumes sometime," said the boy.

"But I do want to hear about them now,"—and she clasped her hands in supplication. "Tell me just about one of them, where she lived and how she got married."

"Some day, when I have time, I'll tell you about a beautiful one."

"How old was she?" interrupted Zorah.

"I should say she was all of twelve,"—this with a quizzical and half-amused expression on the part of Gilbert.

"That's just what I am, all of twelve; I was twelve last May. I was born in May, you know, on the fifth, half-past ten. Mama gave me a birthday party, and Aunt Harriet baked the loveliest birthday cake, and Mr. Pigott, he's my sister Crissie's steady company—and they're going to get married just as soon as he gets a raise in wages; which will be next fall if all signs don't fail—and—what was I saying?"

"You spoke of Mr. Pigott."

"Oh, yes, I remember. Mr. Pigott bought twelve real wax candles, and we stuck them all around the cake, one for each year since I was born, and after supper we lit them and they looked beaut'ful. And Dink blew one out when no one was looking, and bit half of it off for chewing gum. When Crissie tried to take it away from him, he swallowed it, wick and all. Oh, we had a dreadful time with Dink that night. He had pains all over."

The voluble maiden stopped short, from sheer exhaustion of lung power.

"My story," continued Gilbert, "will also tell of an old witch."

"I know," broke in the irrepressible Zorah, "witches dance ring-around-rosy, and say 'Double, double, toil and trouble, fire burn, cal'on bubble.' Crissie and Mr. Pigott saw them at Shakespeare's, and the next night they turned down the parlor lamp and showed our folks just what the witches did, and it was dreadful." She rolled her eyes dramatically.

"Well, the old witch was in the habit of making the little black-haired maiden get up early every morning, wash her face, braid her hair, darn her stockings and sew her frock."

"I sewed my frock when I was only five," explained the little coquette, with an air of superiority. "I couldn't put it on afterward because I sewed it together. Aunt Harriet had to rip it, and mama was so mad she nearly made up her mind to whip me. Wasn't that dreadful?"

Her eyes sparkled with suppressed mischief, and, clasping her hand on Gilbert's arm, she whispered, "Please go on."

"I will tell you the whole story," volunteered the boy, "when we get to my house. Under the trees you can listen and I can remember better."

They met Sandy, and the three sat under a great oak in the grove fronting Colonel Franklin's house. Zorah threw herself full length on the grass, and said:

"Please go on."

Sandy lay with his arms under his neck and gazed toward the heavens, waiting. Gilbert, who had read his favorite stories so often that he knew them almost word for word, now began:

THE STORY OF THE QUEEN OF THE GIPSIES

The King of the Gipsies was sitting on his throne in a shaded nook of the woodland dell. He was old and feeble, and knew that, in a few years, at the most, he would be gathered to sleep with those who had reigned before him.

He summoned a page and commanded him to bid his son, the Heir Apparent, to come before his royal presence. In an instant, the Prince entered the chamber, bowing low.

"Sire, what may be your pleasure?"

He spoke reverently, and with deep filial sympathy, as he beheld his aged and withered royal parent.

"My son, the twilight shadows of life's horizon are closing in upon me, and 'tis but meet that you should prepare to assume the scepter when it falls from my grasp."

"Sadly and sorrowfully do I hear you, Sire," solemnly said the Prince Braveheart, for so he was named.

"Harken unto my voice, oh, my son! We desire that you go forth into the great world and choose the one who is to be your wife and the

Queen of the Gipsies, when I have passed beyond, and you are King."

"Most lovable father and gracious sovereign, I pray that you may continue to reign for many years to come, but, if I must go forth and find the maid who is to be my helpmeet and my Queen, I pray you, what must her virtues be?" And Prince Braveheart knelt before the King.

"By the laws written on the tablets of gold, she who is to be the Gipsy Queen must possess three charms beyond those of any other maid in all the world—the brightest eyes, the blackest hair, and the pearliest teeth."

" 'Tis well," said the Prince, kissing his father's proffered hand, and at the same moment receiving the parental blessing.

"Go, my son."

"I will find her, be the quest never so difficult," —and with great respect and ceremony he withdrew from the royal presence.

Prince Braveheart called for his beautiful black charger, and commanding his faithful Yeoman and his equally faithful Bowman to follow, he immediately set out upon his journey. The party traveled from village to village, from town to town, from city to city, and from country to country, gazing into feminine eyes, scrutinizing feminine ringlets, examining feminine teeth, but all to no avail. Again and again their hopes were raised high, only to be dashed to the earth. Eyes would be found divinely beautiful in one maiden; hair as black as night in another; teeth like rows of pearls in a third, but never was a maid found combining all these three attributes. Wearily they wandered on and on.

One afternoon, the Prince with his Yeoman and his Bowman, dust-stained and hungry, sat beside a spring eating their frugal meal. Just as the Prince leaned over the pool of sparkling water to fill his cup, a merry peal of silvery laughter awoke the silence.

"By my halidom!" he cried, almost tumbling into the spring from excitement, "but that is music to mine ear!"

"It are to mine," said the Yeoman.

"It am to mine," said the Bowman.

At which the observant Prince called the Yeoman's attention to his error in using a singular subject with a plural verb, and the Bowman's attention to his use of the first person instead of the third.

As he finished this criticism there bounded into

his presence a beautiful maiden, who, startled at the sight of strangers, stopped short suddenly.

"By my halidom!" repeated the Prince, "this is a rare adventure." And he assumed a deferential attitude before the maiden.

Shyly, but with a trusting heart, she allowed him to lead her to a rustic bench beside the spring.

The Yeoman and the Bowman kept on eating.

"Fair angel," rapturously cried the Prince, "whence, oh, whence came those beautiful eyes?"

"They were plucked from the heavens above, kind sir, where nightly they twinkled," said she demurely.

"And ah!" exclaimed the Prince, "your hair is as black as the raven's wing."

"I'm told a little blacker, kind sir,"—and she smiled bewitchingly.

"And your teeth, radiant one, are veritable pearls."

"And more evenly set than pearls could ever be, dental men have told me." She spoke with a knowledgeable air.

"I am the Prince Braveheart, beauteous vision. I love you, and would make you my bride." And he knelt before her.

The Yeoman and the Bowman kept on eating.

"Good sir, mayhap 'tis best that you should see my grandmother first, for she is the arbiter of my love affairs. She's a very experienced person."

"Your grandmother! and where might she be found?"

"In her hut, high up on the mountain side, just beyond the Glen of the Four-Fanged Wolf." The maid pointed to a spot at the end of a winding road, thousands of feet above them.

The Prince arose quickly and cried to his servitors:

"What ho!"

At which the Yeoman and the Bowman got up, brushed the crumbs from their clothes, lighted their cigarettes, and led forth the beautiful black charger.

"I will run ahead and tell grandmother you are coming."

"Nay, nay, my treasure," said the Prince, intercepting her. "Mount you upon my beautiful black charger, and I will lead him."

Whereupon the little sprite was placed in the saddle, and with the Prince at the charger's head, and the Yeoman and the Bowman bringing up the rear, they wended their way up the lonely mountain road.

As they rode on, Millicentine, which was the maiden's name, had a splendid opportunity to observe the Prince. He was tall, with fine shoulders, and not stout. His hair was a beautiful red, and his face was dotted with delightful little freckles that lent charm and color most unusual.

Millicentine was deeply impressed, and before they had reached her grandmother's cottage she was already in love with the stranger.

Her grandmother sat dozing in the sitting-room and did not hear them coming up the steps. They walked in without knocking, and the Prince, with hat pressed to his heart, said:

"Madam, I am the Prince Braveheart."

The Yeoman, also with hat pressed to his heart, said:

"Madam, I am the Yeoman to the Prince Braveheart."

Likewise the Bowman, with hat pressed to his heart, said:

"Madam, I am the Bowman to the Prince Braveheart."

And they all sat down.

Without delay the Prince came to the subject of his mission, and in fewest words made known his desire.

The old woman was not a grandmother at all, but a witch; a reformed one, it is true, but still a witch, and heartless and mercenary. With lolling head and closed eyes, she listened as the Prince pleaded for the hand of Millicentine. When he had finished, she said in piping tones:

"That sounds very well for Millicentine, but where do I come in?"

Which was a poser for every one.

The Yeoman looked at the Bowman, the Bowman looked at the Prince, and the Prince looked at Millicentine, who clasped her hands and held her breath.

"Upon what conditions can I claim her as my bride?" asked the Prince of the selfish Witch.

"Fetch me, within a year, a bag of California gold, a bag of Australian gold, and the pigeon-blood ruby that hangs from the neck of the Toltec Queen," said the crafty and cold-blooded old woman.

"That are too high," interposed the Yeoman.

"That am exorbitant," protested the Bowman.

Which slips of speech were unnoticed by the Prince, who, drawing his trusty sword, cried:

"I'll away at once, and before the year is spent shall return to claim my bride."

Gallantly kissing the hand of the lovely Milli-centine, and bowing low to the ugly old Witch, with his Yeoman and his Bowman at his heels, the Prince started in search of the required treasure.

On they wandered, fighting their way through hostile countries, suffering endless hardships, yet ever hopeful. Ten months had already elapsed, and at last they came to the royal city of the Toltecs. The carnival was at its height, and knightly jousts were held before the King and his Court.

Three rich prizes were offered as rewards to the successful competitors: a bag of California gold, to the best lancer; a bag of Australian gold to the best swordsman; and the pigeon-blood ruby worn by the Toltec Queen to the best horseman.

And Prince Braveheart was victor in all the contests.

The Prince, with the ruby placed safely in a locket next to his heart, the Yeoman with the bag of California gold, and the Bowman with the bag of Australian gold, retraced their steps joyously.

During all these months Millicentine was having a very, very hard time of it. As the days passed, and her suitor did not return, the alleged grandmother grew apprehensive, and feared that the Prince had failed to secure the gold and the ruby, and would be so little of a gentleman as to take Millicentine from her by force.

As these thoughts grew and grew within her stony heart, all the mean traits in her character became alive again, and she lapsed into her original state as a full-blown, unblushing Witch, and was really worse than before she reformed.

What does she do but rush down to the wicked Hobgoblin, who lived in a cavern in the Glen of the Four-Fanged Wolf, and confide to him all her fears.

"Aha!" he exclaimed. This was one of his customary expressions, and usually preceded an equally customary remark, made *sotto voce:* "A bird in the hand is worth two in the bush."

And forthwith, poor little Millicentine was chained to a wall in the Hobgoblin's private prison.

She did not know why she was treated thus, though she suspected, but hope did not desert her, even when she heard the Hobgoblin say to the Witch, most mysteriously:

"Aha! She's better in jail than out on bail, and dead men tell no tales."

At this point of our story, which was the last

day for the Prince's return, the conditions were as follows:

Millicentine was kept a prisoner by the Hobgoblin. The old Witch did not believe the Prince could secure the treasure she had demanded, and therefore she would not listen to Millicentine's pleadings to be released, for fear she might run away with the Prince, even though he returned empty-handed.

The Hobgoblin was lying in wait for the Prince, the Yeoman and the Bowman, for he had secret advices that they had secured the treasure and were coming that very day. It was his purpose to kill them, claim the treasure, marry the girl, and snap his fingers at the overreaching old Witch, and he went about, singing low in a minor key:

"She's better in jail than out on bail, and dead men tell no tales."

Millicentine got tired of hearing the miserable creature croak the words all the time. They got on her nerves, and she said:

"He will return sometime and will hear your cackling, and then you'll sing lower still."

But the Hobgoblin's reply always was the very same.

"Aha! She's better in jail than out on bail, and dead men tell no tales."

Hours wore on. Suddenly a solitary horseman was seen slowly proceeding in the direction of the Glen of the Four-Fanged Wolf.

The Hobgoblin opened a peephole, and exclaimed:

"Aha, it is the Yeoman of the Prince, and he carries the bag of California gold!"

When the Yeoman reached the bridge of the Ornithological Lake, which turned into a bird any one falling into it, he was met by the Hobgoblin with profoundest evidences of friendship.

"Has the Prince arrived yet?" inquired the Yeoman, looking at his watch. "I note that he has still twenty-five minutes before the time expires."

"Not yet," chuckled the Hobgoblin.

"We agreed to meet here by the side of the lake, and titivate a bit before proceeding to the abode of the fair Millicentine."

"And you have the gold?" queried the Hobgoblin pointedly.

"We have," proudly replied the Yeoman, "and also the pigeon-blood ruby that hung from the neck of the Toltec Queen. Now, while waiting for the Prince and the Bowman, I believe I will take a bath."

"You need it," said the Hobgoblin, making a horrible attempt to be funny.

Walking to the center of the bridge, the Yeoman gazed into the clear water below, unsuspicious of the treachery of the other, who, creeping up from behind, suddenly gave him a shove, and sent him several fathoms deep into the lake.

When the Yeoman arose to the surface he had been changed into a Whippoorwill, and plaintively calling "Whippoorwill! Whippoorwill!" he flew into a tree, shaking his feathers dry and shivering from fright.

As the transformed Yeoman saw the Hobgoblin seize the bag of California gold and enter the house, he bemoaned his double misfortune. In a moment all was still, then the clang of a horse's hoofs was heard on the road, and the Bowman hove in sight. He dismounted and led his horse to the edge of the lake for a drink. The animal seemed reluctant to approach. So, taking hold of the reins with both hands, the Bowman began to pull, but the harder he strove the more the horse resisted.

Most unexpectedly the Bowman felt a terrific

blow on his knuckles, and, releasing his hands with a cry of pain, he tumbled backward into the lake. When he came to the surface it was observed that he was now a Bob-White, and he immediately flew toward the forest. The Hobgoblin, laughing fiendishly, picked up the bag of Australian gold, exclaiming:

"Nothing remains now but to gain possession of the pigeon-blood ruby which hung from the neck of the Toltec Queen, and which, I conjecture, must certainly be in the possession of the Prince."

Even as the Hobgoblin spoke, the Prince appeared at the cross-road near the Glen of the Four-Fanged Wolf. The sad and depressing notes of the Whippoorwill sounded again and again in his ears, and were answered by the loud clear tones of a Bob-White.

The beautiful black charger stopped, distended his nostrils and whinnied. The Whippoorwill flew about his head, calling incessantly. The charger backed and turned into the right-hand road, and, strive as he might, the Prince could not swerve him in the direction of the Glen of the Four-Fanged Wolf.

"Forward, Sparkles!" said the Prince, touch-

ing the charger gently with his golden spurs, but
Sparkles backed in alarm.

Just then the Bob-White whistled on the right-
hand road, "Bob-white! Bob-white!" and it
seemed to say, "This way, this way."

The Hobgoblin, who was watching with great
interest and greater anxiety, when he saw the
charger take the right-hand road, hissed:

"Am I foiled?" and then he exultingly added:
"Not if I know it."

And, bounding upon the back of the Yeoman's
horse, he rode as hard as he could to intercept the
Prince at the Span of the Black-Hued Demon.
The Hobgoblin hid back of a huge rock at the
entrance to the Span, and poised his lance, preparing to kill the unsuspecting Prince when he approached. The Whippoorwill and the Bob-White
were keeping up a terrific clatter, but the Prince's
thoughts were of Millicentine, and of her alone.
Finally Sparkles refused to budge.

"What *is* the matter?" cried the Prince.

At which his beautiful charger pricked up his
ears and whinnied long and loud. Immediately
came an answering call, and the Yeoman's steed,
on which the Hobgoblin was perched, bounded
into the road.

And there, plainly in view of the Prince, sat the Hobgoblin, with lance upraised.

"By my halidom!" cried the Prince, "this is a rare adventure. Guard thyself, miscreant!"— holding his lance at the charge.

"Aha!" said the Hobgoblin.

And they went at it.

The Whippoorwill and the Bob-White perched themselves on a high limb and watched the contest with great interest.

It was a beautiful fight, but when it ended the Prince's lance was sticking right through the Hobgoblin, who was unhorsed and faintly struggling while breathing his last.

He raised himself on an elbow, and beckoned the Prince to draw near. The Prince knelt by the side of his vanquished opponent, who said:

"In my pocket there is a golden box—it contains two pellets—give one to Bob—" and before he could utter another word he dropped over dead and was done for.

The Prince secured the box, while the Whippoorwill and Bob-White flew down and both perched on his shoulders.

When he raised the lid of the golden-box each of the birds quickly took one of the pellets, and

lo and behold, they were turned back into the
Yeoman and the Bowman, much to their relief.
It took but a moment or two for them to tell the
Prince where Millicentine was, who the Witch
was, and, in fact, everything of interest.

Then, drawing their trusty swords, the Prince
and his servitors started for the private prison of
the Hobgoblin to release the maid. They were
met by a battalion of goblins and gnomes, and
what the Prince and his brave servitors didn't do
to them is not worth recording. When they had
finally put out of business the last goblin, they
had reached the door of the dungeon. There sat
the Witch. They demanded admission; she refused. But the Yeoman and the Bowman, not
having the patience to bandy words, each grabbed
her by an arm, and saying: "Old lady, you'd better cool off," pitched her into the lake.

When the Witch came to the surface, she was
the most miserable looking catbird you ever saw,
and she never got over it.

The Prince rushed into the donjon keep, and
freed the captive maid.

And she, on a beautiful Kentucky-bred horse,
with the Prince on Sparkles, and the Yeoman and
the Bowman on their palfreys, bearing the bags

of gold, all proceeded to the Gipsy country where Millicentine became the bride of the Prince, and, eventually, Queen of the Romany Rye.

And they all lived happy ever after.

"That's an awful nice story," said Zorah.

"Yer don't spec' it's real true, Gil?" asked Sandy.

"Well, I wouldn't vouch for it," replied the little fellow.

Zorah came near to Gilbert, and, looking intently at Sandy, whispered:

"Don't you think Prince Braveheart's hair was a little too red?"

"It might have been had the Prince been a common person, but he was brave and true, and red hair is very becoming to people who are brave and true." said Gilbert.

CHAPTER IX

DOING IT BROWN

Sandy was faithful to his promise, and thus one source of annoyance was spared Mrs. Foley. The rain-barrels were always full and the drudgery of wash-day was thereby considerably lessened.

"I can't make it out," said the widow to Mr. Jebb, "why that boy loves to carry water."

"The Jedge says Sandy is all wool and a yard wide," replied Mr. Jebb, "and loaded to the gunwales with sympathy."

"Sympathy is all right, Mr. Jebb, but it don't go with fillin' rain-barrels. There's a nigger in the wood-pile somewhere."

"Not necessarily, Mrs. Foley." The grocer motioned her to a chair.

"There's that Tom of mine," she continued, "he wouldn't bring a drop to save my soul unless I coaxed him with a cowhide; and Sandy, who ain't no kith or kin of mine, rushes round afore light and brings enough water to float the navy, and then thanks me, if you please, for lettin' him do it. 'Tain't in a boy's nature to do it for nothin'.''

"Perhaps he feels you need his help," returned the grocer.

"Don't yer believe that, Mr. Jebb. If that boy ain't been put up to do it, then his mother ought to send him to a doctor, for he's surely goin' into a decline. Boys don't fill rain-barrels seven times runnin' jest because they hanker after work. The cat will come out of the bag sooner or later, and I know it." Her arms akimbo, she looked at him quizzically, when he discovered suddenly that the counter needed dusting.

"Oh, shucks, it's nothing out of the ordinary," —and he smiled inanely.

"I'll find out; he'll blab it, see if he don't!"— this with mock severity. As she walked away Titcomb watched her, his heart beating faster.

"She is a Juno and no mistake," he soliloquized. "You wouldn't find one woman in a day's travel with such a face and figure. Those blue eyes and that black hair can't be beat in this world." He followed her with his gaze until she disappeared.

"Sandy, Sandy," he shouted, as he saw the lad emerging from the widow's home.

"Hello," responded Sandy, as he came over.

"My boy," said Titcomb, "let's go over your account. I want to settle for the fish."

"All right, Mr. Jebb; I'm ready." Sandy took a small note-book from his pocket, and called off the items.

"Yer owes me fer seventeen catties, thirty-four eels, hundred an' ten yaller perch, hundred an' twenty-eight white perch, twenty-eight rock an' sixteen suckers, which makes three hundred an' thirty-three, or twenty-seven dozen an' nine. At ten cents a dozen that would be two dollars an' seventy-seven cents, which I believe yer'll find correct." He handed the book to Titcomb.

"That's right, and here's your money." The grocer gave the amount to the boy.

"Gee, Mr. Jebb! ain't I gittin' rich? Only took me a week an' two days to make it, an' I ketched most all of 'em Saturday, which was all day."

"Keep right on, Sandy; fill the widow's rain-barrels regularly, and I'll buy all the fish you can catch." The grocer slapped the boy's shoulder approvingly.

"That's all right 'bout the fish, Mr. Jebb, but this lyin' to the widder is orful."

"She doesn't suspect anything, does she, Sandy?"

"She axed me to-day if I wuz so powerful fond of carryin' water as I pertended, an' I sez of course I wuz; then she sez, 'Cross yer heart, if ye are.' I sez I can't do that, an' she sez she knew I couldn't. Then she 'lowed that yer wuz payin' me to do it, an' I didn't say nuthin'. She ups an' sez, 'If Mr. Jebb ain't payin' yer to tote water fer me, cross yer heart,' an' then I was done up. I would ax yer as a favor, Mr. Jebb, to do yer own lyin' hereafter. I ain't no good at it!"

"Was she very mad, Sandy?" earnestly inquired the grocer.

"Not muchee, Mr. Jebb; she wuz most tickled to death an' give me a big lump of bread with butter an' lots o' molasses. She puts her hand on my cocoanut an' sez, soft-like: 'I hope, Sandy, yer will make as fine a man as somebody I could name.' I looked into her pretty face an' squawked: 'Mrs. Foley, 'tain't many that can hope to ekal Mr. Jebb.' 'Go 'long,' she sez, 'I didn't mention Mr. Jebb,' an' she laughed jest like she wuz glad I sed it."

"Sandy, Sandy, you're a great boy, and I think twenty cents a dozen wouldn't be too much for your fish."

"Bully fer you, Mr. Jebb! I likes to say jest

here, if enny fish are left on yer hands, why, yer needn't to pay me fer 'em if yer don't wanter."

"The Lord bless your honest heart, Sandy, I could sell twice as many if I had 'em."

"That's most satisfyin', Mr. Jebb."

"I've never seen such a run on fish before. The day after I agreed to take all you caught, a letter signed 'Treblig,' evidently some great foreign authority, appeared in the *Evening Star*, in which it was stated that, owing to the great amount of phosphorus in fish, it is the most beneficial of all foods for the brain, and ever since everybody's rushing up for fish. Gilbert Franklin came immediately with their cook and spoke for all you caught. On Tuesday, Wednesday, Thursday, Friday, and twice on Saturday, Delia was here to get them."

"I wonder ef the little codger wrote that letter. I know he bought a lot o' *Stars* one day last week. It's jest like him. What did yer say the man's name wuz what wrote it, Mr. Jebb?"

"Treblig," answered the grocer, taking the paper from his desk and handing it to Sandy.

"I never heerd of no man with that 'ere name in the fish bizness, but I'll ask the little codger if he knows him, an' I'm bettin' he does."—scan-

ning the name and spelling it over very carefully.

Sandy wrote out the name in large letters on
a piece of wrapping-paper, and scrutinized it with
great interest. Finally, folding the paper, and
putting it into his pocket, he said: "Mr. Jebb, t-a-t
spells tat anyway yer spells it, but T-r-e-b-l-i-g
don't spell Treblig anyway yer spells it, an' I'm
a-bettin' the little codger knows why."

"Here comes Mrs. Franklin's cook now," called
the grocer, "and I'll bet she'll ask for fish."

In walked Delia.

"Good mawnin', Muster Jebb, has yer got enny
fresh fish?"—this wearily.

"No, Delia, not this morning; yesterday was
Sunday; of course Sandy wouldn't fish then."

"Bress de Lawd fer dat, Muster Jebb! I wah
a-prayin' an' a-hopin' an' a-wishin' dat de supply
o' fresh fish wah used up. Lawd A'mighty, Muster Jebb, dere's done bin terrible doin's in our
house in de fish line all de week. Sence las'
Chuseday, it's fish—fish—fish; fish fo' breakfast;
fish fo' dinner, fish fo' supper; fish all day long,
till yer can't rest fo' fish. Muster Franklin an'
littl' Gil 'scusses fish, an' sez dey gives pussons
brains. I don't 'spute what dey sez, but, laws-

sakes, Muster Jebb, I goes roun' feelin' like I wah a rain-bar'l; fo' dey sez fish'll swim, dead or alive, an' I done drunk de pump dry all de week an' dey are still cryin' fo' mo' watah. I hopes to de Lawd dat de ribber'll run out o' fish, brain or no brain, or dis cullud pusson'll get dropsy sho'."

Sandy hurried to the Jedge to report progress in the financial department.

"Jedge, I've got three dollars an' seven cents, an' I made all of it, 'cept twenty-eight cents, in a week an' two days."

"*Perseverentia omnia vincet,* as scientific men would say," replied the Jedge, "which, to the lower millyun, like me an' you, Sandy, would sound plainer if we jest sez, 'If yer want ter git there, keep a-inchin' along'."

"Jedge, don't yer think we better start buyin' our material an' kind er git ready?"

"That's the talk, my boy, an' if yer'll wait till I put on my alapaky coat, I'll go down to Tom Clark's with yer to select the lumber."

After they had picked the necessary timber for the boat, Sandy proudly took the bill and paid it. He and the Jedge shouldered the planks, and they started away. They met Gilbert and Dink, who lightened their burden, and soon the load was deposited in the Jedge's woodshed. Then a visit was made to a hardware store, where bolts, screws, nails, and so forth, were put aside to be called for, as soon as Sandy had sufficient capital.

"It looks to me," said the Jedge, as they sat on the porch, "that work ought to commence t'morrer. While ye're out on the river fishin', Dink an' me will git the trestles ready, an' spruce up gin'rally fer a starter. Gil kin measure the boards an' see if they're all right, an' everybody kin make themselves useful gin'rally."

"Sandy," said Gilbert, as they left the Jedge's, "my father has given me a set of bcxing-gloves; would you mind coming to the house and showing me a point or two?"

"In course I will. I stands ready to show yer all I knows 'bout how to use 'em," spoke the elder.

"The doctor says boxing is a very healthy exercise, and father is anxious I should learn."

"Jest tell yer father to leave it to me; 'tain't goin' to be hard fer yer to learn. Ye're as quick as greased lightnin' with yer noddle, an' ye've got lots of sand, an' them two things is powerful helps in boxin'."

The boys went to Gilbert's play-room and put on the gloves. Sandy first showed the little fellow the simpler movements, and then the finer ones of side-stepping, countering and dodging, all of which he picked up with surprising quickness. They had boxed intermittently for an hour, and were resting.

"I wants ter caution yer, little feller, 'bout a weakness I've been noticin'." Sandy stood up, and beckoned Gilbert to face him. "Don't wear yerself out tryin' to reach a big feller's mug, when it's beyond yer. Yer'll peter out, an' he'll punch yer sure. There's lots o' fellers what thinks they've got the 'vantage 'cause they're bigger, but every feller is sometimes the littlest in a fight. Now, what yer wants to do, is ter git yer man down to yer size, afore yer think of anythin' else. Jest connive a little, an' the fust chance yer git, whack him in the bread-basket, an' when he doubles up yer'll be pluggin' him in the jaw. It's jest this 'ere way:

"I'm a-recollectin' one Sunday afternoon, I wuz a-walkin' out to Cool Run, jest fer to stretch my pins an' to get a drap of fresh air, an' when I gets round by Swamppoodle, up comes Shanks Robey. It's 'lowed he's a holy terror when he gits started. His Giblets is as tall as a bean-pole, an' a tough customer. He hollered over the street to me: 'I jest heerd ye're the party they call Pipetown Sandy down yer way.'

"I 'lowed that was so an' walked on, not offerin' to argyfy the matter.

"He 'mediately calls out after me: 'I'm a-bettin' anythin' yer wants, I kin chaw yer up in three minits.' I 'peared as if I didn't take no notice of his insultin' bragadocy an' jest walked on, not hurryin', jest walkin'. He came on, follerin' 'bout ten feet erside o' me. I was thinkin' 'bout the song we had in Sunday-school, 'Let dogs delight to bark and bite' an' stopped an' said: 'Shanks, 'tain't no use follerin' me; takes two fer to spat, an' I ain't goin' to spat, leastwise not to-day,'—an' I walked on, not hurryin', understand, jest walkin'. He comes a little closer and yells, 'Fraid-Cat!' I looked at him, sayin', 'Lemme go, Shanks; don't stop me. Don't yer see I'm havin' trouble holdin' myself?'

"He never paid no 'tention to my re-quest, an'-I-hope-I-may-die, if he didn't call me out er my name. I stopped as if I wuz rooted to the spot an' looked at him, not believin' my ears. I turned ag'in an' said slow an' sorrowful like, 'Shanks, did you speak?' He laughed one of them laughs that makes yer so mad yer could bite yer own mother, an' sassed out, 'Did I speak?' an' called me out er my name ag'in.

"I faced right in front er him, an' I-hope-I-may-never-see-the-back-of-my-neck, but he was that tall he could 'a' laid his two fists on my head by jest puttin' his arms out straight. I sez, 'You said yer'd chaw me up in three minits; I'm yer huckleberry;' an' I begins to dance round him. He raised his fists to chop me on the smeller, but I got under, and BIFF! I soaked him one plum' in his bread-basket, an' he come down where I was livin'. Afore he know'd it, I wuz a-playin' a jig on his cocoanut, an' he hollered 'Nuff!' three times afore I heerd him. Well, I ain't sayin' nuthin' 'gainst no feller as can fight like Shanks Robey, but I wuz told he had to take er letter home to his folks afore they agreed 'twuz Shanks."

The next day, work began in earnest on the boat, and there was bustle and activity in the Jedge's back yard.

Between getting up before day to go to the river to fish, filling Mrs. Foley's rain-barrels, and working on his boat, Sandy was beyond question the busiest mortal in Pipetown. The other workers, the Jedge, Gilbert and Dink Dabney, were not idle, either. Gilbert reported faithfully every morning, dinner-pail on his arm, and when the noon hour came he sat as a laboring man in the shade eating his meal.

"An' he does it," said Dink to his folks, "jest as if he wuz a poor boy as had to do it fer his keep."

Gilbert brought the boxing-gloves down to the workshop, and every day after the midday meal he and Sandy would devote ten or fifteen minutes to light sparring.

The days passed and the boat was nearly completed. It had been built and caulked, and one afternoon Gilbert was putting the last coat of white lead on it, while Sandy and Dink were at the carpenter's bench in the shed, shaping the rudder.

The Jedge, seated in a wicker rocker, his eyes gradually closing into sleep, was wholly oblivious of earthly things except when he would brush some persistent fly from his nose. From a soft snore, he changed slowly to a sharp rhythmic grunt.

Snarley Foley came into the yard and noticed Gilbert at work.

"Hello," he called. "Say, lemme paint some?"

"Much obliged, but I guess I can do it without any help," said Gilbert, scarcely looking up from his work.

"Oh, don't be so selfish," continued Snarley, coming over and reaching out for the paint-brush.

"I'm not selfish," replied the little fellow, "but Sandy gave it to me to do."

"Yes, I guess so; yer hang round him so yer don't give him no chance to think fer hisself."

"Well, what of it?"—still painting, and paying no attention to the other boy.

"There's a great deal of it, an' I can't understan' how Sandy puts up with it."

"You had better ask him and find out, if you are so anxious to know," retorted Gilbert, with an angry gleam in his eyes.

"Yer think ye're some pun'kins, don't yer," sneered Snarley, " 'cause yer kin saw catgut, an' wear Sunday clothes? Yer'd better keep a civil tongue in yer head. Fer two shakes of er cow's-tail, I'd punch yer, yer mama's-boy!" snapped Snarley contemptuously.

The boxing-gloves were lying on the floor of the porch where the boys had left them but half an hour before. Gilbert put aside the paint-brush, slowly walked over, picked up the four gloves, went to where Snarley was standing, and threw two of them at his feet.

"Don't yer try to hit me, a-throwin' them gloves at my feet. If yer do I'll give yer a belt in the snoot, yer mama's-boy."

"I'm going to give you a chance to take two of them and belt me, as you say, in the snoot! There are the gloves,—put them on."

"I don't fight with no gloves."

"Well, you'll fight with gloves or without gloves, or you'll apologize for calling me a mama's-boy."

"That ain't callin' yer out er yer name," snarled the bully.

"I think it is; put on the gloves,"—almost as a command, and so loudly that Sandy and Dink came from the shed, and the Jedge woke up.

"What's up?" said Sandy.

"This white-livered cur called me out of my name, and I want him to put on the mitts and settle it," said Gilbert, while Dink helped him on with the gloves.

"Why, Gil, 'tain't fair to let yer fight Snarley; he's 'most twice as big as you are. Let me polish him off," Dink volunteered.

"I don't care if he is four times as big as I

am, he's got to fight or take water," said Gilbert warmly.

"Yes, I'm twice as big as he is an' I shouldn't fight him," shouted Snarley, drawing himself up and trying to appear taller than he really was.

"You can't run around Robin Hood's barn with me. I don't care if you are as big as a house. If you don't put those gloves on, I'll pull your nose, and boot you all over town besides," cried Gilbert, his eyes flashing fire and his face expressing contempt.

" 'Tain't no use, Snarley; ye've riled the little feller an' ye've got to fight him, square up an' down, three rounds. Here's the gloves,"—and Sandy forced them on Foley's hands, and laced them carefully. "Yer called the little codger out er his name, an' it would spile his temper if he didn't try to lick yer fer it."

"Sandy," said the Jedge, "I don't think it's right to let the little feller fight that big lummux."

"Jedge, it's all right," said Sandy decisively, "ef yer got any sympathy lyin' round loose, jest give it to Snarley Foley, fer the little feller'll knock him galley-west jest as sure as cats is cats."

"Understan' now, boys, I excuses yer fer a-fightin' in my back yard, 'cause one of yer called the other out er his name, an' wouldn't take it back."

Sandy went over to Gilbert and whispered, "Remember Shanks Robey!"

If the lad was excited, he showed no signs of it, and came up facing his taller and stronger opponent, cool and absolutely fearless. He ran around the bigger boy, cat-like.

His movements evidently worried and rattled Snarley. Gilbert made a feint, as if to strike with his left hand, then he side-stepped. The big boy, lumbering and awkward, threw out his elbow wildly, and unexpectedly gave Gilbert a terrific jab on the nose. The blood spurted in streams, and the little fellow's anger was fully aroused.

Taking advantage of the opening his antagonist had left, he planted, with lightning speed, blow after blow. Suddenly he landed with both fists, and doubled Foley up. The bully was too badly scared and whipped to call "Enough," and screaming, "Murder! Help! Don't let him kill me!" he rushed from the yard, waving his arms like windmills.

Gilbert took off his gloves, went into the kitchen, washed the blood from his face, returned to the yard, and resumed his work on the boat.

Words just then were not adequate, so all were silent. The Jedge, Sandy and Dink were thoroughly satisfied, and looked at the little fellow with intense admiration.

Sandy sent Dink for the boxing-gloves that Snarley in his hurry had forgotten to leave. Dink returned shortly with them, and reported:

"Snarley looks like he had been used fer a choppin' block, an' he hops along kind er lopsided, 'cause one eye's in mournin', an' when I holler'd 'Giddy giddy gout,' he jest beller'd, an' didn't say nuthin'."

"I guess he's found out he got the wrong pig by the ear," observed the Jedge, chuckling as he resumed work on a hickory rod.

As Sandy and Gilbert separated at the Corner that evening, the older boy put his hand on the little fellow's shoulder, and said:

"I know'd you'd 'a' done it an' done it brown, but yer done it browner than that."

CHAPTER X

JUNO WENT A-SAILING

The *Lillian* was finished at last.   Painted a beautiful ultramarine, a broad stripe of white edging her gunwales, her rudder and oar-blades a brilliant red, she rested on the trestles ready for shipment to the river,—an object of admiration to every boy in Pipetown.

Her name, in letters of gold, was stretched across the stern, the handiwork of Gilbert.

"Gil," said Sandy, as the former stood off viewing the boat critically, "I wants ter ax yer a favor."

"All right, Sandy!" The little fellow turned to the older boy, waiting for him to speak.

"Yer knows Jim Cook, my second cousin?"

"He's a sailor, isn't he?" asked Gilbert.

"Yes, that's him."

"Of course I know him."

"I seen him this mornin', an' he tol' me that in the navy, when they launches a new boat, Uncle Sam invites er lot o' people an' a purty young lady to come an' help christen it, an' Jim sez, when the boat slides inter the water the lady takes er bottle o' champagne an' cracks it on the bow, sayin' at the same time the name the boat is goin' by. An' Jim sez the win' jammers strike up *The Star Spangled Banner,* an' the people hurrah."

"I think I know what you're driving at," said Gilbert, "and we ought to christen the *Lillian* that way."

"That's jest what I wuz a-comin' to, little codger. D'yer think yer can git yer little sister to come an' do it?"

"Of course; she will be delighted."

"In course, we can't 'ford no champagne, but my mother has some home-made blackberry wine, an' mebbe that'll do."

"I think soda pop is better, Sandy. My father says the only difference is, that champagne has more 'fizz' and costs five dollars a bottle."

"That settles it; soda pop's the baptizin' fluid. I'll git a bottle at Jebb's."

"Instead of a band, I'll bring my fiddle and play the tunes," said the younger.

"Bully fer you, little codger! Now it's all settled, an' we'll have it Saturday afternoon. We'll give her a great send-off an' no mistake."

Saturday morning the boat was hauled to the river, and after the midday meal, Lillian, dressed as the Goddess of Liberty, went with her brother to take part in the proposed function.

Sandy, Dink and Gilbert shoved the jumper down the whitened beach and into the clear water. The Jedge escorted Lillian to the bow of the boat, and the child, holding the bottle of soda pop in her hand, began the ceremony:

"I christen you *Lillian*,"—and pop! went the soda.

Gilbert struck up *The Star Spangled Banner*, Lillian waved a tiny flag, and the rest of the company joined in the song.

"She sets as quiet-like as possible; she's cert'nly stanch, Sandy. Take the oars, boys, an' see if she's got any speed,"—and the Jedge and Lillian sat in the stern, Sandy took the stroke and Dink the bow oar, while Gilbert sat forward, playing.

They turned upstream, and with measured stroke and feathered oars, they sent her through the water like a veritable racer. After speeding for about two miles they ran ashore, stepped the mast and raised the sail, with Sandy as skipper.

She soon caught the wind, keeling beautifully, while the spray dashed over her bow.

"She's a daisy an' no mistake," enthusiastically exclaimed the Jedge, "an' I'll bet there ain't a jumper this side of Jericho kin tech her." The Jedge bounded everything by Jericho, north, east, south or west, and therefore the *Lillian*, in his opinion, was without a peer.

The wind gradually died away and the boat drifted slowly down the river toward her moorings. To those on shore, there came, wafted over the summer waves, the sweet voice of Gilbert's violin. *Home Sweet Home* and *The Old Folks, Annie Lisle* and *The Mocking-bird* palpitated upon the quiet air, melodies that have been heard on a thousand similar occasions, and will be heard as long as the American heart is attuned to thoughts of home or to thoughts of love.

The youthful voices joined in with the violin, and even the Jedge put in an occasional note that he called "the second."

Before the sun was hidden behind the western hills the *Lillian* was at anchor, her sail furled, oars and oar-locks safely stored, and the party was homeward bound, happy in the memory of a perfect day.

"Sandy, the boat's a great success," said the Jedge. "Boats sometimes, under the most carefullest buildin', turn out bad, in which particular they are like boys. I've seen boys whose folks could trace their pedigree 'way back to prehistoric times, as scientific men would say, an' afore you'd know anythin' they'd butt their nozzle ag'in a rock, an' down they'd go, rumsoaked an' busted. But the *Lillian* is O K, copper-bottomed, an' we are all proud of her."

When Gilbert and Lillian reached home, they recited with glowing enthusiasm every detail of the launching, rowing and sailing, and were loud in their praise of Sandy's skill.

The Jedge went to Jebb's store that night and informed the "faithfuls" that "Sandy reminded him more of hisself when he wuz Sandy's age, than anybody he had ever seen."

"Of course, in them days I had also the mentality, as scientific men would say, which is peculiar to Gil Franklin," he continued, "but take me by an' large, as I wuz when I wuz a boy, in l'arnin', eddication, help yerself an' git there, I wuz a twin brother to them two boys."

After supper Sandy sauntered into the grocer's and received the congratulations of all hands on his success in building the boat. Calling Jebb aside. he said:

"I'm very much 'bliged to yer fer buyin' my fish, Mr. Jebb, an' I wants ter ax yer somethin'."

"Go ahead, Sandy; I'm all attention," said the grocer good-naturedly.

"Wouldn't yer like to go out sailin' in the *Lillian,* say next Tuesday afternoon? The Jedge'll tend store for yer, an' I'd be mighty pleased if you'd let me take yer up as far as the Sycamores, an' then when the sun's goin' down, jest come back."

"It will be a great pleasure, Sandy," replied Mr. Jebb politely, "if I can arrange my business affairs."

"But, Mr. Jebb, yer store won't run 'way while the Jedge is watchin'," said the boy earnestly.

"Yes, I understand that, Sandy, but I have some very, very important matters to attend to on Tuesday, but I'll let you know whether I can go, if you'll come around later."

"All right, Mr. Jebb, I'll come, but I'm afeerd I can't count on yer." Sandy walked to the front of the store, picked up a few raisins out of a box, and then very carelessly said:

"Oh, Mr. Jebb, I fergot. If yer conclude that yer could go, would yer mind if somebody else went along?"

"Certainly not, Sandy, but do not count on me, as I'm likely to be very busy next week."

"Well, I wuz jest 'bout to say that on my way here I stopped at the widder's an' invited her to go sailin' with me on Tuesday, an' she said she'd positive go, rain or shine, but if ye're too busy, don't say nuthin' more 'bout it, an' I'll take her all by myself." Sandy was half-way out of the door.

"Wait a minute, boy, don't hurry so. Did you say the widow was going?" Titcomb spoke excitedly.

"That wuz my remark." Sandy continued to move away slowly.

"Come back here a minute; don't hurry off before I have a chance to talk to you. My! you hop about just like the Irishman's flea. On second thought, I'm sure I can arrange my business affairs to go with you."

"Oh, don't put yerself out, Mr. Jebb; if yer can't go, don't hesitate to say so. I kin take yer any other day."

"You said Tuesday, didn't you, Sandy?" questioned the grocer eagerly.

"Tuesday was what I sed."

"I'm afraid I didn't quite catch the day, when

you first spoke. I am so absent-minded sometimes, but I remember now, Tuesday is my easiest
day off. I've nothing to do on Tuesday, and I'll
go; you can count on me."

"I'm glad you've arranged yer business affairs,
Mr. Jebb. I'll stop an' tell the widder I've invited you. I don't know whether she'll like it or
not, but I'll chance it. Now be sure an' don't
fool me,"—and Sandy, laughing roguishly, left
the store.

The grocer immediately went to his desk, and
hours after the store was closed he was still writing. His task was finished, and he had added
a new poem to his collection. That night he
dreamed of an aquatic Juno.

On Tuesday Sandy came punctually. Titcomb
was waiting for him, and together they went to
the widow's house. She was in the little parlor
ready for them. Dressed in her best gray delaine,
with white collar and mitts, a black silk shawl and
a "kiss-me-quick" bonnet, she looked most be-
witching. The trio left the house and started
toward the river.

"I've asked Gil to go 'long to help sail the
boat," spoke Sandy, "an' he'll meet us at the
landin'. He's went ahead some time ago."

After they had gone a block or so, Sandy whispered slyly:

"Mr. Jebb, if yer don't mind, I'd like to run on an' git things ready by the time yer git there,"—and away he went, before the grocer could reply.

Jebb walked proudly by the side of Mrs. Foley, and the knowledge that the woman he loved was near him filled his soul with a wild exultation. He was almost afraid to speak lest it might be only a dream, and the sound of his voice dispel the illusion. The widow had her thoughts, too. When they reached the river, Sandy and Gilbert had everything in readiness.

"We'll sail up as far as the Sycamores, Mr. Jebb, if you an' Mrs. Foley's willin', an' then stay there an' watch the sun go down."

"I've been told," said Titcomb, "that the sunset viewed from the Sycamores is very beautiful, and that in imagination you could picture Paradise itself in the many hues of the dying day."

"I've watched it go down lots o' times when I've been yankin' fish in the cove, an' I tell yer it's no slouch of a sun, anyway," added Sandy, with just a suggestion of the melodramatic.

"The river is delightful up there," added Gilbert with animation.

"The river is delightful anywhere, Gilbert, and I know the Sycamores are fine, if you say so," remarked the widow.

The *Lillian* glided into the stream; Gilbert sat in front of the mast, his feet hanging over the bow; the widow and Titcomb occupied the middle seat, and Sandy was at the helm. Up by the Magazine they sailed. Rounding into the Devil's Elbow, they passed beyond the big marsh under the shadow of the Banks, and soon reached the Sycamores.

As the boat grated against the pebbly beach, Gilbert stood ready to jump ashore and pull her up. After all were out, Sandy took a hatchet, and giving one to Gilbert, said:

"Mr. Jebb, the Jedge axed me to cut him some hick'ry poles fer fishin'-rods. There's some bully good uns up on the shore, t'other side of Turtle Creek, an' if you an' Mrs. Foley don't mind, me an' Gil 'll go up to the head of the creek an' cross over. That'll take us 'bout an hour an' a half, an' if yer'll jest row the boat up to the mouth of the creek, me an' Gil 'll be there waitin' fer yer. Don't hurry, 'cause it'll take at least that long afore we kin cut 'em an' fetch 'em down. Yer kin sail up if yer wants to, but I don't advise yer to, unless yer know all 'bout the river, specially if it should blow. On second thought, I guess you'd better row; it's safer."

The boys disappeared up a path leading to the creek, leaving Titcomb and Mrs. Foley alone with the birds and flowers.

The grocer carefully brushed the sand from a board that had been washed ashore, and improvised a seat for the widow. He threw himself, with an air of abandon, on a green mound near-by.

"I presumed on your good nature," he began. "I have brought some of my verses and will read them, if it pleases you."

"I'm jest dyin' to hear some more of your po'try pieces, Mr. Jebb; specially 'bout Juno, whoever she may be." The widow leaned forward, looking inquiringly into his face, and the poor lovelorn grocer could scarcely refrain from declaring his passion then and there without more delay.

"This wayward thought,"—his voice trembled with suppressed emotion,—"was written last Saturday night just after Sandy told me that you had accepted his invitation for to-day. I have named it *Juno Went A-sailing.*"

"Juno went a-sailing where the rippling waters flow,
  Up the stream and down the stream, a-gliding she did go.
  The summer day was mild and sweet, the sun was in a
      glow,
When Juno sailed upon the river.

My love, my love, my love, I love you so;
My love, my love, oh, listen ere you go;
Juno went a-sailing where the rippling waters flow,
And I am dreaming on the river.

Juno, proud and lofty, oh, I feel you do not know
My heart is longing for you as I wander to and fro;
Tho' I scorch in Africa or freeze in Arctic snow,
I love you, sailing on the river.

My love, my love, my love, I love you so,
My love, my love, oh, listen ere you go;
Juno went a-sailing where the rippling waters flow,
And I am dreaming on the river."

"Law sakes, Mr. Jebb, that is too pretty for words. It ought to be sung to."

"It can be sung to, Mrs. Foley. It adapts itself to the tune of *Marching Through Georgia.*"

"I wish you would teach it to me, and I kind er think it would be awful nice to sing when you're alone, an' all worn down to a frazzle."

"Nothing would give me greater pleasure," he replied proudly.

The widow beckoned Titcomb: "If you don't mind, come set down here by me, and let me sing off the words with you."

They began softly and with a decided tremor in their voices, but gradually growing more confident, they sang louder and louder, and the hills sent back the echo.

"My love, my love, my love, I love you so."

When they had finished, the widow turned and looked wistfully at the silently-flowing water, then sighed.

"I hope the song has not made you unhappy," almost whispered Titcomb.

"Unhappy, Mr. Jebb? This is the first happy day I've known these many years."

"Let us hope this is but the beginning of many happy days," he spoke with insinuating sympathy.

"How is it?" she interrupted, "that all them pieces of po'try you write are about a lady named Juno; who is she that you are so powerful fond of her?"

"Can't you guess?" his eyes trying to convey the thought rampant in his brain.

"I can't guess, 'cept that her name is Juno," said the widow dubiously.

He turned, and grasping both her hands, cried passionately:

"You are Juno! Who but you could be Juno? You are the one woman in all the world I love, I idolize, I would die for."

She withdrew her hands quickly, and covered her face.

"No, no, Mr. Jebb, you mustn't, you mustn't. I'm a respectable woman."

"Of course you are; do you think I believe you otherwise?" He kneeled before her, and tried to grasp her hands.

Holding him aloof, she cried:

"No, no, Mr. Jebb, I can't, I can't. God knows I can't."

Faintly over the water came the clear voice of Gilbert:

> "Maxwelton's braes are bonny,
> Where early falls the dew,
> And 'twas there that Annie Laurie
> Gave me her promise true.
> Gave me her promise true,
> Which ne'er forgot will be,
> And for bonnie Annie Laurie,
> I'd lay me down and die."

Looking into her face, he exclaimed in love-laden accents: "You hear that song—'And for bonnie Annie Laurie I'd lay me down and die.'

That's what my heart says to you. You are my Annie Laurie, you are my Juno, you are my everything on earth."

"Mr. Jebb, Mr. Jebb, you don't understand me. Heaven knows I believe you, but I can't, can't listen to you, as I am an honest woman."

"What do you mean?" he implored.

"Mr. Jebb, I don't know whether I am married or single."

"Married or single? I do not understand!" he exclaimed.

"Neither do I, and I have never met any one who does. Listen!"

He came back to his seat by her.

"Just after the war broke out my husband went off, not because he wanted to, but because some one gave him money to shoulder a musket. He was a worthless drunkard, if there ever lived one. He was first on the Confederate side, then deserted his people and went North. I tracked him out for a while, but I haven't seen him for nearly five years, and I don't know whether he is alive or dead."

"After all these years, it seems hardly probable, if he were alive, that you wouldn't have heard from him," said the grocer.

"But I haven't," she replied, "so what can I do? I bear his name; he is the father of my son, and I can't encourage no other man while I'm in doubt."

"Hallo-o-a! Hallo-o-a! Mr. Jebb! Mr. Jebb!" Sandy's voice came over the water from the direction of Turtle Creek.

"I do declare, we've been so busy talking we forgot all about the time," said Titcomb, "why, it's nearly six o'clock."

"It's gettin' dark, too. It looks like a storm was comin'," said Mrs. Foley, noticing heavy clouds gathering over the hills.

"Hallo-o-a! Hallo-o-a!" came again.

"We'd better go," said Jebb. The rain began to fall slightly. A distant rumbling of thunder and a flash of lightning caused them to hurry. The grocer helped the widow into the boat and started to hoist the sail.

"Hallo-o-a! Hallo-o-a!" the boy called once more.

"Sandy said I'd better row, but I'm sure we can make better time sailing. I don't know much about a boat, but it is not far and we will be there in a few minutes." Titcomb was uncertain of his ability to handle the craft.

He shoved the *Lillian* off and she scudded

toward the mouth of the creek. The clouds grew blacker and blacker, the lightning began to play incessantly and all heaven's artillery was in action. The rain poured in torrents, and the boat shipped water and lurched violently. The boys were standing on a point projecting into the river and they noticed, with grave apprehension, the erratic steering of the grocer.

"I don't like things," said Sandy. "I tol' Mr. Jebb not to sail her, because I don't believe he knows any more 'bout a boat than a hog does 'bout Latin. Hallo-o-a! Mr. Jebb; lower that sail as quick as yer can. Great Jehoshaphat, she can't stand ev'rythin'. Gil, run up the bank there, an' git that bateau out an' bring it down. I'd go myself, if I wuzn't afeerd to git out o' sight o' Jebb an' the widder."

Titcomb was standing up. Something was amiss with the sail, and he was evidently at a loss what to do. Suddenly the boat made a short turn, swung around quickly, and keeled over in the white-capped water. The boom, swinging out, struck the two occupants, and swept them off their feet into the river.

Off went Sandy's shoes, hat and coat, and shouting at the top of his voice, "Don't give up,

I'm comin'," he plunged in and swam swiftly toward the struggling couple.

As he reached them, the grocer, though exhausted, was trying to keep the widow from sinking. Calling to Sandy, he said faintly:

"Don't mind me, I'm almost done for; but save her."

Mrs. Foley was going down for the second time. Sandy dived, and when he came to the surface, he was holding her by the collar. Then he urged Jebb:

"Swim over here, old man; we're all right if yer don't git scared. Here comes Gil with a boat, an' I'll have yer in it in a jiffy."

Gilbert came abreast the trio, and helped the widow into the bateau, and then assisted Titcomb. Finally Sandy scrambled in.

The *Lillian,* meantime, had righted herself, caught the wind, and dashed into a soft mud-bank a few hundred yards away. The boys rowed over, lowered her sail and took her back to the Sycamores. The storm subsided nearly as quickly as it had come, and the wet and tired quartet started homeward.

Everybody praised Sandy and Gilbert for their brave rescue of Titcomb and Mary, but the lads preferred to talk of the splendid behavior of the *Lillian*.

"She's a beauty an' no mistake," declared Sandy emphatically, "I don't believe if it blow'd all out-doors she'd turn'd turtle. She's a daisy with a large yaller center. When I seen the boom strike Mrs. Foley an' Mr. Jebb, I tho't it wuz four o'clock fer both of 'em. Mr. Jebb held on ter the widder like grim death to a mop-stick. It's mighty lucky that Gil jest brought that 'ere bateau in the nick o' time, fer I-hope-I-may-die, when they went over, I tho't it wuz four o'clock fer both of 'em, but whichever way it would er wound up, yer can't beat my *Lillian*."

CHAPTER XI

"I'VE BIN FIGHTIN'"

Our national game! What an enemy to nepotism, paternalism, or any other "ism" that thrives on favor or influence!

Oh, base-ball! thou art truly the embodiment of purest democracy; like love, thou dost level all ranks!

Of what avail is distinguished ancestry, pre-Adamite origin, cerulean blood or stainless escutcheon, when one is at the bat and strikes out! Intellectual superiority, physical perfection, social status, wealth or poverty count for nothing, if you fail to bring in the winning run.

The game was in full blast in Pipetown. Every afternoon the boys gathered on the common, and the sound of the umpire's voice was abroad in the land.

The Eagles were champions of their class, and the tri-colored pennant floated proudly from the flag-pole on their grounds. Of all rivals they feared most the Smithsonian Rangers, and the three games with them were the great events of each base-ball season.

At this time Sandy was captain and pitcher of the Eagles, and day by day his club improved in batting, base running, catching and team work. One position alone was weak—that of first base. Five or six boys had been tried there but all had proved unsatisfactory, and Sandy was worried. "If we don't git a first base that can hold it down," he said to Gilbert, after a hard practice game, "the Rangers'll knock the tar out er us, sure."

"Where will you find him?" queried Gilbert. "You've tried every boy in the neighborhood, and not one has been worth shucks. It puzzles me where you are to find the right man for the position."

"I wish I could tell yer, Gil," was Sandy's reply, "but I don't know. Yer kin bet I'm hard pushed when I puts a boy like Snarley Foley on first bag. He ain't got sense 'nough to pour water out er a boot. He's the biggest butter-fingers of the lot. I didn't think a feller could muff so much. If I'd 'a' kept him on, I'd had to give him a clo'es-basket to ketch the ball in; nuthin' smaller would 'a' done. Lor' knows where I'll git a first baseman. But I ain't give up by no manner o' means."

Therefore Sandy persevered until by mere accident he found the player he sought.

As an interested spectator at the practice games, he had frequently noticed a handsome, dark-complexioned, well-dressed boy of perhaps sixteen years. He was as tall as Sandy himself, slightly heavier in build and evidently a new-comer in the neighborhood. Clearly he understood the game, for he never failed to applaud a brilliant play.

About a week before the Eagles' first match game with the Rangers, the stranger was as usual on the field, and showed keen interest in the work of the team. There was a crowd of small boys, upon whom Tom Foley and Fatty Beeks were playing all sorts of practical jokes. One of their favorite tricks, that furnished great sport to every one but the victim, was to have Foley creep up on hands and knees behind some unsuspecting lad, while Fatty with a push sent him sprawling backward over the crouching fellow conspirator. The joke had been worn threadbare that afternoon, and it was becoming difficult to find new material to work on.

The stranger had noticed this rough horse-play,

but was so wrapped up in the ball game that he paid little attention to it. Evidently the two jokers believed he would be a good subject, and going through a hurried pantomime they went cautiously toward him; but no sooner had they bumped against the youth, than out shot his right arm, and, grabbing the surprised Fatty by the collar, with lightning rapidity he reached for Foley, jerked him to a standing position, and, holding each in a vise-like grip, banged the heads of the two frightened jokers together, and then threw them to the ground.

A shout of delight came from the lookers-on, and the cowardly rascals, seeing the tables turned upon them, sneaked away. Sandy laughed boisterously, then walked over and said:

"That's bully; yer whacked their cocoanuts so hard they'd 'a' cracked, if they wuzn't made o' mush."

"I don't like practical jokes," said the newcomer.

"Well, yer can bet yer bottom dollar, Snarley and Fatty won't monkey with you no more."

"I don't think so, either," said the other convincingly.

"Do yer ever play ball?" asked Sandy.

"Oh, yes, I'm first base on our nine at school," was the reply.

"Where is yer school?"

"In New York City," said the other.

"Well, New York City, what's yer t'uther name?"

"My name is Leander Daindridge."

"My name's Sandy Coggles, an' I wish yer'd go out an' hold down fust bag fer us," said Sandy, shaking hands cordially with him.

Young Daindridge took off his coat, turned up the sleeves of his shirt and went toward the base, where for an hour he surprised the team with his fine work in catching, base running, batting and throwing.

As Sandy and Gilbert strolled homeward after the game, the older boy broke a long silence with, "I don' understand it, Gil."

"Don't understand what?" asked the little fellow.

"I don't understand it at all. That Leander's the fust boy I ever seen what wore Sunday clo'es on a week-day, an' could do anythin',"—and Sandy shook his head as if greatly puzzled.

"Over the river," he said, and the two boys parted.

Next day Leander was permanently installed as first baseman on the Eagles. The youth had all the qualities of a real American boy. He was brave and gentle, unassuming and courteous, and soon became a general favorite.

The day of the great match with the Rangers was at hand. The Pipetowns consisted of Tub Dykes, catcher; Sandy, pitcher; Leander, first base; Lefty Sparrow, second base; Dink Dabney, short stop; Ernie Crawford, third base; Pat Corrigan, left field; Curley Harris, center field, and Sloppy Sowders, right field, and the nine was the strongest the club had ever mustered. The players' ages ranged from fifteen to sixteen. Gilbert was secretary, treasurer and official scorer all in one.

The day of the game was the glorious Fourth. Sandy won the toss and sent his team into the field, with the parting words: "Don't fergit, boys, this game's fer blood, an' if we lose, we needn't die ag'in."

The contest was a hot one, and it was any one's game until the last player had been called out in the ninth inning. But victory was with the Eagles. This was happiness enough for Pipetown, and every man, woman and child went to bed at peace with all the world and their neighbors. Sandy and Leander were the favorites of the event.

On the evening after the match, as the twilight shadows were growing deeper and the soft-faced stars were heralding the coming night, the boys of the victorious ball club were circled about a hollowed place on the old chip bank by the river. The memorable contest was reviewed again and again. Leander's wonderful stop in the fifth inning and Sandy's home run in the ninth, were enthusiastically commented upon, and many prophecies were ventured on the result of the second game.

Dink insisted that the next time the Rangers wouldn't be knee-high to a grasshopper with the Eagles, and he "didn't blow no bazoo nuther."

Changing the subject, Ernie Crawford said: "Gil, spin us a yarn."

"Yes, a story," shouted the others.

"No, I'd rather not to-night," replied the lad. "I've told so many I should think you'd be tired of them."

"Sandy, Sandy'll tell a story," shouted Ernie.

"Oh, pshaw! I don't know no stories. I've never been nowhere. I'm no account in that 'ere line, as I tol' yer afore lots er times."

"Yes, you are," retorted Gilbert. "Now think of something you've heard or seen."

Sandy gazed vacantly for some time, then began: "The only thing I kin think of that might do at all, is when the army come home."

"That's it; tell us about the great review of the Army of the Potomac. I've heard you say you saw it; so tell us all about it," urged Gilbert.

"Well, here goes!" said Sandy falteringly. "If yer boys gits tired, jest say so, an' I'll stop."

WHEN THE ARMY CAME HOME

'Twas three years ago last May, jest a little while after Gen'ral Grant an' Gen'ral Lee had their great confab at Appermattox, an' settled things. I guess everybody wuz mighty glad they talked it over an' made up their minds to quit an' stop fightin' each other.

My father wuz readin' the *Evening Star* after supper, an' he ups an' sez, "Jennie, I sees by this 'ere paper that the army is comin' home." "The Lor' be praised fer that," sez mum, "an' I hopes an' prays they'll stay home, an' never go off fightin' ag'in," at which my dad sez, "Amen."

"Jennie," he sez, "I'm a-feelin' it's almost 'Lights out' with me, but if the Lor' wills to let me stay till the army comes back, I'm a-goin' to put on my uniform, an' jest go out an' see 'em marchin' up the street."

My old dad was ailin' a terrible lot jest then. Between three or four lead slugs that had never been dug out, an' his sawed-off leg, he was full of mis'ry, but he never croaked. The only way we knowed he wuz sufferin' wuz when he'd holler in his sleep, an' then he wouldn't 'low he did, when we tol' him. He'd say he was jest dreamin' o' nothin' in partic'lar, but, in course, we know'd better.

Sure 'nuff, the corporation begins cleanin' the streets an' hangin' out buntin' an' flags an' evergreens, an' there wuz stuck up ev'rywheres signs what said: "Welcome to the Nation's Heroes," "Welcome to the Army of the Potomac," "Welcome to the Gallant Fifth and Sheridan's Invincibles," an' sich like.

The old man gits his uniform out an' has mum to sew up the bullet-holes, so people wouldn't think it was moth-eaten or worn out, an' when the day come, he spruces up, an' me an' him legs it up town to see the sojers come back.

When we gits up by the capitol, the school children wuz standin' aroun' on all sides a-waitin'.

The gals wuz all dressed in white an' the boys had duck pants on an' blue jackets, an' all of 'em had red, white an' blue rosettes pinned to their shirts. Some of 'em had bo'kets an' things like that to give to the sojers when they come along.

We stan's there a little while an' hears 'em sing *Rally Round the Flag*, an' *When Johnny Comes Marchin' Home*, then the old man sez, a-startin' off: "Let's mosey along to where Andy Johnson an' Grant's goin' to review the boys."

We kep' on a-walkin' until we got up by the President's house, an' we steps up, brash as yer please, on a stand, jest across from the place where Andy Johnson, Gen'ral Grant and the other big guns wuz goin' to sit an' look. Nobody said nuthin' to us, so we squats right down an' watches the people come a-pilin' in.

It wuz Guv'ner this, an' Guv'ner that, an' Guv'ner t'other; it wuz jest rainin' guv'ners. We warn't no guv'ners, an' we know'd we didn't b'long there, but we didn't holler it out so folks could hear us, an' nobody noticed the diff'rence. Afore long ther' wuz some clappin' an' shoutin', an' Andy Johnson and the Gen'ral comes out on the stand opposite. Then a lot er high-up officers, an' sich folk, hustles on, lookin' mighty well-kept an' important. There wuz two boys 'mong that crowd, an' somebody sez they're the Gen'ral's children. I spec' they wuz orful proud o' their daddy, fer yer could hear the people hollerin', "Grant, Grant! Hurray fer Grant!" more'n anythin' else jest then.

Well, sir, we hears a rumblin' down the street an' we know'd the Army wuz comin'. There wuz a fine-lookin' gen'ral ridin' in front. One of the pack er guv'ners sez, "There's Meade!" I'd never seen him afore, but I took the guv'ner's word fer it. Then come a lot 'er officers, some clean an' new-lookin', an' 't'others consid'rably s'iled, an' as they passed the President, they s'luted with their swords an' kep' right on.

I wuz jest wishin' it would get a little excitin', when, lickety-split, the devil's own horse comes tearin' up the street fer all he wuz worth. He cert'nly did look bad. The crowd stops cacklin' an' rose up like bees a-swarmin', an' strains their necks peekin'. There wuz 'n officer on the horse, with no hat on. His long lightish hair wuz jest blowin' ev'ryway; ther' wuz a great wreath swung on his left arm, an' that 'ere horse wuz runnin' as if Satan hisself wuz chasin' it. I wuz so scared I jest kep' my mouth shet fer fear I'd spit out my heart. My father grabs my arm tight as a vise; yer could see the place a week afterwards.

"My God, he 'll be dashed to pieces!" hollers a lady, holdin' on to the rail.

"Who is it?" shouts a guv'ner, shakin' like a aspen leaf.

"It's Custer!" bellers er officer, jumpin' on a chair, mos' dead from excitement.

"That's all right!" yells my daddy, as loud as he knows how. "Set down, an' enj'y yerself."

Jest then the horse rears up, an' when he come down I tho't he wuz goin' heels over head.

"Oh!" cries all the people at onct, a-shudderin'.

"Set down!" yells my dad ag'in. "Set down; it's Custer, an' it's all right. He don't ride a horse 'cause he has to; he rides 'cause he kin."

Fer a minute yer could hear a pin drop. An' lo an' behold, we sees the Gen'ral comin' back, an' his horse was steppin' soft an' actin' as gentle as a parson's nag on Sunday. Custer was a-bowin' to Andy an' Grant an' the ladies as he passes, an' he wuz jest as ca'm an' smilin' as if he wuz in a parlor.

Oh, my, how that crowd did clap an' hurray! Yer'd a-tho't it wuz a house er-fire. My dad said he felt like he had hair clean down his back, an' ev'ry one a-standin' up, when he seen that horse runnin' away, but when he heard it was Custer he jest lay back, an' could er snoozed, he felt so peaceful like. Pop sed Custer wouldn't know how to start gittin' scared.

Pretty soon along comes his cav'lry, an' they cert'nly did look scrumptious with their carbines, an' sabers an' red scarfs a-danglin' sassy-like round their necks. They had a band, an' it was tootin' chunes that ev'rybody was keepin' time to, an' even dad was a-pumpin' up an' down with his cork leg.

After a while the Zoo-Zoos comes by, all in red trimmin's, an' red tassels on the caps, an' it wuz jest great, an' the *Tramp, Tramp, Tramp, the Boys are Marchin'*, stayed with me till I got home. Lots of the flags had crape on 'em. One of the guv'ners sed it wuz 'cause Mr. Lincoln had died, an' that wuz mighty sorrowful to ev'rybody, aroun', to say nuthin' of poor ol' dad.

When dad an' mum an' me was sittin' talkin' 'bout it that night, pop sez: "It wuz fine, an' no mistake." But after he had lit his pipe, he sez: "Jest wait till to-morrer, an' then yer'll see somethin' that yer'll see. My Army is comin'. The Bummers with Uncle Billy an' Black Jack'll be

marchin' in, an' they'll make Rome howl!" Pop
was powerful fond of Uncle Billy an' Black Jack,
an' proud he'd been with The Bummers. When
he wuz argufyin' he'd say it might be a matter
o' dooty fer a sojer to lose his leg with any army,
but with The Bummers it wuz a pleasure, an' I
don't believe he'd a-taken it back if hell had froze
over.

Well, sir, nex' mornin', bright an' early, me an'
dad starts up, an' when we gits to the Botanical
Gardens by the Tiber Creek bridge, we finds a pile
o' bricks, an' as they looks handy to set on, we
perempts 'em, an' we could see hunky-dory.

At nine o'clock, "Boom!" goes the signal gun,
an' afore yer got tired waitin' along comes The
Bummers. They looked like they had been mos'
too busy to change their fightin' clo'es. Their
broad-brimmed hats looked great, an' the crowd
got stuck on 'em mighty soon.

Officers come 'long with wreaths on their
horses' necks, an' lots an' lots er the sojers had
bo'kets stuck in their guns, an' Lor' alive, but they
did hoof it. Yer could hear 'em plunk, plunk,
plunk, the boys are marchin', till yer couldn't
rest.

Well, sir, here comes a sojer marchin' 'long

with his comp'ny, an' I-hope-I may-die, if he
didn't have a racoon a-settin' on his shoulder.
That racoon jest put his face down by the side
of the sojer's cheek an' looked out at the crowd,
jest as sharp an' bright as yer please, an' it
seemed to me he was sayin':

"I've bin there, I've bin there; I've been
fightin'."

The crowd clapped an' laughed to split their
sides. Then up comes a tall sojer carryin' a flag
pole, an' the flag was faded an' shot to pieces.
There wuz stains on it that look'd like blood, an'
all at once the breeze jest flung that flag out,
proud an' defiant like, an' I thought it sed, plain
as possible:

"I've bin there, I've bin there; I've bin
fightin'."

The crowd clapped till the flag was out er sight,
an' pretty soon along comes mules, an' donkeys,
an' goats, an' dogs, an' cows, an' I-hope-I-may-
die if there wuzn't a rooster perched on a horse's
back an' a-crowin':

"I've bin there, I've bin there; I've bin
fightin'."

And we jest went crazy, clappin'.

When the sappers an' miners comes, their

blouses tucked in their pants an' their belts tightened, an' shoulderin' their shovels, picks an' axes, we knowed they'd bin there. We knowed they had chopped, had dug, had shoveled their way to vict'ry, an' to Glory Hallelujah. An' when they pass'd, the line comes to a halt fer a minute. My ol' dad wuz keepin' both eyes open, an' all of a sudden I seen a sojer lookin' at dad, an' he hollers out:

"Well, I'll be damned; there's Dan Coggles!" And afore yer could say Jack Robinson, he tosses his gun to another feller, an' rushed over to dad, an' honest-to-goodness, if they didn't hug each other like they wuz two mothers.

"I tho't yer wuz dead, Dan," said the sojer, as if he wuz goin' to cry.

"I heerd you wuz, Sam," said dad, an' he wuz a-blubberin'.

"No; I'm all right," said Sam, laughin' happy like an' pattin' my cocoanut.

"An' I'm all right, too," said dad. He wuzn't, but he didn't let on.

And then I know'd the sojer was Sam Dickson, who had gone to the war with dad, an' they had marched an' starved an' almost died together. I know'd it, fer one of the other sojers told me.

Well, sir, what must we do, but dad jest takes his place in that 'ere company right 'long side o' Sam, an' Sam handed his gun to me, an' I walked in front a-totin' it at right-shoulder-shift, jest like all the sojers in the reg'ment.

An' *Tramp, Tramp, Tramp, the Boys Are Marchin'*, we went up the Av'nue. Dad stepped out jest as if he hadn't enny cork leg, an' I stretched my shanks fer all I wuz worth.

The people clapped an' clapped, an' give me a bo'ket, an' dad got a lot o' 'em, an' the officer who wuz marchin' right in front er the comp'ny kep' his eyes glued ahead, an' pretendin' he didn't see nuthin', which cert'nly was mighty white er him.

We wheeled round the corner. Jest as we got to the gran' stan' the officers shouted out their orders. Me an' The Bummers presented arms, an' dad s'luted as we passed the President. The crowd seemed jest crazy happy, but I wuz orful lonesome, 'cause I wuz the only one in that 'ere hull review who couldn't say:

"I've bin there, I've bin there; I've bin fightin'."

CHAPTER XII

SANDY AND LEANDER HAVE IT OUT

"I think you're a mean old thing, so there!"

Zorah laughed in rippling coquetry and waited for Sandy to speak. The boy was busy repairing the weather-beaten arbor that extended from the street to the front door of his little home. He stopped working and looked inquiringly in the direction of the speaker.

"I mean just what I say," continued the maid, assuming an air of mock gravity.

"What have I been an' done?" asked Sandy.

"To think you built a boat and never so much as said to me, 'Won't you go sailing?'" and she shook her finger at him reprovingly. "I'll never, never forgive you."

"In course," said Sandy apologetically, "I inten' to take ev'rybody out sailin' in the *Lillian,* sooner or later."

"Sooner or later don't suit me at all, an' if you had any gumption you'd know that, too,"—tossing her head scornfully.

"I spec's that's so; I ain't got no noddle for gals," faltered the boy.

"Oh, you mustn't act as if you don't know enough to come in when it's raining. You've got gumption enough to ask others to go in your boat."

"They wuzn't no gals I asked: they wuz only the Jedge, an' Dink, an' Gil, an' his little sister Lillian."

"Well, if you thought of Lillian, why didn't you think of me?"

"Mebbe I should have, but I ain't got no noddle fer gals, generally," drawled Sandy, perplexed.

"Oh, tell that to the marines. A boom-e-laddy wouldn't believe it," said Zorah, with a disdainful shake of her head.

"Gals never pays no 'tention to me," retorted Sandy, now on the defensive.

"I suppose you want them to kneel down in front of you and say, "Oh, Mr. Coggles, won't you take me out sailing?' "—and Zorah pantomimed the action most extravagantly.

"If a gal did that I'd think her looney," replied the boy.

"Of course you would. Leander was surprised when I told him I hadn't been in your boat."

She spoke as if a great wrong had been done her.

"Mebbe yer'd like to go sailin' with him," Sandy suggested, with a touch of impatience.

"That would be simply delightful." The little coquette clasped her hands fervently, and looked heavenward.

"If yer wants to, I'll lend him my boat."

"No, thank you," quickly answered the torment; "I don't go in borrowed boats."

"A borrowed boat is better'n no boat at t'all," fired back Sandy hotly.

"Oh, I don't know about that; somebody I know has a new boat,"—this in a tantalizing tone.

"D'yer mean Leander?" questioned Sandy in surprise.

"You can go up head; you guessed right the first time,"—and Zorah laughed triumphantly.

"When did he git a boat?"

"His uncle, the Commodore, gave him a regular beauty this morning."

"Who told yer?" asked Sandy.

"Leander told me so himself. You know he's awfully fond of calling at our house, and we do love to have him, he's so bright and cheerful. He's got such fine hair and peachy skin. Crissie says any girl would be proud of such a beautiful, clear complexion; not a freckle, as we can see,"— and Zorah dwelt on the word "freckle" as though it were a bitter morsel.

"I s'pose that's so; but what's the name o' the boat?"

"Leander hasn't named it yet, but he expects to call it the Zorah."

The boy started violently, and, slightly flushed, asked huskily: "Did he say he'd call it the Zorah?"

"No, not exactly; but he said he thought Zorah would be an awful nice name for it. I said so first, and then he said so," volunteered the tantalizer.

"Would yer let a plumb stranger name his boat fer yer?"

"What has that got to do with it?"

"Lots an' lots," answered the other. "A total stranger's got no business to use names like Zorah, when he knows gals at home with other names."

"I can't see how that concerns you."

"I thought yer had too much pride to 'low it," hotly exclaimed the boy.

"It's just because I have pride, that I want a boat called Zorah."

"If yer wanted my boat called Zorah, why didn't yer say so?"

"If you wanted to call your boat Zorah, why didn't you say so?"

"I didn't want to."

"Then you have no right to object, if Leander does."

"Yer hinted him into doin' it," said the boy stoutly.

"That's more than I could do with you."

"Yer didn't try," exclaimed Sandy.

"What's the use? A brick house would have to fall before you'd take a hint."

"Mebbe ye're right, Zorah. I axes yer pard'n fer gittin' excited an' fergittin' myself; but I calls my boat the *Lillian,* 'cause I likes Gil's little sister an' she likes me, an' she told me so the very fust time I seen her."

"I suppose if everybody told you they liked you the first time they saw you, your boat would have as many names as a city directory?"

"I didn't say so," answered the boy.

"Well, I think it would, and I am very much obliged to you for not calling your boat Zorah, 'cause everybody will know that you don't like me, and that is delightful."

" 'Tain't true,"—Sandy shook his head solemnly.

"How do I know it ain't true?"

" 'Cause I sez it."

"Well, it's the first time you said it, and I hope you feel better," exclaimed Zorah maliciously.

Gilbert came at this moment and looked at his friends amusedly.

"What's the matter with you two—quarreling again?" he asked.

"I 'spect I've been makin' a monkey o' myself," said Sandy.

"How is it you can't be together five minutes without being at daggers' points?" said Gilbert.

"Sandy's awful hard to get along with," spoke Zorah sadly.

"Mebbe that's so. I ain't got them soft ways that goes with gals," Sandy admitted regretfully.

"Of course you have, but Zorah simply doesn't understand you," said Gilbert encouragingly.

"I certainly don't," answered Zorah firmly.

"Now let's see," said Gilbert, "if we can't get up a conversation between you without ending in a fight. Sit down Zorah,"—and he pointed to a bench inside the arbor.

The little maid seated herself most demurely.

"Sandy, you sit there,"—pointing to the other end of the bench. "I'll sit between you and direct the conversation. Now, Sandy, you begin, and say what I say."

"I'll say anythin' yer sez, little codger."

"So will I," repeated the chatterbox, not to be outdone.

"Now, we'll start," said Gilbert. Imitating Sandy's voice he began:

"Good morning, Zorah." Sandy solemnly repeated the words after him.

"Good morning, Sandy,"—and Zorah mimicked Gilbert, all the time suppressing her mirth.

Gilbert intoned the following sentences, which were alternately repeated by Sandy and Zorah, much in the style of the Litany.

"I hope your mother's well."

"Very well, thank you."

"Mine has been sick."

"How sad! nothing serious, I hope?"

"Oh, no; just a slight ailment."

"There were a million cats in our back yard last night, Sandy."

"A million?"

"Well, a thousand."

"A thousand?"

"Well, a hundred."

"A hundred?"

"Well, our Tom and another cat."

"Oh!" This exclamation was long drawn-out by the children, and then the absurd dialogue was broken by loud and uncontrolled laughter on the part of all of them.

"Now, you see how easy it is to get along without quarreling," remarked Gilbert.

"Don't yer think we might git them speeches down by heart, an' jest say 'em to each other when we meets, an' nuthin' else?" queried Sandy soberly.

"Yes, that's a great idea, Sandy," replied the little maid. "But let's start with five million cats, and then it will take a little longer." Zorah looked roguishly at the elder boy. "I guess I must go now," she continued.

"I've been tryin' to see Leander all day," interposed Sandy.

"I'm going to see him the first thing in the morning," volunteered Zorah.

"I've bin to his house twict already to-day an' they sed he'd gone to Georgetown an' wouldn't be back till late to-night," continued Sandy. "I wants him to know that the game with the Rangers is to-morrer. They had ter move it up a day sooner on 'count of some shenanagin 'bout the grounds. Will yer please tell him about it, Zorah, so he won't make no mistake?"

"Certainly," she replied; "you can depend upon me."

"Did Leander surely say he'd go sailin' in the mornin'?" questioned Sandy very earnestly.

"No, not 'specially. I said so first, and then he said it after me."

"Well, tell him if he does go to be sure and be back in time fer the game, fer we needs him mighty bad and we'd be in a orful hole if he didn't show up."

"Trust me, and good-by. Trust me to tell him what you said,"—and Zorah departed.

"Sandy," said Gilbert, as they watched the little minx disappear, "mother wants a hornet's nest for the parlor, and the Jedge has promised to go with me for it day after to-morrow. He says he knows where the yellow-jackets build every year and we can get a cracking good one."

"I'd like to go with yer, little codger, but I've got a lot er hustlin' to do to-morrer an' the next day; if I git through in time, though, I'll meet yer down by the Burnt Bridge."

"All right, I'll expect to see you when the Jedge and I reach there on our way back."

The two boys picked up hammer and nails, and work was resumed on the arbor.

"Zorah made me mad clean through this mornin'," put in Sandy, " 'cause she said I fergot to take her out in the *Lillian*. She'd orter know I'd a-called my boat Zorah if yer'd never had no little sister. Girls kin rile yer, can't they?"

"I wouldn't mind Zorah if I were you," said Gilbert; "she's a regular little pill-garlic. I'm sure she likes you better than anybody else, and loves to put on luggs just for the fun of it."

"Mebbe that's all right, but I don't think she orter let a plumb stranger gobble up her name fer his boat,"—this with just a tinge of petulance.

"I wouldn't mind that," was Gilbert's soothing comment. "My father says that women never reason when they're angry, and I guess Zorah was put out because she felt herself slighted."

Next morning Aunt Harriet, Crissie and Zorah went to the Yard to meet Leander. He led the way to the wharf, and they embarked for the trip.

"We'll go down the river," he said, "cross over to Four-Mile Run. have our lunch and return about two." Then he raised the sail and the boat glided out into the stream.

They had a delightful time, the luncheon was most enjoyable, and it was Zorah's pleasure to christen the new boat after herself, "Not with soda pop, but with real champagne," her aunt explained the next day, with satirical emphasis.

On the way homeward, the wind was such that Leander found it necessary to tack continually. When opposite Giesboro Point the boat suddenly ran on a bar, stuck hard and fast, and, in spite of the boy's efforts, she would not budge. Worse yet, the water was receding.

"This is tough, and no mistake," said Leander. "We must make the best of it, and wait until the tide changes and floats us off."

"How long will that be?" anxiously questioned Zorah.

"I should say in three or four hours," replied the boy.

"Oh, I forgot to tell you; Sandy gave me a message," remembered the maid suddenly.

"What was it?" asked Leander.

"He said to be sure and not forget that the game with the Rangers was this afternoon at three."

"This afternoon? I thought the game was to-morrow," he said.

"They made it one day sooner, 'cause of a mix-up about the grounds, and Sandy asked me to tell you without fail."

"I'll never get there now," said the boy, much worried; "I'm awfully sorry, for Sandy hasn't any one to play first base, and that makes it mighty bad for the Eagles."

"I meant to tell you when we started, but I for-got," excused the girl, beginning to realize the trouble her forgetfulness might cause.

"I do wish you had," Leander said with great earnestness. "I wouldn't have missed the game for anything, and you know we could have gone sailing any other day. I hope Sandy will under-stand I didn't keep away for lack of interest in the club."

For three hours they sat, watching the tide re-cede, reach its ebb, and begin slowly to return. At last the boat floated off, but it was beyond night-fall when Leander and his party arrived at the anchorage.

At Zorah's home they heard the discouraging news that the Rangers had defeated the Eagles, because, as Dink said, "Sandy had ter put Snarley

Foley on first base, an' he was the rottenest yer ever seen."

Among the "faithfuls" that night at Jebb's store, the principal topic of conversation was the ball game and Leander's contemptible action in not appearing.

"It's a blamed shame," said the Jedge. "The Rangers couldn't beat the Eagles onct in a thousand years if they had their full nine on hand. Here's poor Sandy workin' like a yeller nigger to git 'em inter shape, an' Leander throws him down an' never shows up."

"Yer never can put no confidence in them 'ere boys that wears Sunday clo'es on week-days, an' sez 'if yer please' an' 'I begs yer pardon,' every five minits," snarled Tom Foley.

"We don't want no free-gratis-fer-nuthin' advice from you, Snarley," said Sandy. "We'd a won that game if Leander'd held down first base. When I puts yer on the base I know'd we wuz as good as done fer, but I had ter do it, 'cause there wuzn't 'nother snoozer round that knew straight up an' down."

"Yer ain't got no right ter sock me," whined Foley. "Yer turned me off, an' didn't gimme no chance ter practise."

"I turned yer off 'cause I knowed if I kep' yer on we'd a-stood as much chance as a sausage in a dog house," retorted Sandy. "An' that's all the chance we did have."

"Well, I ain't a reg'lar stickin' plaster round gals, anyway," blurted Foley.

"Who's a stickin' plaster?" asked Sandy.

"Leander Daindridge is," sneered Snarley. "He jest goes off with Zorah Dabney a-sailin' down the river, an' don't care a tinker's darn whether the Eagles lose er win, so long as he kin stick near a petticoat."

"If that's so, I'll tell him what I think of him," said Sandy angrily.

"Tell him he's a stickin' plaster, an' see how he likes it," dared the other, feeding Sandy's indignation.

"I'll tell him; don't fash yerself."

"He know'd yer wuz goin' ter play, so he goes off an' ties hisself to a piece er calico. Enny galoot what cares more fer calico than he does fer his word is no 'count nohow."

"No, I wouldn't give a picayune fer a feller as goes back on his pals," emphasized Sandy.

"Yer wouldn't tell him that to his face," hissed Tom.

"I would, if it wuz the last word I ever spoke," asserted the angry lad with determination.

"Let's see if yer do"—and with that as a parting shot, Snarley walked out of the store.

The next day Leander went to explain, but was told that Sandy was not at home; he had gone down to the old Burnt Bridge to meet Gilbert. As Leander sauntered in the direction of the river, he was met by Tom Foley, who shot the question at him at once.

"Why didn't yer come ter the game yesterday?"

"Well, first of all, I didn't know there was one until it was too late, and when I found it out, my boat was stuck on a bar, and it was impossible to move her until nearly dark."

"That's all right," said Tom, in his most irritating tone, "yer might tell that ter the man in the moon, but I wouldn't say it to a feller who'd cut his eye teeth an' know'd a thing er two."

"What do you mean?" demanded Leander.

"Yer knows yer wuz out with the prettiest piece er calico round here, an' yer couldn't keep away frum it."

"Nonsense. I wouldn't have missed the game for anything," insisted Leander.

"That's all in me eye, sez Betty Martin. Ye're stuck on the gals, an' the gals is stuck on you."

"You flatter me, Tom," laughingly replied Leander.

"Well, Sandy notices it, an' he sez yer nuthin' but a stickin' plaster."

"When did he say that?" Leander's tone had lost its laughter.

"Yesterday after the game, an' he sed a lot more things that wouldn't sound well in Sunday-school, an' he 'lowed he wouldn't give a tinker's darn fer no boy ez would stick to a petticoat an' go back on his pals."

"Did Sandy say that?" Leander's face flushed violently, and anger shot from his eye.

"Them's his very words, as-I-hope-fer-salvation," said Foley.

"I'll give him a chance to tell me that to my face,"—and Leander's teeth closed tightly, as he clenched his fists.

"That's jest what I sez to him, jest exactly," piled on Foley, "I sez to him, 'Yer won't tell him that to his face.' "

By this time the two boys were near the Burnt Bridge.

There they saw Sandy, with nine or ten companions, who were heatedly discussing the match of the day before.

Leander walked toward the group, and with great deliberation, said:

"Coggles, I've been told you said something about me yesterday."

"Well, what of it?" asked Sandy half savagely.

"There is this much of it,"—Leander spoke without a tremor, and with commanding gesture, —"you've got to take it back."

"I don't take nuthin' back," eying the other boy from head to foot, and folding his arms in an attitude of defiance.

"Then you've got to whip me, or I'll whip you." Leander spoke slowly and emphatically.

"That suits me to a T," said Sandy, taking off his jacket, rolling up his trousers and pulling off his outer shirt.

Leander slowly removed his tie, collar and shirt, and converted his suspenders into a belt.

Both boys threw their caps on the pile of discarded clothes.

"Enny kickin'?" asked Sandy.

"I never kick," answered Leander.

"Nuther does I. Enny bitin'?"

"I never bite."

"Nuther does I," replied Sandy. "Enny wras-'lin'?"

"As much as you like."

"Then it's square up an' down, no hittin' under the belt, an' wras'lin', as I understands it," said Sandy.

The boys present formed a ring, watched with breathless interest every movement, and heard with strained ears each word that passed between the combatants. The comparative prowess of these two had been cause for argument and dispute from the day of Leander's advent. As the opponents stood facing each other, the contrast in their general build was easily discerned.

Leander was quite as tall as Sandy, possibly ten pounds heavier, with broader shoulders, head finely poised, and his black hair giving him the appearance of a Greek youth of the time when Athens was the Mecca for the lovers of sports.

Sandy was longer-armed, and appeared to be only muscle and bone. His red hair glinted in the sunlight and his blue eyes seemed brightness itself.

Of fear there appeared no trace in either boy.

Leander put up his defense first, and Sandy began slowly to circle around him, each boy sparring lightly and feeling his way with extreme caution.

The onlookers held their breath and the tension was keen.

Suddenly Sandy's left swung in a semicircle and caught Leander just above the eye, raising a "goose-egg" almost immediately. Leander rushed in to clinch, but Sandy side-stepped and avoided a malicious straight blow from Leander's right.

They moved about and again Sandy lunged for his opponent's eye, but fell short and received a terrific counter which closed his right eye. Sandy's face puffed out perceptibly. Leander tried to rush him again, but without success. The red-headed boy was feeling for Leander's nose, and, with dexterous in-fighting jabs, adroitly landed plump and square on that organ, damaging it and setting the blood flowing freely.

For the next two minutes they became more and more wary in their tactics, blocking, dodging and dropping cleverly. Then Leander attempted to wear out the lighter boy by falling heavily against him in clinches, but Sandy was too nimble for him. Another clash, and Sandy reached Leander's left eye, which was soon closed. It was give and take for the next three minutes, with honors easy as to points and punishment.

Sandy was playing for Leander's left ear and almost immediately had it swollen and discolored, while Sandy's blind side was continually catching it from Leander's terrific rushes. Leander tried to reach Sandy's jaw, when the freckle-faced boy closed in, hooking a blow on the other's good eye, which went rapidly into mourning. With both optics closing fast, Leander rushed again and clinched. Sandy wanted to shake himself free but could not, and, throwing his arms over the heavier boy to protect himself from harm, rolled over on the grass with Leander.

The fighters were nearly used up, but too game to give in. They struggled to pin each other's shoulders to the ground, but at every endeavor one or the other would squirm out and the battle be renewed.

A small row-boat landed at the bridge abutment, and the Jedge and Gilbert stepped out. The latter, taking a tightly-closed basket on his arm, walked toward the crowd, which had attracted his attention as the boat neared the shore. He saw that something unusual was going on, but at his distance could not tell just what it was.

Once at the ring, though, the Jedge and Gilbert speedily realized what the cause of the excitement was, and, rushing in between the combatants, they grasped them by the shoulders and tried to separate them. Very much excited, Gilbert dropped his basket and begged Sandy and Leander to stop. The fighters, still struggling, staggered to their feet, but again they went over, striking the basket with all their weight.

Out flew a swarm of angry yellow-jackets, and in an instant there was a wild rush on the part of everybody to escape from the hornets' stings.

Five minutes later, the Jedge and Gilbert helped Sandy and Leander to wash the blood and mud from their faces. Bruised, battered and stung, the late fighters, with their two friends, sat down on the river-bank.

"What wuz yer fightin' 'bout?" asked the Jedge.

"Hanged if I know," answered Sandy.

"Neither do I," said Leander, trying to smile through his bruises.

"I'll bet some liar sed somethin' to start yer," suggested the Jedge.

"Well, Tom Foley—" began Leander.

" 'Tain't necessary to say nuthin' else," interrupted the Jedge, "if Tom Foley sed it, yer can bet it's a lie. Shake hands, an' say ye're sorry yer started to bang each other."

"I'm willing," agreed Leander, extending his hand.

"So am I,"—and Sandy grasped Leander's hand with all the warmth of true friendship.

CHAPTER XIII

JEBB AND SHAKESPEARE

A marked change had come over Mrs. Foley from the day Titcomb Jebb had made the avowal of his love up by the Sycamores, along the banks of the beautiful river. The years of weary toil, since the desertion of her husband, had driven the iron deep into her soul, and her temper had suffered accordingly. She had been sullen, morose, and easily aroused to violent anger, particularly by the escapades of her scapegrace son.

Now, however, she was transformed into a quiet, non-assertive being, whose voice was never raised in passion, and who went about her work in a spirit of complete resignation. She was no longer enveloped in the mist of distrust, because deep love and the joy of living were budding in her heart.

The one thing that interfered with her complete happiness was a conscientious scruple against divorce. While the grocer felt that Mrs. Foley was not indifferent to him, he was unsuccessful when he tried to persuade her to secure her freedom in a court of law. One evening, when he attempted to argue the matter with her, Mrs. Foley's answer was:

"Mr. Jebb, I don't believe I could marry unless I knew Dennis was dead, divorce or no divorce. 'Tain't for my sake that I take this stand. God knows, if I was free I'd be the happiest woman in the world to be your wife. 'Tain't fair to you. S'pose that bummer'd turn up. Ornery as he is, he'd cook up some yarn to get folks' sympathy, and you'd never get any peace on this earth, and I'd blame myself for bringin' that mis'ry on you."

"Then we must make every effort to learn something definite about him."

"That's what I think; but how are you goin' to do it? This is a large country, and he might be tucked away ever so far, and dead or alive, we couldn't find him," she answered.

"Suppose we go and see Colonel Franklin tonight, take him into our confidence and ask his advice."

"I think that's a good idea. Just wait till I get my bonnet and shawl and I'll go with you."

They found the Colonel in his study, and in few words Titcomb explained the object of their visit.

"How long has your husband been gone?" asked the lawyer.

"Five years, comin' Christmas," answered the widow.

"Did he say when he left that he would not return to live with you?"

"No, not exactly. After Tom was born Dennis would go off a year or two at a time, then come back and say he was sorry. And I, like a fool, would always believe him. But the night he went for good, he had just got a lot of money from a Richmond gentleman for enlistin' in the Southern Army, and when I asked him for some of it to pay the butcher and the baker and the candlestick-maker, he ups and hit me, and that's the last I ever seen of him. Times got so hard down our way, that work as I would, I couldn't make both ends meet, and I wrote to the Confederate authorities at Richmond askin' about Dennis. After a while I got a letter which said that he was a deserter, and had escaped through the Union lines."

"Did you ever try to find him?" questioned the Colonel, now thoroughly interested.

"I did, but it was nearly six months later before I heard anything about him. An exchanged prisoner,—I knew him because he was born down my way,—told me that Dennis was makin' a lot of money as a bounty jumper, an' livin' in clover, an' that he'd seen him in Baltimore."

"A bold rascal he must have been," interrupted the Colonel.

"I took my boy and walked clear to Baltimore, determined to make him support us."

"Did you see him there?" interposed Jebb.

"No, I found the provost-marshal had nabbed him, and sent him to the front. Finally, I traced out his regiment and wrote to his commander."

"And what was the reply?" queried Colonel Franklin.

"Why, the officer answered that by the records of the regiment, Dennis Foley was missin' after the first skirmish, and that nothin' had been seen of him since."

"Perhaps he was killed," ventured Jebb.

"No such good luck, I don't think. When the war was over, I met some soldiers from his company, and they said they were sure he had skedaddled."

"And what then?" laconically asked the lawyer.

"I've never heard another word about him. one

way or the other," said the widow, as she concluded her story.

"Now, Mrs. Foley," began the Colonel, "there are two ways open for you to be free, even though your husband should be alive. Under the statutes, three years of wilful desertion entitle you to a divorce, or, if you have not heard from him within five years, the law assumes a civil death, and you may legally remarry."

"But I can't set my heart on marryin' one man while the other may be alive an' kickin'. It seems to me to be sinful," said the widow, shaking her head.

"But these laws were made to cover just such cases as yours. He may never turn up. He may be dead. Even if he's alive, he may be married. If you love Mr. Jebb, it is your duty to make him happy by becoming his wife. And that duty is stronger than any weak scruple you may have about a man turning up who legally has forfeited his claim as a husband."

"That may all be true, Colonel Franklin, but if I marry and that rapscallion turns up, I'd never forgive myself for bringin' disgrace into Mr. Jebb's life."

"There is one thing more we can do," suggested the Colonel. "Suppose we put advertisements in the leading newspapers of New York, Chicago, Washington, Richmond and New Orleans, asking for information regarding your husband."

"That's the very thing I intended to suggest," said Jebb, brightening up. "If he's dead, some of his former comrades may know it and communicate with us."

"But suppose we hear he's alive?" faltered the widow.

"In that case all doubt would be dispelled, and you would be in a position to act intelligently, which seems almost impossible under present conditions," explained the lawyer.

"And if we find out he's dead, we can be married right off, can't we?" exclaimed Jebb impetuously.

"I want mighty good proof, Mr. Jebb," laughed Mrs. Foley. "I've been married once, and I know men use different colored spectacles after they're spliced than they do before."

"I'll prepare the advertisements," continued the Colonel, "and we'll see what comes of it."

"Very well, and as soon as you hear anythin', please let us know," concluded the widow, who then arose, bade the lawyer good night, and left in company with Jebb.

When the couple reached Mrs. Foley's house they tarried a while at the door, then she asked invitingly: "Won't you come in and have a glass of lemonade? It's pretty sultry to-night, and I think you'll enjoy it."

Delighted at the invitation, he went in.

The little parlor bore evidence not only of frugality, but of neatness and taste. The widow served the lemonade, and with it some cake, and the two chatted for a few minutes.

"Have you thought of all I said to you the other day?" began Jebb, recurring to the one subject ever present in his mind.

"Yes, Mr. Jebb, I've thought of it a thousand times. But don't talk to me like that again until I'm free to listen."

"There can be no harm in speaking about it."

"But, Mr. Jebb, it's jest misery to hear you say them lovin' things, ev'ry one of them entitled to an answer. I would jest like to scream out what my heart sez, but then I remember Dennis, and I freeze up."

"But, surely, the day must come when you can listen and speak."

"Let us hope so. Suppose, when you want to say somethin' real nice, you jest talk to Juno and I'll answer for her, bein' that she ain't here," suggested the widow.

"That's splendid," he said, "and reminds me, I have a wayward thought written only yesterday, and with Juno's kind permission, I'll read it."

"Do, Mr. Jebb. I've jest been hungry to hear about Juno. I mean Juno has been hungry to hear about Juno, for more than a week."

"I call this—"

"Mr. Jebb, jest a minute," she broke in, "before you read your new piece of po'try to me I want to ask you a promise."

"Ask me," he cried, delighted to have the opportunity to serve her. "Ask me, command me. There's nothing I wouldn't do for you and do it gladly."

"Mr. Jebb, what I ask is, whichever way this thing comes out 'bout Dennis, even if the Lord wills you and I must separate an' go our own ways, I want to ask you,"—her voice lowered,— "that you don't let anybody else be Juno."

"Any one else be Juno!" he exclaimed passionately, "any one else be Juno! There's no one in the world that could be Juno but you."

"Oh, no, Mr. Jebb," Mrs. Foley replied, "you'll make me stuck up if you talk that way. I know the world's world is very big and mine is very small, but whatever happens let me be to you Juno till I die."

"You shall be Juno till I die, till you die, and till the Judgment Day." He spoke in all earnestness.

"Excuse me, Mr. Jebb, for interruptin', jest as I always do. Juno's waiting; hurry 'long." She sat in an attitude of eager expectancy.

"I call this *Juno's Confession*," he said, "descriptive, as it were, of certain incidents in our lives lately enacted!"

> "Oh my heart was full of anguish,
> And a tear rolled down my cheek,
> As I heard your sad confession,
> Made on Tuesday of last week.
> There was no balm in Gilead,
> When I heard you sadly say
> That you must not, dare not, listen
> To my loving roundelay.
>
>> Juno, oh how I love thee,
>> Juno, oh how I love,
>> Juno,
>> You know,
>> To know
>> Juno,
>> Is like a dream from above.

On that most eventful Tuesday,
Sandy showed what he could do,
With the help of little Gilbert,
I was saved and so were you.
From the dark and angry waters,
We were yanked without delay.
'Twould have been quite awkward for us
If the boys had kept away.

        Juno, oh how I love you,
        Juno, oh how I love,
        Juno,
        You know,
        To know
        Juno,
        Is like a dream from above."

"I do declare, Mr. Jebb, you orter been one of them reporters on the newspapers; you tell a thing jest as it happens, and that's more'n they do mostly. And while you're tellin' it, it's still beautiful po'try, all the time. I could go on a list'nin' to you till the cows come home. I can see Sandy a-swimmin' for dear life and a-hollerin', 'Keep up, Mr. Jebb; don't get scared, Mrs. Foley.' When you were readin', it seemed like as if we were in the water flounderin' round and swallerin' a gallon ev'ry minute. It's a mystery how you can tell it so clear and never forget it's po'try."

"Modesty forbids me speaking, Mrs. Foley, but you know what Shakespeare says:

"'The form of things unknown the poet's pen
   Turns them to shapes, and gives to airy nothingness
   A local habitation and a name.'"

Jebb was floating on air because the one soul he loved appreciated his poetic efforts.

"Shakespeare's all right, but I don't ketch his pieces like I do yours. It beats me how you can do it," the widow said wonderingly. "Nothin' seems po'try in this world till you write about it. Them words like 'roundelay' and 'well-a-day' are mighty soothin' to a tired woman, and I jest say them over and over at night, and drop to sleep afore I know it, and that on the top of a hard day's wash, too. It's simply wonderful."

He rose and clasped her hands. Her full ripe lips and limpid eyes would have tempted an anchorite. To him she seemed the embodiment of all that was beautiful. With a sudden, uncontrollable impulse, he pressed forward as if to kiss her.

"No, no, Mr. Jebb," she cried, shielding her face, "not yet, not yet. If I'm ever to be kissed again it will be by you, but I can't now, you know I can't. Please go now; don't you see I'm blushing?"—and she laughed confusedly.

The widow stood at the door until his footsteps

died in the distance.   An hour later she was on
her knees, and let us hope that God in His wisdom
was listening to her prayer, so beautiful in its sim-
plicity, so pure in its sentiment.

CHAPTER XIV

About three weeks after Colonel Franklin had inserted the newspaper advertisements asking for information regarding Dennis Foley, the law firm of Franklin and Hayes received the following letter:

Dere sur   i red a pece in a chicago Paper bout a man whos name wuz denis foley who wuz a old frend of mine   denis foley who i node was born down on the patuxin river in merrylan an tole me so over and over agin   he had a wife merry but he called her molly an a sun named tomas which wuz the only sun he had an he called him tom likewise the only child he had as he had no gals and never had none   he tole me over an over agin that that wuz so   he went south an jined the army but didnt like the grub an konkluded hed leeve wich he did do the fust chance he got wich wuz one nite when he wuz dooin pickit dooty   he went up north after he wuz south an jined the northern army   as the grub didnt sute him he left an kame west me bein

239

with him an me an him traveld togethur it is a
sad story but i am sorry to say i kant say no more
bout him until i here from you an i am yourz
trooly   J or John Hildey.

  p s eny further infermashun will be cherfuly
tolld you to yure fase i am a pore man an need
muny mity bad you can rite me care of J or John
Hildey council bluffs ioway

Colonel Franklin sent for Jebb and the widow
at once, and read them the letter.

"This man's description tallies to a dot with
Dennis, and I'm sure he must know him," said
the widow.

"I will write immediately and ask him to come
on," said the Colonel.

"I'm afraid I'm more trouble than I'm worth,"
half-heartedly faltered the widow.

"Not at all," said Mr. Jebb. "It may be possible to find out from this man whether Foley is
still alive, and thus clear up the doubt in your
mind."

It was agreed that Colonel Franklin should send
a letter to Hildey, requesting him to come to Pipetown. He did so and received this reply:

dere sur   yure letter i reseavd wich you want
to no bout denis foley my ole frend and komrad
ime a very por man an kant aford to do nuthin
fur nothin but if U will garante to pay me 2 hunderd dolors an me expences to yure plais an back
i will kum on an tel you all bout denis foley
what he tole me over an over agin an what I no
anser as before an yurze trooly

> J or John Hildey

The lawyer answered with an offer to pay Hildey's expenses on arrival, and two hundred dollars for the information he claimed to have. The
return post brought the following:

i will kum on an tel you what I no bout denis
foley if U will sen me a ralerode ticket an muny
fer my bed an grub fer the time i luze an 2 hunderd dolors befor i start to tel U my story in yure
hous dont rite no more unles U mene biznes my
time is to valable to waist it ritin leterz fer nuthin
yurze trooley J or John Hildey adres as befor

The Colonel acted at once, and despatched the
following letters:

Messrs. Smith & Burnsy, Atty's at Law, Council
Bluffs, Ia.:

Gentlemen: There is a man residing in your
city named John Hildey, with whom we have
been in communication regarding certain facts
required by us.

It is necessary for him to come here and give
the information in person. We enclose draft for
One Hundred Dollars which we request that you
apply to the purchase of his railroad ticket and
necessary expenses for traveling. Kindly protect
us in this outlay to the best of your ability.

Very sincerely yours,

Franklin & Hayes, Attorneys at Law.

Mr. John Hildey, Council Bluffs, Ia.:

Dear Sir: Kindly call upon Messrs. Smith &
Burnsy, Attorneys at Law, of your city, who will
furnish you with transportation here and necessary expenses for traveling. We request that you
start at once. We agree to pay you Two Hundred Dollars for the information you say you can
give.   Very sincerely,

Franklin & Hayes.

These letters called forth the following replies:

Messrs. Franklin & Hayes, Attorneys at Law.

Dear Sirs: The party named in your inclosure of the 28th came to our office to-day. We have arranged for him to leave on the midnight train, and have placed his ticket and traveling expenses in the hands of the passenger agent of the road in this city. We also gave him Ten Dollars as pocket money, and hope he will turn up all right, although we are positive he belongs to the genus, "old bum," and therefore is a most unreliable customer. He showed us a letter in which you agreed to pay him Two Hundred Dollars for certain information he possesses, and insisted before he would consent to go, that we give him a letter indorsing you as a thoroughly reliable firm, which we did.   Very truly,

                              Smith & Burnsy.

P. S. In addition, we took upon ourselves the purchase of a suit of clothes for him, as he was most unpresentable when he came to our office.

mister franklin an hayes esq dere surs i am kuming on the ralerode an hope U will have the 2 hundred dolors reddy when i git thair. J or John Hildey council bluffs ioway

Five days later the office boy announced to Colonel Franklin a man named Hildey.

"Show him in," said the lawyer.

An unkempt specimen of humanity slouched into the office and stood hat in hand, waiting to be addressed.

"You are John Hildey, of Council Bluffs?"

"That's me name, Guv'ner, an' I got yer letters regardin' me fr'en' Dennis Foley, an' this 'ere one from the lawyers in my town. It sez yer responsible to cough up the two hundred bones yer promised."

"It's all right, Hildey; you'll get your two hundred at the proper time. But sit down; I want to talk to you, and expect you to answer me truthfully."

"How about the rhino?" inquired the visitor.

"Don't worry about that, I've given my word that I'll pay you for certain information, and I'll do it; but first I must ask you a few questions."

"That's all right, Guv'ner, fer you; but I gits lock-jawed when I don't see de tin," blared out the bum.

"The one question, the all important one; the one we brought you here for is, whether Foley is alive or dead."

"I'm no foo-foo, yer don't s'pose I'se goin' ter tell yer that, afore I sees the color of yer money, do yer?" rasped the stranger.

"No, nor do I intend to ask that question before I give you the money. What I want to know, for the present, is more about Dennis Foley. First of all, I must be absolutely sure that the man whom you knew as Dennis Foley is the one we are seeking."

"Fire away, Guv'ner, spout yer questions. I've got my ear to the groun'."

"Tell me anything you know about Dennis Foley, beyond what you stated in your letter."

"Well, Guv'ner, I fust met Dennis up in Philadelphy. He jest vamoosed from de Confed'rit Army an' skipped from Ohio, where he worked de bounty racket until it got too hot fer him. Then he landed in Philadelphy wher' I met him an' we gits to be great fr'en's. We kind er got together in a minit, fer we seemed borned fer each other; our dispositions was so tender-hearted. We worked up a little plan to make some money easy. I played bounty broker an' he played bounty jumper, an' we jest raked in the rhino an' had a great time. He must 'a' enlisted in ev'ry city from Baltimore to Boston

an' back, afore the provost-marshal grabbed him
an' sent him to the front, an' me a-goin' wid him
out er fr'endly feelin's.

"Our reg'ment laid round waitin' to git into a
scrimmage, an' one night when nobody wuz
lookin' an' we wuz doin' pickit duty, we seen the
Johnny Rebs a-crawlin' up, an' we makes a bee
line fer nowher' in partic'lar. 'Twuz a mighty
good thing fer us that we did, fer them Johnny
Rebs got clean up an' knocked the spots out er
our reg'ment."

"You don't mean to say that you ran away
without sounding an alarm, and arousing your
comrades?" asked Colonel Franklin, shocked at
this avowal of cowardice.

"We jes' got 'way, that's all, an' let the other
fellers fin' out the Johnny Rebs wuz comin'," volunteered the fellow, unabashed. "Then me an'
Dennis traveled all over the country, many a night
hidin' in a haystack, or some other cozy corner.
He tol' me 'bout his ol' home on the Pawtuxin
River; 'bout his wife who wuz pretty, an' that she
had blue eyes an' black hair, an' wuz put up like the
picture of the Goddess o' Liberty, an' that he had
a boy by the name of Tom; that his wife's maiden
name wuz Molly Madigan, an' she wuz born in

Maryland, an' that he had run away with her
when she wuz still goin' to school, an' the boy
wuz born before she wuz eighteen."

"There seems to be no doubt that this Dennis
Foley you describe is the very man we want. Now
if you will come here to-night at eight o'clock, I
will have the money for you; also the two persons who are most interested in this matter."

"All right, Guv'ner, I'll be here on time,"—
and the tramp shuffled out.

The lawyer immediately communicated with
Mr. Jebb and Mrs. Foley, and at the hour named
the four were seated in his office. Colonel Franklin spoke first.

"Mrs. Foley, this man, John Hildey, I am confident, knows, or did know, your husband thoroughly. His story coincides with yours, and I
now propose to ask him certain questions." Then
turning to the vagabond, he asked:

"Do you know, at this time, whether Dennis
Foley is dead or alive?"

"I cert'nly do, Guv'ner, an' when I sees the coin
I'll tell yer."

"And you'll give all further knowledge you
possess on this subject?"

"That's it, Boss; I'se got all the knowledge

right here in my coco'nut, an' jest as soon as I sees the rhino, I'll open my potato trap an' give it to yer, gospel truth."

The Colonel counted out two hundred dollars, and handed them to Hildey.

"As a Notary Public, Hildey, I ask that you be sworn. Do you, John Hildey, swear that what you say is the truth, the whole truth and nothing but the truth,—so help you, God?"

"I do," said the fellow with mock solemnity.

"Do you or did you know Dennis Foley of Maryland, born near Nottingham on the Patuxant River?"

"I know'd him well."

"Were you in the Northern Army together?"

"We wuz that."

"Did you leave the Army about the same time?"

"We cert'nly did do that."

"Did you travel together?"

"We wuz as close as a postage stamp on a watermelon."

"Tell us what you know of Dennis Foley, from the day you left the Army until the present time." Franklin sat back in the chair, awaiting the narrative.

"Well, sir, me an' Dennis concluded to travel West—'Go West, young man, go West'—sez Horace Greeley, so we goes West. We wuz havin' a mighty fine time seein' the sights, when one night it was snowin' an' jest as cold as charity, an' poor Dennis got chilled a-ridin' on a slow freight. Pneumoney sets in, an' I nussed an' nussed him but he didn't git no better, an' in a little while he drooped an' calls me to him, an' sez: 'Pard, 'tain't fer me to stay here longer in this vale of tears; 'tain't fer me to see my Molly, or my little chil', which we calls Tom, no more. Pard, cut off a lock o' me hair, an' if yer ever sees my Molly, give it to her with my love.' An' then he falls back a-moanin', sayin', 'Molly, Mary, Tom, I'm a-comin, I'm a-comin',' an' then he wuz dead an' dun fer." The old bum wiped the tears from his eyes, and added, "He wuz me only fren'."

He brought from his inside pocket a little leather bag, which he opened and handed to Mrs. Foley. It contained a lock of hair.

She looked at it intently, the tears welling in her eyes, and with great emotion, she said:

"God knows, that's his hair. I could tell it among a thousand. The Lord rest his soul, and may he sleep in peace."

"Amen!" religiously whispered the old vagabond.

"You were with him when he died?" asked
Jebb softly, moved by the stranger's touching
story.

"A holdin' him in me arms," said Hildey, apparently choking with emotion.

"How long since he died?" asked the Colonel
gravely.

"Must be about two years, now," said the
tramp, tapping his forehead.

"Where is he buried?"

"Please don't ask me that."

"Why not?" said Franklin, wondering.

Hildey leaned over, looked theatrically into
the faces of the listening group, and said in a
hoarse whisper:

"Grave robbers! Night doctors!"

"Horrible!" they all cried, and the widow
buried her face in her hands. For a moment
there was silence, which Colonel Franklin broke
with the words:

"I will put your statements into legal form, and
have you swear to them. Then, to-morrow, I
want you to go with me and see the Judge of the
Orphans' Court."

"All right, Guv'ner; in course yer pays me fer extry work?" said the visitor.

"Yes, I'll pay you for any service that you render."

Jebb and the widow talked long and earnestly with Hildey, and Mrs. Foley questioned him over and over again. Shortly after, she and the grocer arrived at her little home, and both went in.

"Mr. Jebb," said she, "there ain't no doubt from what we have heard to-night that Dennis has gone to his long home. He was away from me so much, from almost after Tom was born, that he has left nothin' but the recollection of a very unhappy life. I have always felt that divorce was wrong, and have allowed, as you makes your bed in the beginnin', so you lays in it to the bitter end. If he was alive an' kickin', I wouldn't touch him with a forty-foot pole, but, honest Injun, I don't believe you could have ever persuaded me to marry you, if we hadn't found out Dennis was dead. Mr. Jebb, you said a lot o' cheerin' and lovin' words to me, and the world seems much brighter since you started to sayin' 'em, now I'm goin' to say somethin' to you.

"When I first knew you, I was pleased when you sat next to me in the hoss-cars goin' up to market, but now I'd be proud to sit by your side on a curbstone and not a-goin' nowhere. You love me, and I know it, and I ain't goin' to pull away from you now, and I am yours for the askin'."

She leaned forward, her wonderful eyes tender in their gaze, her cheeks aglow and warm in the strength of her simple life, and thereupon they became engaged.

When John Hildey left the Colonel's office he went direct to his lodgings near the railroad station and started to write a letter. After a long struggle it was finished, and the envelop bore this address:

Mr. Dennis Foley, Esq.,
                  To be called fer,
                        Post Orfise,
                              Council Bluffs.

CHAPTER XV

Dennis Foley was a self-elected Ishmaelite, his hand against every man and every man's hand against him. He was of the lowest stratum of that peripatetic community that sprang into existence after the Civil War, now known as "tramps." In the cases of some of these aimless wanderers there may have been extenuating circumstances, for perhaps, through no fault of their own, they found themselves out of tune with the new conditions. But Foley was a vagabond, bummer and thief from choice.

The advertisement asking for information concerning himself came to his notice, as, in company with Hildey, he was working Council Bluffs in the many ways known to the gentry of the road. The scheme of answering the advertisement and of having Hildey go to Pipetown to announce him as dead was of Foley's own concoction.

Hildey had been gone fully two weeks, and Foley was becoming impatient for news from him. From morning till night he haunted the post-office, until at last a letter was handed him and with it he hurried back to the miserable shanty where he slept. With feverish eagerness he tore open the missive which read thus:

my old pard as i never brakes no promis i rites to tel yer all about it   when i get hear i sees the bloke as rote me the letters he is a lawer an started to ax me all bout U he sez bekauze he wanted to be shure U waz the man i gave him yer histry jest as U tole me without no hitch an it tallied with his to a t he had yure wife an a galoot they call jeb to kum to his orfise an with the tearze kumin to my eyze i sez pore denis foley is ded these 2 yerze jest as U tole me to say an when I gave them the lock of yure hair yure gal jest cride an sed god res his sole an may he sleep in pece i axed them why they wanted to no an i foun out the groser wants ter mary yure wife shes a hummer jest as U sed she wuz an as purty as a painted post yer wife wuz willin to mary him provided she new U wuz ded so there goin to git maryd kauze yer ded but she wouldener if U werent ded an she tole me that hersef over an over agin i seed yer boy tom hes jest like you

as 2 pees in a pod if yer wasnt ded i wood luv
to tel him so.   yure old fren

John 399 N. J. ave this place.

Foley looked through the envelop carefully,
shook it, swore a chain of linked blasphemy, and
then exclaimed:

"Durn his soul; he don't say nuthin' 'bout the
rhino.   'Tain't no use, yer can't trust nobody.
I'll jest send him a scorcher an' if he don't come
back an' pony up my share, I'll go on an' break his
infernal neck, if I has to swing fer it."

Several letters passed between the scamps, but
in his replies Hildey was careful to say nothing
of the money, and Foley became desperate.   He
determined to go to Pipetown.

About a month after Hildey's interview with
Colonel Franklin, Dennis Foley, half-drunk, and
quarrelsome, confronted his chum at his miserable lodging house.

"Where's me money?" he shouted, trying to
grasp his partner by the throat.

Hildey eluded him, and began to talk in a
soothing tone.

"Set down, pard; don't git excited. Let me
tell yer all 'bout it, but afore we go ahead, take a

drink of good old buck-juice,"—and he handed a long black bottle to Foley, who drank deeply.

"Yer a nice pardner," sneered Foley. "I puts yer on the track to make a honest penny, an' yer goes back on me an' don't divvy as yer orter have."

"I wuz a-goin' to bring yer all the rhino, Dennis, s'elp me bob, I wuz, if I hadn't had a dream. I dreams three times han' runnin' I wuz a-ridin' on a golden chariot, with beautiful white horses an' the prettiest tails yer ever seen."

"Well, what's that got to do with it?" said the other.

"Nuthin', as I kin see now, but a lot jest then. I wuz on my way to the railroad station to come out ter yer with the tin an' I runs up ag'inst a policy shop, an' right afore my eyes comes the dream ag'in, an' so I sez, why not bring Dennis twict as much? I goes in an' plays a hunderd on 'horses' an' loses; then I plays t'other hunderd on 'gigs,' an' durned if I didn't lose ag'in, an' then I wuz broke. I can't get it through my coco'nut, no way I looks at it, 'bout that 'ere dream. It wuz horses an' chariots, an' it means yer can't lose if yer plays 'em right. But when I tells the policy man 'bout it, he sed mebbe it was a steam engine I dreamed an' no numbers didn't go with that."

"Yer a liar, an' yer knows it; yer blow'd the money in on whisky, an' yer ain't man 'nuff to say so. I've got half a mind to break yer bloody neck,"—and Foley arose, as if he meant mischief.

"Don't do nuthin' brash, Dennis, 'cause yer'd be awful sorry if yer hurt yer old pard," pleaded Hildey.

"What yer doin' now to keep a-goin'?" queried the other, quieting down for the moment.

"As far as the galoot an' the lawyer is concerned, I've milked 'em dry, but I'm doin' a little in the sneak line, an' with your help, we may pick up some good things round here in the houses. 'Tain't no use tryin' the German count driven from home, or the Irish lord what can't go back, 'cause the peelers grab yer here an' run yer in the chain-gang, even if yer sed yer wuz the Czar of Rooshy. I've seen some invitin' houses which don't have no padlocks on their back doors, where we might do some bizness."

"But have yer seen this man what wants ter marry my gal, or the lawyer what wrote, sence yer tol' 'em I wuz dead?"

"That feller what's goin' ter splice with yer

gal wuz mighty 'commodatin' at first, gives me lots o' grub an' knickknacks, an' treats me mighty white, but I comes into his place full as a goat four nights runnin', an' one night when he wuzn't lookin' I tho't I'd tap his till fer a bundle of shin plasters, an' while he didn't have me pulled in, he invited me to stay 'way."

"How 'bout the lawyer, that snoozer Franklin?"

"He's a heartless feller. He's got no 'preciation of a hard-workin' citizen like me. After I had got some money outer him, five or six times, he seemed to drap to me, an' last week when I went to his office, he booted me out. Jest think of it, booted me clean out to the gutter, and me a gentleman, born an' bred!" The rum-soaked loafer spoke in an aggrieved tone, and shook his arm wildly.

"I think yer durn foolishness has sp'ilt the whole game fer me, an' I ain't got a red out o' it yet," angrily cried Foley.

"They don't know nuthin' 'bout you, pard, but they're on ter me. Whatever yer do, I gives yer a clean start, fer ye're dead up to this time, as fur as they knows. My influence round here don't 'mount to much, jest now. Why, that bloke

Franklin sez to me, when I wuz sneakin' in his hallway after dark an' near scared the women out'n their wits, he sez, a-grabbin' me by the collar, an' whackin' me as if I wuz the bull drum in a nigger band—'If. I ever sees yer aroun' here ag'in, I'll have yer sent up!'—an' he chases me clean round the corner, a-kickin' me, an' me a gentleman born an' bred."

"You a gentleman born an' bred! If yer had a know'd yer bizness we might 'a' worked this thing right along, a-sayin' I wuz dead one month an' alive the next, but yer never will be nobody," —and Foley drank long at the bottle.

" 'Tain't too late, yer old gal ain't taken on ag'in yet."

"When does she git married?" asked Foley.

"Tom tol' me, yer son Tom,—he's a fine boy, so much like his dad! Yer orter git acquaint'd to him, Dennis, he's one of us, jest as nacherel as if he had been bro't up to it," Hildey mumbled garrulously.

"Durn the boy! When does the old gal git hitched?"

"That's what I wuz comin' to; Tom sez the weddin' takes place on Christmas Eve."

"Christmas Eve?" mused Foley. "It wuz

Christmas Eve when I skedaddled; lemme see,"
—he took another drink from the bottle, and
looked into space. "Yes, jest five years gone.
I remember it as if it wuz yesterday. I got
a lot o' money from Colonel Glenn to shoulder a musket fer Jeff Davis, an' I had a row
with Molly 'cause the rent wuz due, an' the
groc'ry bill wuz due, an' her shoes were all
worn out, an' she sed she wuz workin' like a
nigger, an' tol' me that I wuz a whisky sot.
I tol' her I didn't 'low no woman to talk to me
that 'ere way, an' I bangs her in the eye, an' starts
up stairs to git my duds. When I comes down, I
sees her a-trimmin' a Christmas tree fer the boy.
I sneaks out, 'cause if I hadn't I'd 'a' banged her
other eye, an' as I passes the winder she was
kneelin' down with her arms aroun' Tom's neck,
an' a-sayin' prayers. I almos' busted, a-tryin' to
keep from laffin', fer while she was a-cryin' an'
a-prayin', Tom wuz jest a-yankin' things off'n
that tree, an' she never noticed it. It wuz funny,
an' I laffed over it many times, thinkin' how Tom
fooled her."

"That's Tom all over," said Hildey. "He's
goin' to be a great man, an' orter git purty high
in the world,"—and with drunken familiarity, he

slapped the proud father's back playfully but with a heavy hand.

"Not too high, pard; not too high," said the other, now drunk.

"No, not too high; not as high as a gallus."

"What d'yer mean by gallus?" said Foley, grasping the neck of the bottle menacingly.

"I was jest a-thinkin' of somethin' high, and gallus seemed to be nacherel."

"What does Tom say about this shameful marriage?" queried the other.

"He's flabbergasted. He sez 'tain't decent, an' he's willin' to swear on a stack o' Bibles a mile high that his mother has been talked into it by that bloke Franklin. Drat him fer meddlin' in other people's affairs, an' durn him fer kickin' me, —yes, kickin' me three times,—d'yer hear,—me, a gentleman born and bred."

"Did yer tell Tom I wuz erlive?"

"No, I wouldn't tell him that; he might blab it, an' I'd have to skip mighty fast. But he sez to me, t'other night—wouldn't it be funny if my dad'd just turn up an' spile the ol' woman's scandalous conduct."

"But I can't turn up. I'd be nabbed fer a deserter."

"Bosh! The war's over, an' they ain't botherin' much jest now 'bout deserters, yer kin bet. If yer show yerself, an' worst comes to worst, yer could cook up a yarn 'bout havin' been tak'n pris'- ner by the rebs an' dump'd down in Cuby, or some other place, an' this is the fust chance yer had to git back."

"Did you think o' that?" questioned Foley.

"Naw, that's Tom's idee. He sez a hundred times, 'I jest wisht the ol' man wuzn't ded.' 'But he is,' I sez; 'ded as a door nail.' He sez 'I wisht dad wuz erlive, if only for a long 'nuff time to come on an' break up mum's weddin';' but I tells him, if yer wuz alive, yer wouldn't dast show yer- self as yer ran away from the Army. An' then he sez, 'Why, if dad hadn't turn'd up his toes, and he show'd up here now, he could cook up a yarn that half of the galoots roun' here would think wuz true,' an' Tom sed he wouldn't be surprised if the gov'nment would give yer a pension, and Congress vote yer some thanks fer yer devotion to the Union. Tom sez it's a blamed shame yer kick'd the bucket, when yer chances look so good."

"That Tom mus' be a cute boy, an' if they ever gits the nippers on me, I'll use Tom's idee, an' make 'em weep when I tells how I fit an' bled for my country,"—and he drained the last drop from his glass.

" Was Tom sorry I wuz dead?"

"He wuz, fer truth," said the other, going over to his bed and extracting from between the mattresses another long-necked bottle. Pulling the cork he took a long swig and handed the bottle to Foley.

"That's mighty good whisky, beau; wher'd yer git it?" asked Dennis, smacking his lips.

"Me an' Tom's been workin' the little stores round here, an' we ain't los' no time."

"How does yer do it?"

"Me an' Tom goes into a store with a tin can an' asks fer a pint o' 'lasses, an' I goes down with the ol' woman into the cellar to help draw it, an' yer know how mighty slow 'lasses is. Tom picks up anythin' handy, like a bottle of whisky, or ef the money drawer ain't locked, a dollar or two, but we makes the pickin's so light that we works the same store three times a week."

"That's all right, pard; so jest fork over my share o' the swag."

"Dennis, old pard, as I'm a gentleman born an' bred, I ain't got more'n a dollar to my soul.

I wuz so stuck on them white horses an' chariots, that I've played policy ev'ry day, hopin' to git me money back. But if yer lets up on me, I'll tote fair from this time out."

"I'll see that yer do. If yer do me dirt ag'in, I'll kill yer. Here I am, an' I ain't in nuthin' fer bein' dead. 'Cordin' to my countin', I ain't dead, an' I ain't dead fer nuthin', an' they'll find it out, curse 'em!" Foley rolled over on the bed, clutching the bottle tightly, and soon fell asleep.

Hildey took a long drink, and mumblingly said: "That bloke wouldn't help a pore man, curse him! an' kicked me out inter the gutter,—a gentleman born and bred, an' so I sez curse him!" The sot crept over against his partner, and almost immediately began to snore.

CHAPTER XVI

THE NOCATCHTANK CLUB

The season for shooting ortolan and other marsh-birds was drawing to a close in Pipetown. The reed-bird had begun his journey southward, and the monotonous "click-click" of this ornithological glutton was scarcely heard in the fields.

Ye, who live only to eat, ponder while ye may! Bow ye not to the gastronomic idol, hanker ye not for the delights of the festal board! Verily, I say, ponder in fear and trembling as ye view the speedy degeneration of this foolish bird, victim of his own voracious appetite!

In the glad springtime, what song more joyous, what voice more musical than the bobolink's?

Love is in his heart; love tones gush from his melodic throat. For him the day is fair, the sun is bright, and all the world is wocing.

Darting here and there among the buds that blossom in the orchard, he plays at hide-and-seek with his mate, happy from dawn to dusk. He builds his nest in sweetest meadow-land, and rears his young in great joy to the strains of ecstatic trills.

But soon there comes a change.

His song is hushed, his once happy home deserted.

Neighbors begin to whisper.

Mrs. Blue Jay, in confidence, tells Mrs. Catbird, who informs Mrs. Robin, who in turn asserts to little Miss Wren, that something is wrong with the Bobolinks.

They have reason for this gossip. The once well-groomed bird allows its black and buff plumage to grow seedy, and when finally the feathery Mrs. Grundy puts him outside the pale of polite society, he vanishes in a night. Southward he flies, with the one desire paramount,—to eat.

His garb has become an ashen yellow, and in his downward path he changes his name, and now is known as the Reed-bird. His beauty and symmetry of form have disappeared, and in their place is a decided aldermanic *cmbonpoint*.

At the coming of autumn's first chill winds, he departs hastily for the fields of Carolina, and, from daylight to dark, gorges himself, and, wholly forgetful of ancestral pride, assumes another name, the Rice Bunting.

Under this alias his voracity leads him still farther southward, until he reaches the Isles of the Summer Sea, a lazy lump of yellow fat.

Now he is the Butter Bird, *sans* song, *sans* sentiment, *sans* plumage, *sans* everything, but mighty fine broiled on toast.

During the season's shooting Gilbert was frequently Sandy's companion, and had acquired considerable skill and accuracy as a wing shot. This was attested by the liberal number of sora or ortolan, reed, sprig-tails and blue-wings he had brought home. It was an unwritten law among Pipetown hunters never to shoot at a sitting bird, and Gilbert was ever scrupulously faithful to this tradition.

Sandy, Leander, Dink and Gilbert were to meet by appointment at the Jedge's to discuss a hunting and camping trip. Sandy arrived first, and Gilbert's shooting became the source of conversation.

"He's got a nacheral eye," said Sandy to the Jedge, describing some particularly fine shot Gilbert had made. "When he hits, he does it jest as clean as a hound's tooth. 'Tain't many cripplers with him; jest close shootin', an' I enjoys a-showin' him how."

"I'm mighty glad to hear he ain't one er them fellers as closes his eyes and let's the Lor' direct the shot," said the old man approvingly.

"No sirree, Jedge, if the birds carried bells, he'd ring 'em lots o' times, he shoots so close."

Gilbert, Leander and Dink finally came, and the pleasure trip was discussed.

"I should say," remarked the Jedge, " 'bout the best time to camp out would be Thanksgivin' week. The river orter be loaded down with canvas-backs, red-heads, mallards, an' all sorts of trash ducks. Uplands an' yeller shanks are apt to be plentiful, an' there ain't no tellin' but what we might be able to pick up a good many snipe an' woodcock. An' fer a change, it 'pears to me, judgin' by the dry summer, there orter be lots an' lots o' partridges in the stubble, an' cottontails so thick that they'll trip yer up."

"Well, Jedge, the time is all right, but we don't want no big gang of fellers goin' 'long, d'ye think?" inquired Sandy.

"Ye're right, a big gang's always in the way. A party orter be congenial, leastwise to themselves, to say nuthin' o' common politeness to each other," said the Jedge in his most conclusive manner.

"I've made a list; see how this will suit," spoke Gilbert.

Captain and Executive Officer, ...	The Jedge.
Adjutant and Flag Lieutenant, ...	Sandy Coggles.
Sergeant Major and Master at Arms, .	Leander Daindridge.
First Private and Able Seaman, . . .	Dink Dabney.
Second Private and Ordinary Seaman,	Gilbert Franklin.
Striker and Mess Attendant, ...	Matt Johnson.

"That strikes me jest about right, with one 'ception," said the Jedge. "I 'low it orter read this 'ere way—Second Private and Walkin' Dictionary, Gilbert Franklin. Yer see, Gil, we might need yer book-l'arnin' to straighten things out, an' 'twouldn't be fair to the rest to call on a second private 'less he wuz 'titled to that 'ere position."

The Jedge resumed his seat and pipe, amid applause.

"I votes with the Jedge's 'mendment that it passes," said Dink. The resolution was unanimously carried.

"Now, Jedge, what must we take along?" asked Gilbert.

"As a starter, one Sibley tent and one bell tent."

"I'll get those," said Leander. "I am sure my uncle, the Commodore, will lend them to me from the Government stores at the Yard."

"Two lanterns," continued the Jedge.

"I'll get those, too," added Leander.

"Groceries an' sich, to last a week," went on the old man.

"My father promised to buy all the provisions we'll need, so I'll take care of that item," said Gilbert.

"Fishin' tackle, decoys, an' skiffs will be supplied by Yours Truly,"—this from the Jedge.

"Me an' Dink'll git the tin plates fer to eat out'er, an' a ax an' hatchets, so don't worry 'bout them," assured Sandy.

"Everybody brings his own gun, ammernition, knife, knapsack, blankets and rubber boots, an' I'll bring fryin' pan, chowder-pot, coffee-pot, an' skillets, so that orter be 'nuff," said the old hunter.

"If there's anything we've forgotten, and any one happens to think of it, he'd better jot it down and bring it up at the next meeting," added Gilbert.

"Now, remember boys," spoke the Jedge, "we start at four o'clock A. M. afore light, from Jebb's Corner, Monday mornin' of Thanksgivin' week, rain or shine, in this year of our Lord."

"Hold on, just a minute!" said Gilbert, standing in the center of a little group. "My father says, before the white man discovered this country there was a powerful tribe of Indians that lived on the banks of our river. From Pencote up and beyond Oyster Shell Landing, the shores of the stream were dotted with the wigwams of the red men. They hunted and fished and—did everything—before our ancestors drove them away. Let's call ourselves after them: the 'Nocatchtank Hunting and Fishing Club'."

"I seconds that with 'mendments, which is this," said the Jedge; "the title to be the Nocatchtank Huntin' an' Fishin' Club, Gilbert Franklin, Little Admiral, an' the other officers to remain as they wuz. It is already carried 'nanermous an' the meetin' is adjourned."

The days following were busy ones for the boys. Everything needed for the trip was carried to the boat-house and stored.

On the specified day the little party started, accompanied by the Jedge's two setters, Sandy's water spaniel, and Matt's 'possum dog, Blinkey. The Jedge, Leander, Dink, Matt and the dogs went in the *Lillian*. Sandy and Gilbert paddled up in the skiff *Dolly*. They reached their destination, Licking Banks, by eight, and the boys immediately began preparations for camping. Poles were cut on which to hang the coffee-pot, and soon a fire was burning brightly.

"Boys, I hereby elects myself cook o' the occasion, an' will prepare yer one o' my five-minute breakfasts, celebrated from here to Jericho. Ev'rybody stir yer stumps! Gimme the eggs, Matt; grease the pan, Dink; slice the bolony, Sandy; chop off a bit of bacon, Leander; pour in the milk, Gil, while I hold the pan over the coals." The Jedge lapsed into silence and watched the contents of the pan begin to cook.

The rest of the party were interested lookers-on and the air was soon filled with appetizing odors.

"Whoa," said the Jedge, taking a fork, and tasting the dish as it sizzled. "It's all right, boys, O K, copper-bottomed, an' a dish fit fer Apolly Belvidery, or enny other gentleman. Take that coffee off, Sandy, she's b'ilin' over. The rest of yer boys git plates an' things, an' bread an' butter. In one minit we eats."

And eat they did.

After the meal the tents were carried ashore and erected beneath the bluffs. In a couple of hours everything was ship-shape, and the Jedge made his assignments for the day.

Sandy and Gilbert went to hunt for grass-ducks at Piney Run in the *Dolly*.   With them was Prince, the water spaniel. After they had paddled up stream for some distance, Gilbert whispered suddenly, "Mark left."

Far ahead and to the north were flying a flock of mallards. The boys turned their skiff into a tiny creek, and watched with breathless interest. The big, strong-flying ducks began to circle. At each turn they came nearer the ground, and, after a cautious outlook, rose and darted downward again and again, finally settling in a pool in a large zizania marsh, a long distance ahead.

"I know jest where they went down," said Sandy, "an' if we work right we'll git a crack at 'em."

Silently the skiff was pushed into deep water.

"I'll bet they're up in Piney Run," whispered Sandy. "Jest as soon as we git inside the mouth of the creek, put away yer paddle as soft as possible an' git out yer creepers. Don't make no noise, fer a mallard's got the best hearin' an' the sharpest eyes of ennything that flies."

In due time the boys reached the Run. They were crouching low and Gilbert was using the creepers, much as a fish does his fins. Gun in hand, the older boy sat watching for the ducks at every turn in the creek. Not a sound was uttered. Occasionally a terrapin, sunning himself on the bank, would topple over into the water with a faint splash.

The boys had glided at least a mile through the circuitous creek, when Sandy put a warning finger to his lip. They turned the corner, when "Quack! quack!" up rose the bunch of mallards, not forty yards away. The surprised flock jumped against the wind, and as they wheeled, Sandy let them have both barrels, and down tumbled nine ducks.

The strain was over, and the boys gave way to loud shouts of joy. It was Gilbert's first experience at grass-duck shooting, and he was wild with excitement.

"I got nine with two barrels," exulted Sandy, "and there's two cripplers gone down ahead. We'll have to push fer 'em."

" 'Twould be too bad to lose them," spoke the other.

"Prince'll git 'em if he hasn't lost his nose," said Sandy with confidence, lovingly patting the dog on the head.

Prince looked up and wagged his tail as if to say, "Depend on me, I'll find them."

After the dead ducks were gathered into the skiff, Sandy took the shoving pole and Gilbert sat in the gunner's seat. The older boy punted the *Dolly* through the marsh, in the direction where the wounded ducks had gone down. The spaniel kept his nose well over the bow, alert and ready. Suddenly there was a rustling in the weeds, and up came a crippler, flying strong.

"Shoot him!" shouted Sandy.

Gilbert banged with his first barrel and missed, but almost instantly he fired again, this time bringing down his quarry. Then out jumped Prince, and retrieved the fallen duck.

The second crippler was not so easily found. He had evidently hidden in one of the numerous muskrat houses which dotted the marsh. The boys had about given him up, when the dog unexpectedly darted from the boat, and up scampered a beautiful black mallard, with wing broken, but still exceedingly active.

Prince was in hot pursuit. Through reeds, over clear places, and everywhere the mallard ran, swam and hopped. He could not fly and he could not remain long under water. For fifteen minutes the boys watched this exciting exhibition of hide-and-seek, until finally the dog cornered the duck in a bunch of matted grass, seized it, and carried it carefully to the skiff.

As the lads paddled slowly down the main channel, Gilbert noticed a number of little objects bobbing on the water and asked excitedly, "Do you see anything?"

"I think I do," said the older. "Jest turn in this 'ere creek for a minit, Gil. We'll have to make a blind if it's ducks."

They ran the boat ashore, got out and cut a number of cedar boughs, which they piled up in the bow of their tiny craft.

"Yer see, it's this 'ere way," said Sandy. "When there ain't any ice on the river, yer can creep on a white-back or a red-head, if yer jest hide yerself 'hind somethin' green; an' when there is ice on the river, if yer hide yerself 'hind somethin' white, the chances is yer can git within shootin' distance er the game." Sandy brought out the creepers, and lying flat again, the boys moved the skiff slowly toward the black objects.

"Ducks, an' no mistake!" whispered Sandy, as they came near enough to see them swimming and diving in the open water.

"'Take yer first shot when they jump, an' give 'em bally-hooly when they double," cautioned Sandy quietly.

Nearer and nearer the *Dolly* drifted, while the waterfowl, warned by their instinctive sense of danger, swam toward a common center, and crowded together so closely that a large blanket might have covered them completely from sight. Apparently by concerted action, they rose in a body.

"Paste 'em, Gil!" shouted Sandy in great excitement.

From some unexpected cause, which he never could explain, Gilbert pulled the trigger before he got the gun to his shoulder, and the recoil struck him full and square in the nose. Then, to make his misfortune worse, he lost his balance, and overboard went dead ducks, dog, and both boys.

Gilbert swam to the overturned boat and held on for dear life. Sandy came up out of the water some ten feet behind, and quickly joined his companion. Together they shoved the tiny craft into a shallow place and righted it. The gun Sandy secured by diving, while the scattered ducks were retrieved by the spaniel.

"What became of the ducks I started to shoot?" asked Gilbert, pulling off his boots and emptying them of water.

"I guess they wuz too busy to stay," laughed Sandy. "When they seen us go kerflop they felt so sorry that they put on extry steam an' went home to tell their mothers all 'bout it."

"Golly, but I'm wet!" said the little fellow, with teeth chattering.

"Don't mind that, jest take a double paddle an' work it fer all ye're worth, an' yer'll be as warm as a bug in a rug."

Reëntering the skiff they shoved off and soon reached the camp. It did not take them long to put on dry clothes, and, none the worse for the adventure, barring Gilbert's battered nose, they were soon relating their experience. The Jedge congratulated them on their fortunate escape, and then said:

"Don't ever ag'in put yer finger on the trigger, Gil, until ye're ready to shoot off your gun, an' know what ye're shootin' at. Lots o' people on this earth git inter trouble by shootin' off their mouth before they knows what they're aimin' at. Ye're mighty lucky to git off so easy."

During the giving of this advice, Leander and

Dink returned from Succabel's Cove where they had been hunting woodcock. A bare half-dozen constituted their bag.

"Hunting woodcock isn't the thing it's cracked up to be, Jedge," lamented Leander.

"No, that's true; there's a powerful lot o' room outside o' woodcock," chuckled the old man.

" 'Tain't tellin' anythin' out'n the way," chimed in Dink, "when I sez we misses four woodcock fer every one we git, when we do git 'em. They look dead easy, but they keep yer wonderin' how they kin go right on after yer shoot at 'em. But they do, an' no joke."

"The woodcock is a noble bird," said the Jedge, "but he is shot at so much, he jest gits used to it. It's a wonder to me he hasn't lost confidence in the world an' passed in his checks, a-goin' where the wicked cease from trouble an' the weary are at rest."

"They git mighty brash sometimes, though," said Dink. "Honest-to-goodness, if one didn't turn round this mornin' an' make a bee-line fer Leander. I thought he wuz goin' to take Leander's gun away from him, an' it scared me so I hollered fer my mother."

"Yer must have been born under a lucky star,

Leander," laughed the Jedge. "'Twas only yer luck saved yer gun. Ye're certainly lucky. I spec' if yer tumbled overboard yer'd come up dusty."

Supper was nearly ready,—the potatoes were roasting in the ashes, the fish were frying, and the ducks were broiling on the spit.

Matt, the darky, had built a table during the day, and the Jedge, with the boys, gathered round it for their evening meal. Matt sat by the fire, a huge piece of bacon, some sweet potatoes and a can of steaming coffee before him. Blinkey, his dog, was dozing near by.

"I spec's, Matt," said the Jedge, "that yer like hog-meat better'n mos' anything else, don't yer?"

"I 'knowledges the co'n, Jedge; I'se powerful fond o' hog-meat. But if yer wants this culled pusson to be right in heaven, jest gimme roas' 'possum.'"

Blinkey opened his eyes, raised his head, and listened attentively.

"'Possum?" queried Leander.

"'Possum's what I sez," repeated the darky, and his dog looked around sharply.

"'Possum, stuffed with sweet potatoes, is jest about right," said the Jedge.

" 'Possum, sah! 'tain't nuthin' like 'possum; 'tain't nuthin' like 'possum! It's de bestest an' mos' appetizin'ist thing in de wo'ld, an' dat's 'possum, sah, 'possum, an' jest 'possum."

The reiteration of 'possum had some effect on the dog. He became restless and suddenly disappeared. Before Matt had finished expatiating on the beauties of 'possum, the dog was heard vigorously barking in the woods. Everybody was alert.

"That sounds mighty like 'possum," said the Jedge, listening intently.

"Dat sounds jest like 'possum," said Matt, and taking a lantern he led the way into the timber, directed by the sounds coming from Blinkey.

"Dar's a 'possum, sho',"—and up the tree the darky shinned.

"Dar he is, out'n dat limb, a-makin' out he's sleepy. Gimme yo'h hatchet." Sandy immediately climbed up to Matt and handed it to him. In an instant the darky had cut the limb. Down came Mr. 'Possum, and fell among the group, lying motionless and grinning like a simpleton. Quick as a flash, Blinkey had mastered him, and in triumph the animal was brought to the camp.

"I sho'ly hoped we'd git a 'possum sometime,

but, hones' nigger, I didn't spec' to hev one so soon,"—and Matt patted his dog's head approvingly.

"That 'ere exhibition of Blinkey's is what scientific men calls 'canine intelligence,'" expounded the Jedge. "He listened to us talkin' 'bout 'possum, an' he made up his mind we wanted one."

"I'se been a-hankerin' ar'ter 'possum sence away befoh' las' grass," said the darky.

"Speakin' o' canine intelligence, I used ter have a dog what had more of it than yer could shake a stick at."

"When was that, Jedge?" asked Leander. The Jedge needed only an interlocutor.

"It wuz before the war," the Jedge commenced, and every one around the fire listened intently.

THE JEDGE'S STORY

I wuz settin' home one mornin', jest pinin' 'cause my rheumatiz wuz troublin' me, a ruminatin' on the vicissitudes of life, as scientific men would say, when along comes one of them furriners with a shingle up his back, they call valets.

He ups and sez, "I understand ye're the party

this note is intended fer," an' hands me a letter, addressed an' superscribed to me.

It was from a gentleman in Philadelphy I know'd. It sez he would be much 'bliged if I'd give his fren', C. Johnson-Johnson, Esquire, a good hunt, an' furnish him with a dog an' a guide, if I wuz person'lly unable to go.

I told the party to say to Mr. C. Johnson-Johnson, Esquire, that the dog an' guide would be ready fer him any time he would call. He said his guv'ner would be down the nex' mornin'.

Well, sir, nex' mornin' 'bout nine, in walks C. Johnson-Johnson, Esquire. He wuz one of them sweet-scented roosters whose nose seemed huntin' fer a smell all the time. He wore green goggles an' put on 'nuff luggs fer a peacock with two tails. He wuz arrayed as never wuz Daniel Boone in the dark an' bloody groun's: moccasins, buck-skin pants with tossels up the side, fur coat, an' squirrel cap. He weighed 'bout as much as a bar o' soap after a hard day's wash, an' he wuz nervous as the St. Vitus dance.

I sed, "C. Johnson-Johnson, Esquire, ye're certainly rigged up fer keeps. We don't hunt pa'-tridges and cotton-tails in that 'ere kind o' garb down here."

"But I desires to," says the sassiety tad, mighty pompous.

"Enny way yer likes, as the turkey sed when he was asked how he wanted to be cooked," I whacked back.

"I propose to go as I wish," he barked like he had a double chin.

Sez I, "Are yer a good shot?"

He looks at me cantankerous like an' drawls, "I never miss."

I ups an' sez, "That's all right, Mr. Philadelphy. If yer never miss, I've got the dog an' nigger to go with yer, an' they'll show yer more birds in a day than yer ever seen afore in yer life. But remember, it's no use o' takin' that 'ere dog along if yer misses. He don't like it an' he's powerful partic'lar who he hunts with."

"I told you that I never miss," sez the sassiety tad, almost a-hollerin' at me.

I whistles fer my dog, an' Bob comes out, lookin' at the stranger, curious like.

"What breed was the dog, Jedge?" queried Leander.

He hadn't no special breed, jest plain dog. I guess his pedigree wuz all breeds 'cept pug. I never had no use fer a pug. Pugs always riled me. My dog never riled me, so I kalkerlate he never had no pug in him.

Well, as I wuz sayin', I sez, "Here's the dog. His name's Bob, an' he'll stay with yer as long as yer hit. But if yer miss three times runnin', I won't guarantee him."

"I told you I never miss," bellered the sassiety tad, a-stampin' with his foot. Then he asked, bossy-like, "Are you goin' as my guide?"

"I would like to, jest to see yer pop 'em over, only my rheumatiz is so bad I can't walk," I sez, "but I've got a kidney-foot nigger, named Ebenezer, who knows ev'ry inch of groun' in these 'ere parts,"—and I whistles fer Ebenezer, who wuz snoozin' 'cross the street.

When he comes over I tells him I wants him to go with the gentleman an' give him a good hunt; an' so Ebenezer sed good-by to his folks an' got ready to start. I called the dog an' the nigger over to me an' I sez, "I've lent yer to this 'ere gentleman, C. Johnson-Johnson, Esquire, for to go huntin'. He sez he never misses, so yer orter have er continual round o' pleasure."

Bob looked at the stranger, an' I hope I may die if the dog didn't shake his head, sorrowful like. Ebenezer didn't say nuthin', but he pop-eyed so at

the tad I kicked him twict on the shins afore he'd
let go a-lookin'.

"Be mighty keerful of both of 'em, 'specially the
dog," I sez, as the sassiety tad picked up his gun.

"Come, Bob," sez he, shoulderin' his firearm,
which was a britch-loader, an' the fust that me an'
Bob an' the nigger'd ever seen.

Bob looked at the tad an' grabbed him by the
coat-tail an' was pullin' him back. The man got
awful scared an' hid behind me.

"Jest wait till I finds out what the trouble is," I
sez. Bob kep' jumpin' up as though he wanted to
reach the gun.

"Come on!" sez Mr. Philadelphy, startin' once
more. The dog grabs his coat-tails ag'in an'
hangs on. "Somethin's wrong," I sez. I calls
the dog off, an' patted him on the head. He took
hold o' my sleeve an' led me over to the corner
of the room where my ol' muzzle loader was
restin', an' rubbed his nose ag'in the ramrod four
or five times.

It jest come to me in a minit what the trouble
wuz. Bob noticed the stranger's gun hadn't no
ramrod, bein' a britch-loader, an' he didn't understan' it. I sez to the stranger, "You can't
blame him: he ain't never seen a britch-loader

afore an' he knows a ramrod is indispensable to a gun gener'lly." I jest took the stranger's gun an' showed Bob how it worked, an' he walked off with the tad, waggin' his tail satisfied like, an' they wuz soon out o' sight, goin' toward the country.

Well, sir, about two o'clock, I wuz sittin' on the back porch takin' a little siesta, as scientific men calls snoozin' after dinner, when who should I see a-humpin' up the street but Bob.

When he gits to me, he squats down an' looks in my face, expectin' me to ask him somethin'. "What's the trouble, Bob?" I sez.

With that he straightens out like as if he wuz p'intin' birds, then barks twice an' runs like mad up the street, comes back an' squats in front of me ag'in, an' then he does the same thing two times runnin'.

I gits it through my coco'nut what he meant, an' patted him on the head, an' he went out to his kennel to have a sleep.

A little while after, along comes Ebenezer, a-limpin' like he wuz lame all over. When he gits to the gate, he sez, "Marse Jedge, please 'scuse me, I'se powerful uncomf'table. Dat fool man sed he could shoot round a corner, but it didn't work, an' now I'se gwine down to de doctor to git him to dig de shot out'n my carcass. I'se 'fraid I'se done fer, fer settin' down,"—an' Ebenezer hobbled away.

Well, sir, in about two hours along comes C. Johnson-Johnson, Esquire. "What luck?" sez I. "Only fair," sez he, showin' two catbirds, a crow an' a sparrow. "Where's the nigger?" sez I. "Oh, asleep somewhere in the woods," sez he. "He jest strolled off, an' I ain't seen him," sez the sassiety tad. "I hopes he didn't take nuthin' of your'n away with him," I sez, jest a little bit riled. "No, he didn't," he answered. "Yes, he did," I sez, "he carried off a load o' yer shot, an' jest as soon as the doctor gits through pickin' 'em out'er him, he'll give 'em back to yer."

"Why, the last I saw of him he wuz goin' over a fence," sez Mr. Tad. "Yes, an' you helped him over with four drams o' powder an' two ounces of number ten," I shouts. "You surprise me!" said the sweet-scented rooster. "Where's the dog?" I asks, innercent like. "Oh, he ain't no good," sez the tad, "I couldn't do nuthin' with him; he's gun-shy, an' flushed the birds an' ain't got no nose, nohow."

Honest-to-goodness, but out comes Bob, an'

a-lookin' at the stranger, he barks, "Liar! liar! liar!" jest as plain as speakin', an' then starts up the street a-hoofin' it fer the B. and O. depot.

"That dog acts like he wuz mad," sez Mr. Tad.

"He's got reason to be," I whacked back. "You shoot?" I shouted, my dander up. "I bet yer couldn't hit er flock o' barn-doors in a month."

"Sir!" he sez, "yer shock me."

"Shock yer? If it wasn't fer my rheumatiz I'd shock yer till yer tho't I wuz a galvanic battery. I'd break yer neck," I sez, itchin' to git my hands on him, fer bullyraggin' my dog, when presto! I sees Bob a-comin' helter-skelter, with somethin' in his mouth. When he gits to us, he drops it in front of the sassiety tad. It wuz a railroad time-table, an' C. Johnson-Johnson, Esquire, takes the next train for Philadelphy.

"Boys, it's time to turn in. It'll be nine o'clock sooner than yer think, an' yer all orter be a-snoozin' afore that time," said the Jedge. "I'll take a fresh chaw of kinnikinick an' a few puffs on my ol' dudeen an' I'll be there before yer know it."

It took but a moment for the youngsters to get into the tent, and, rolling themselves snugly in

their blankets, before long they were fast asleep.
Matt found a cozy place in the smaller tent, and
shortly after the Jedge, too, sought rest for the
night.

At five next morning the camp was astir again.
In an hour breakfast was over, and the assignments for the day were made. And thus it continued all the week. On Saturday afternoon
stakes were drawn, camp was broken, and with a
generous bag of quail, rabbits, squirrels, ducks,
snipe, and a fine haul of fish, the party slowly
glided down the river. By dark they had reached
the *Lillian's* anchorage.

Men and boys were happy and contented, better for their outing, and proud of the success of
the first expedition of the Nocatchtank Hunting
and Fishing Club.

CHAPER XVII

"TWO GENTLEMEN, BORN AN' BRED"

It was midday when Dennis Foley awoke from his drunken stupor; he was in an ugly frame of mind, and ready to quarrel at the slightest provocation.

"Bein' a deader without gittin' nuthin' fer it ain't what it's cracked up to be, Cul," he said. "If my bein' a stiff wuz worth them shellin' out two hundred, seems to me we orter git more if they know'd I wuz alive an' kickin'."

"I don't think that 'ud help yer much," said Hildey.

"Why not?" asked the other.

" 'Cause if yer show yer mug, the jig 'ud be up."

"How d'yer figure that?" queried Foley savagely.

"I've been thinkin' it over, an' I don' believe it'd work for yer to show yerself, even if Tom thinks it would be all right. That man Franklin is a holy terror, an' it wouldn't take him long to git on ter yer game, an' what he wouldn't do to us for foolin' him, I ain't a-sayin'."

"But if I turned up 'live, that 'ere man Jebb orter shell out big to git rid o' me an' let him marry the ol' gal."

"I s'pose he would," agreed Hildey, "if yer wife wuzn't so cantankerous, but she tol' me she wouldn't marry the best man that ever lived, if she knew yer wuz alive."

"Mebbe she's still gone on me, pard, an' jest expectin' I'll come an' say: 'Come to me arms, me little ducky darlin','"—and Foley laughed hilariously at the very thought.

"Don't fool yerself 'bout that, Dennis. I axed her if yer wuzn't dead, would she be glad to see yer, an' she yells at me, 'I wouldn't tech him with a forty-foot pole, if ther' wuzn't 'nother man in the world.'"

"Did she have the gall to say that?" Foley inquired angrily.

"That's what she said, an' she meant it, too. Yer don't stand no more chanst with her than a feather in the fi'ry furnace."

"If she talks that 'ere way, durn her, I won't let her marry no man, if I swings fer it a minit after."

"Don't be rash an' let 'em know ye're alive, Dennis, though it's my 'pinion that we orter git even with the hull caboodle of 'em, fer interferin' with two peaceful gentlemen born an' bred, an' bringin' us all the way on here, fer only a measly two hunderd plunks."

"Yes, an' durn yer skin," cried Foley, rising and shaking his fist in Hildey's face, "I ain't seen a red cent of it."

"Don't be hard on me, beau," pleaded Hildey, "'cause I fergot meself once. Yer mark my words, ther's a lot o' fine pickin' roun' here, an' yer'll say so when yer gits yer bearin's."

"Well, yer can bet I didn't come here for nuthin'," said Foley, bringing his hand down heavily on the table.

"Now yer shoutin'," exclaimed Hildey.

"I'm goin' out now," grunted Foley; "I'm feelin' like a bear with a sore head. I'll look round an' see the lay o' the lan'."

Promising to return shortly, Foley put on his slouch hat and started on his tour of investigation.

It was long past dusk when he shambled back.

"How does things look to yer?" was Hildey's first question.

"Dead open an' shet," chuckled Dennis. "I saw the hull caboodle—Molly an' Jebb an' Franklin. They didn't see me, an' I guess they wouldn't 'a' know'd me if they had. I wuz a-talkin' to a bloke to fin' out what he'd say 'bout Mary. He ups an' sez: 'It's a mighty good thing that Dennis Foley's dead, fer if he wuz alive an' come round here botherin' the widder, the boys 'ud jest tar an' feather him, an' throw him inter the river.' An' then the feller tells me my own hist'ry, an' I sez, 'How d'er know that's so?' And he sez, 'Colonel Franklin has let ev'rybody know what an onery cuss Dennis Foley wuz, an' what the Colonel sez, goes.'

"I sez, pretendin' not to be interested, 'What hez Colonel Franklin got ag'in a dead man?'

"The Colonel sez, he sez to me, 'The devil cert'nly orter have Dennis Foley, for he wuz a traitor, an' a deserter, an' a wife beater, an' the dirtiest coward what ever lived.'

"I jest b'iled over an' walked away, but I made up my mind I'd git even with that Franklin, an' the hull gang."

"What's yer plan, pard?" asked Hildey.

"Fust of all, we wants ter pick up what we kin in the way er spondulix to git even with them

people round here fer their poor 'pinion of us,"
Foley replied. "Second, I wants ter sock it good
an' hard to the ol' gal fer fergettin' to keep my
mem'ry green; an' third, I wants to make that
bilk Franklin feel I ain't so dead as he thinks.
But, beau, yer needn't go in cahoots with me 'less
yer got nerve, fer it's goin' to take nerve to do it.
Are yer in?"

"Count on me," was Hildey's quick reply. "I
ain't makin' no highfalutin' bluffs, but I'll stick by
yer like yer shadder, Dennis, old pard, 'specially
if I kin git a whack at that old stick-in-the-mud
who booted me, a gentleman—"

"Never mind that now," interrupted Foley.
"This is me plan," he continued. "To-morrer we
must git a place to live, where the old Nick hisself can't find us, an' then we'll jest work out
things carefully."

"I knows the very spot to hide," said Hildey.
"I was a-hoofin' it from a cop one day, an' jest
stumbled on it, lucky like. It's a big cave under
a bluff on the river, right back of a ol' cemetery,
an' yer kin only git inter it under a rotten wharf
what ain't been used fer years. I'll take yer down
an' show it to yer to-morrer, an' if ye're thinkin'
it's all right, we'll move there fust chance we gits."

"Sounds all right," replied Dennis, "an' I'll see it soon as I kin."

"What d'yer say to takin' yer son Tom in as a pardner?" suggested Hildey. "He knows these diggin's round here better than we does, an' he might come in handy."

" 'Tain't the thing yet to let him know I'm still on deck," objected Dennis, "he'd blab it sure as eggs is eggs. I wants him to think I'm dead, yet a while."

"Jest as yer say, pard, but he's with us," responded Hildey. "Whenever I talk to him he jest gets riled about yer ol' gal marryin' an' keeps on a-sayin', 'I'd give a hull lot if dad wuz here an' cooked her goose.' "

"He's got no right to hate his mother," interrupted Foley with emphasis.

"Well, I don't know," said the other slowly. "She's no better'n she ought to be, I'm a-thinkin'."

"What d'yer mean by you're a-thinkin?" asked Foley sharply.

"Yer knows what I mean. She'd jest let anything that wears pants an' galluses toddle after her."

This attack on his deserted spouse roused Foley's pride as the woman's husband, and, jumping up, he caught Hildey by the throat, pushed him toward the wall and shouted:

"Ye're a liar! Don't say nuthin' 'gainst my Molly; there's no guess comin' 'bout her. She's my wife, whether er no, an if yer says 'nother word ag'in her I'll beat yer to a pulp."

"I didn't mean nuthin' 'g'in her character, Dennis," said Hildey, wriggling away, "but she's no spring chicken an' wouldn't crack under the wings, an' she orter know better 'n to let a galoot hang round her afore she know'd yer wuz dead."

"Mebbe yer right 'bout that," mused the other after a long pause, "I seen her to-day a-walkin' with that bloke what wants her. I wuz restin' in a park, layin' on a bench, so they couldn't tell who I wuz, an' I heerd him say to her, 'I'm a-countin' de days when I can take yer to my heart an' call yer my own,' an' she answered, 'So am I, Mr. Jebb,' a-blushin', jest like she done when I fust knew her, durn her carcass!

"But I'm goin' to git even with her an' ev'rybody what's interfered in my fam'ly 'fairs. Nobody's got no right to come between me an' my lawful wedded wife. If they hadn't I wouldn't be dead now, an' she wouldn't be a-list'nin' to that fool a-talkin' love. It's a mighty poor world when a man can't be away five years without some one coaxin' his wife off. What are we comin' to, ennyhow? But I'll make 'em toe the mark, see if I don't."

Conditions now confronting Foley had become an exemplification of the old adage, "Blessings brighten as they take their flight." Mary Foley had suddenly assumed an importance her husband had never realized before; because another man loved and wanted to marry her the miserable wretch was determined upon revenge, and this feeling extended to every one who was friendly to her.

"John," he said, after a long pull at his second bottle, "yer remember that little job we put up at Evansville two years ago?"

"Yer mean the one where we swiped the kid, an' held out fer big money?" asked his pal.

"Exac'ly! It was dead easy, the way we worked it."

"Yer bet! Nuthin' like a stolen kid to keep the peelers off, an' let yer transact yer bizness with the principals fust hand."

"I noticed a brat to-day runnin' round the yard er that 'ere man, Franklin. The black wench, what tends her, calls her Lily. If we could kidnap that gal, I'd be hittin' two birds with one stone; git revenge an' have a barrel er rhino, besides."

"It's risky bizness, pard," whispered Hildey, looking around nervously, "means lynch law 'mong these 'ere Southerners, if they nab yer."

"Southerners ain't no quicker at nabbin' than enny other folks. An' we ain't goin' to be nabbed. We'll do the job so slick that we'll keep right on stayin' round here with no one no wiser."

"How yer goin' to work it?" asked the other curiously.

"It's dirt easy," chuckled Foley.

"All right, pard. I've always been with yer, an' if we're ketched, we'll jest say it's four o'clock with both of us, an' take our medicine like two gentlemen born an' bred."

"Two nuthin'," sneered Foley, snapping his fingers. "In a town like this the newspaper tells yer even what folks has fer dinner, an' how many kids has got the colic. Sooner or later that man Franklin will git out er town on bizness, and the paper'll say so, an' then, with only the wimmin folks an' the brats in the house, 'tain't nuthin' that's goin' to stop us."

The two vagabonds had now drawn their heads close together, and were engaged in earnest conversation that became almost imperceptibly faint, save for occasional words—"dog-button," "chloroform," "how much," "kid."

Then as the dim and flickering candle burned to its end, Foley and Hildey, grinning hideously, clasped hands, and a moment later were enveloped in the darkness of the room.

CHAPTER XVIII

SANDY ON THE WATCH

For the two weeks following Dennis Foley's advent, the police of Pipetown were very much exercised at the daily reports of robberies committed in the vicinity. Jebb's store was entered twice, and money and valuables were taken. The work showed the evidence of experts, and, so far, every clue worked upon by the detectives had come to naught.

The townspeople had heretofore been careless on account of their supposed immunity from thieves and burglars, but they now realized that it was necessary to secure windows and doors. Every one was on the alert, but completely mystified that the robbers had so far eluded detection.

One evening on returning from his office, Colonel Franklin said to his wife as the family gathered around the supper table:

"Nannie, my sister Sophie writes that Amelia is to be married on Thursday. They are going to have a house wedding, and she is very anxious that mother, you, Edith, and myself should attend."

"Whom does she marry?" said the grandmother, with sentimental interest.

"Oh, Cad Wilkins, son of General Wilkins, who lives at Grimes' Four Corners. He comes of one of the oldest and best families of southern Maryland."

"I've met him," said the lady, "he will make a very good husband for Amelia, I'm sure."

"I think it will be our duty as well as our pleasure to attend," said the Colonel. "We can drive, leaving here at ten o'clock Thursday morning, and reach there by three. The wedding is to take place at five, and there'll be a reception and an old-fashioned country dance that night at Sophie's house."

"I do hope we can go," said Mrs. Franklin, "I know there'll be so many of our old friends there, and we'll surely meet many acquaintances we haven't seen in years."

It was thereupon settled that they would make the trip. So at a quarter to ten on Thursday morning Matt had the carriage at the door, and waited for the three ladies and Colonel Franklin to appear. As the colored man stood at the horse's head, he noticed a shaggy-bearded, stoop-shouldered rag-picker, who was plying his vocation in front of the house, gathering bits of rags, scraps of paper, bones and old iron from the gutters and the roadway.

· Gilbert, Lillian and Delia came out with the rest of the household. After the wedding party had entered the carriage and the children had been kissed good-by the father said to them:

"Now, be very good and don't worry Delia. We'll be home to-morrow, sometime. And, Delia, be sure to lock up securely to-night, and unchain Lion before you turn in." After a few more cheery parting words from the parents the carriage rolled away.

The rag-picker continued his labors until the vehicle had disappeared in the distance. Then he suddenly lost interest in his work, and shuffled slowly away in the direction of the river. He finally reached a lonely spot back of an old cemetery, and, crawling under a dilapidated wharf, found the entrance to a cave, well within the hill. He whispered softly and was answered by a voice, inquiring:

"Is that you, pard?"

Pulling off his disguise, Dennis Foley, stoop-

ing beneath the low roof, groped his way to a
dim light some distance inside.

"What d'yer fin' out, Dennis?" asked Hildey
anxiously.

"Jest what the paper said las' night,—that
Franklin an' the wimmin folks wuz a-goin' down
to Marylan' fer a weddin' an' wouldn't be back
till ter-morrer."

"Why pard, it's comin' out jest as if it wuz pus-
sonly 'ranged fer us."

"It looks like the easiest job we ever tackled.
There's nobody left in the house, but that black
wench, an' the boy an' the kid, an' if we can't bag
the brat, we ain't got no right to be in the bizness.
Have yer got the dog-button ready?"

"Yep, I've fixed it up good an' strong."

"That galoot, Franklin, tol' the wench to be
sure an' unchain the bow-wow, an' that's jest
what we wants. An' the cullud lady looks as if
she'd snooze like a house afire. She orter be dead
easy. I guess a little 'go-ter-sleep' on a han'k'-
chief will do the hull trick in less time than a pig's
whistle."

After the departure of Colonel Franklin and his
party, Gilbert went to Sandy's house and found
his chum all alone. Mrs. Coggles was visiting

relatives in Baltimore, and was not expected back for a week. After much persuasion, Sandy finally accepted Gilbert's invitation to spend the days until his mother's return at the Franklin home.

"You see, Sandy," said Gilbert, "Lillian, Delia and I are keeping house all by ourselves, and it would be fine to have you come and boss things."

"Boss yer gran'mother," laughed Sandy; "but if yer really wants me, little codger, I'll come," —and the two started off.

Lillian, acting as hostess, welcomed Sandy with charming imitative graciousness, and put him wholly at his ease. The afternoon was quickly passed with books and games.

When supper was over, Gilbert played his violin, with Lillian and Sandy as the only auditors, and after a half-hour of backgammon, Delia came in and suggested bed-time.

She took Lillian to her room in the nursery on the second floor, and then, after unchaining Lion, a magnificent Newfoundland dog, and a part of the family, Delia and the boys fastened doors and windows for the night. Sandy and Gilbert went to the latter's room on the third floor, and after the colored woman had washed the supper dishes and put them away, she retired to her room in the

back of the house. In a very short time all the
lights were out, and everybody was fast asleep.

The bells of St. Peter's chimed out midnight.
Sandy was awakened by the low, deep growling
of the dog. He listened intently, and thought he
heard the animal walk on the porch at the rear of
the house. But the boy closed his eyes again and
soon dozed off.

In a little while he was startled again, this time
by the cry of a child. He jumped out of bed and
drew on his clothes hastily, his ears strained to
catch the slightest sound, and his mind filled with
some foreboding of evil. He heard Lillian speak:

"Is that you, Gil?"

"Gil, Gil!" whispered Sandy, shaking the sleeping boy.

"What is it?" said the younger, rubbing his
eyes and sitting up.

"Gil, Gil, I heard yer little sister call yer, mebbe
she wants somethin'."

Gilbert went to the head of the stairs and called
down: "Lily, do you want me?"

"Are you up there, Gil? I thought you were
down here. Somebody's walking round my
room."

"I'll come right down, dearie," said the little

fellow, striking a match to light the gas.

"Gil, come quick!" screamed the child, at the top of her voice.

"Damn yer!" came through the darkness. It was a man's voice, and the boys heard some one hastily descending the stairs.

Down dashed Sandy, three steps at a time. When he came to the first floor he groped in the darkness toward the door. Just as he reached it, a bull's-eye lantern was flashed in his face. Like a tiger he jumped for the light, and grappled with the intruder. His onslaught was so sudden that the lantern was shifted for an instant, and Sandy caught a glimpse of Dennis Foley.

There was a short scuffle, a cry of "Take that, yer fool!" and Foley struck the boy a terrific blow with a sling-shot. Sandy grabbed wildly, then fell in an unconscious heap on the floor.

Opening the door, Foley rushed out and joined Hildey, who had been waiting under the shadow of a near-by tree.

"Hustle fer all yer worth. The bloke's tumbled an' the game's up fer to-night. I'll meet yer at the place,"—and away they ran in different directions.

As soon as Gilbert had quieted the fears of his

frightened sister, he awakened Delia, and then hurried to the stairway, calling for Sandy. No response came.

"I guess Sandy is chasing that man out on the street," said the little fellow, as he slowly felt his way down stairs. Unexpectedly he stumbled on a prostrate form. He stooped, and in an instant knew it was Sandy.

"Sandy, Sandy," he called, "speak to me. Are you hurt? What has happened?"

In the darkness he placed his hand under the head of the senseless boy and felt the warm blood oozing from a deep wound. In agony and despair, he cried out:

"Oh, God, don't let him die! don't let him die!" Then he shouted, "Delia, Delia come quick; Sandy's hurt."

The servant hurried down, lighted the gas at the landing and in the room, and, with the help of Gilbert, raised the unconscious boy and gently placed him on a couch. Gilbert put his ear over Sandy's heart, and whispered joyously:

"It's beating, Delia; it's beating!" The colored woman gently sponged the blood from the ugly wound just above the boy's temple.

Sandy moved slightly, groaned, as if in great

pain, murmured some incoherent words, and slowly opened his eyes. Gilbert knelt by him, and said softly:

"Sandy, tell me; what is it? how did it happen? Who did it?"

Sandy looked around for a moment, and then the light of reason came back once more into his face.

"Golly, but that wuz a whack!" he said faintly, trying to smile through his pain. "That feller what banged me is a dirty coward. He jest hid back of the door till I got down, an' didn't gimme no chance fer my white alley. I seen his face an' I seen his hand with only three fingers on it, an' I pulled a button off his coat when I went fer him. I'll know him ag'in, if I don't see him for a thousand years."

Then the boy sank back again, thoroughly exhausted from the loss of blood. Gilbert hurriedly dressed and ran for the doctor, who came in all possible haste. After dressing the wound the surgeon said gravely:

"It's a mighty lucky thing for you, young man, that that blow didn't catch you half an inch lower. I shouldn't like to say what might have happened."

"I ain't a-sayin' nuthin'," said the wounded boy, "but if I ever see that feller ag'in, I'll know him, an' he'll know I know him."

The next morning the dead body of the faithful dog was found, outside the kitchen door. He had died at his post, while trying to guard those whom he loved and who loved him.

CHAPTER XIX

CHRISTMAS EVE

It was the day before Christmas. At four o'clock the wedding of Mr. Jebb and Mrs. Foley was to be solemnized at the old G Street church. The local papers had contained pleasant notices of the coming event, and had referred to certain episodes in Mrs. Foley's personal history, among them the manner in which the death of her former husband had been finally established.

A short bridal tour was to be made, and the grocer had planned, with the coming of the New Year, to move into a cozy little cottage which he had presented to his bride-elect.

The usual neighborhood interest in occasions of this character was plainly in evidence at the church, which was filled to overflowing.

The Jedge appeared in a high choker, white cravat, and a long black coat of the old *régime*, and had gone so far, even, as to wear white cotton gloves. He moved about like a master of ceremonies, radiating geniality.

"These 'ere occasions," he said, as he led Grandmother Franklin to a seat, "these 'ere occasions are progressive steps in the upward trend o' modern civilization, as scientific men would say. Jest think o' the Hottentots, the Cannabiles, an' others too numerous to mention. Did they go to a church to git hitched? Not on yer tintype. Ef Mr. Jebb had been one of them aberigines, he'd er jest hid round the corner, with a shillalie in his hand an' when the widder come 'long, thinkin' o' nuthin' in partic'lar, he'd creep up behind, an' BIFF! When she'd come to, she'd be Mrs. Jebb, 'cordin' to law. Things *do* change!" concluded the old man, with deep conviction.

As the morning paper stated the following day, "The wedding guests were regaled with a superb musical program by the organist, and finally, as Mendelssohn's *Wedding March* reverberated through the sacred edifice, the high contracting parties, Mr. Jebb and Mrs. Foley, came up the aisle and stood before the chancel."

The minister began the service: "Dearly beloved, we are gathered together here in the sight of God, and in the face of this company, to join together this man and this woman in holy matrimony; which is commended of St. Paul to be honorable among all men: and therefore is not by any to be entered into unadvisedly or lightly; but reverently, discreetly, advisedly, soberly, and in the fear of God. Into this holy estate these two persons present come now to be joined. If any man can show just cause why they may not lawfully be joined together, let him now speak, or else hereafter for ever hold his peace."

"Hold on!" shouted a rough voice from the direction of the gallery.

The clergyman stopped, and the startled congregation turned to see from whom the words had come. In the little gallery above, with his hands grasping the railing and leaning far over, stood an unkempt, unshaven figure, a malignant gleam in his snaky eyes.

"What does this mean?" inquired the minister.

"I kin show cause why they can't marry," triumphantly exclaimed the stranger.

"God forgive me!" cried the bride, clasping her hands, "that's Dennis Foley talking."

"I ask again, what does this mean?" said the clergyman.

"It means," roared Foley, "that she can't marry that galoot, 'cause she b'longs ter me."

"It's true, it's true," moaned the unhappy

woman, and, sinking on her knees, her hands clinging to the chancel, moaningly she repeated: "Oh, God in Heaven, let me die—let me die!"

The clergyman raised his hand, stilling the surprised and excited people.

"Brethren, I can not proceed with this ceremony until these charges are properly investigated."

Jebb knelt by the stricken figure, and tried to whisper words of comfort. The clergyman bent toward the kneeling woman and raised her to her feet, conversed with her a moment, and then said aloud:

"Mrs. Foley states to me that the man who interrupted this ceremony is her lawful husband."

"That's right," came the voice from the gallery, "I'm her husband. She's my lorful wedded wife, an' I ain't goin' to give her up ter nobody."

"I would suggest that the guests retire," said the clergyman.

The congregation filed slowly from the church, and in the murmur of excited comment, it could be noted that sympathy was clearly with Mr. Jebb and Mrs. Foley. They, with the minister, remained in the church, while in the gallery Foley stood, waiting for some sign from those below.

As the Jedge walked slowly down the aisle, the grocer hurried to him and asked him to remain. When the church had been cleared, Jebb said to the minister:

"We had every reason to suppose that Dennis Foley was dead." Then he explained what had been done by Colonel Franklin and himself to secure information, telling also of the sworn statement of Hildey as to Foley's death.

"As there was no apparent object why he should lie," continued Jebb, "we believed his statement, and thought we had a clear right to marry, until this development to-day."

The Jedge called up: "Foley, come down here, we wants to talk to yer."

"I'll be down, durn quick."

When Foley had walked up the aisle, the Jedge asked him sharply: "Where've yer bin all these years, an' why d'yer turn up jest now?"

"I've bin down in Cuby where the Johnnie Rebs sent me, an' I couldn't git back afore," said the tramp, grinning at the recollection of Tom's idea.

"That's lie number one," burst out the Jedge. "How'd yer know this weddin' wuz to take place?"

"I read it in the sassiety papers," tauntingly said Foley.

"If yer read it in the papers, why didn't yer go to yer wife like a man an' tell her yer wuz alive?"

"I wuz afear'd it might make her nerv'us," with a sneer.

"Lie number two! Ye're a scoundrel, an' I believe yer did it 'cause yer wanted ter make her feel like the little end o' nuthin'."

"I ain't got no good blood fer her failin' to keep my mem'ry green. Yer can't blame me fer sockin' it to her, fer fergettin' a man like me,— a gentleman born an' bred,—to marry a snoozer like that. I heerd she sed she wouldn't tech me with a forty-foot pole. I'll be durned if she'll tech any one else with one. An' that's the reason I give yer all a surprise party."

"An' I bet yer expect to make some money out er it."

"That's my lay, Guv'ner; yer struck the nail right on the head. If I wuz dead an' done fer, there'd be nuthin' comin' to me, but she's my wife an' she can't deny it."

"I don't deny it. I consented to marry 'cause I believed you dead. I wish I was, and the shame and sorrow of this day buried with me,"—and the widow covered her face with her hands.

"Don't talk that way, Molly. Ain't yer goin' to give a howdy-do kiss to yer hubby?"

"Oh, keep away; don't touch me!" cried the unhappy woman, shrinking back.

"Is that the way to treat yer long-lost darlin'?" wailed the reprobate in a mocking tone.

The Jedge's blood was up. He grasped Foley by the collar, and shook him till his teeth rattled.

"I knows this ain't no picnic o' mine," he said, "but if yer open yer potater trap, 'less yer spoken to, in the presence o' the widder, durn yer, I'll break yer in two, an' scatter the pieces!"

A word from the minister, and the Jedge released his hold.

"'Tain't no affair o' your'n to meddle 'tween husban' an' wife," whined the tramp, but he kept well out of the Jedge's reach.

"I'll make it my affair, yer rum-soaked loafer, you, an' if yer open yer mouth ag'in, when I git through with yer, there won't be no mistake 'bout the widder bein' a widder."

The preacher and Jebb begged the Jedge to sit down, and not excite himself. The old fellow was finally quieted.

"What's to be done?" asked the grocer, anxiously.

"Nothing can be done at present," said the clergyman. "There's no doubt that this man is Mrs. Foley's husband. She can remarry only when death or the law intervenes."

"That's jest it, parson," said Foley. "Now, what'll the feller what wants ter step in my boots gimme, if I go 'way an' never come back no more, an' let Molly git a divorce?"

"He'll give you nuthin'," said the wife, "I wouldn't let him pay you a cent to have me free, if you lived to be as old as Methus'lem."

"All right, Molly, I'll hang roun' here an' make myself to hum, which I has a right to, an' if yer don't treat me like a faithful wife should, I'll have the law on yer."

The Jedge began to boil again, and, rising, said:

"I've made it a rule never to interfere in fam'ly 'fairs, an' I don't perpose to begin now, but as a man what desires to keep the moral atmosphere of this 'ere town clean, as scientific men would say, I'm goin' to make it my bizness to watch yer in this burg, an' if yer look cross-eyed, I'll lam the life out er yer, an' if yer don't git out er here quick, I'll start right now."

Foley, fearing the indignation of the Jedge, walked down the aisle and out of the church, with the parting shot:

"I'll be round fer supper, Molly, so be sure an' put the kettle on."

Standing in the church-yard was a group of men and boys, and the subject of their conversation was the unhappy ending of the ceremony. In the gathering were Gilbert and Sandy, the latter with his head still bandaged. As Foley came slouching into view, the crowd looked at him curiously.

Sandy eyed him with absorbing and ever-increasing interest. With a cry, "That's him, that's the man," he darted under the fellow's upraised arm, and, clutching his windpipe, tripped Foley, and held him a prisoner.

"Yer dirty coward!" shouted the boy, "you're the bum what whacked me t'other night."

In a moment the Jedge, who had come out of the church, together with a number of friends, held the man prisoner, while Gilbert rushed for a policeman. Shortly afterward Foley, with nippers on his wrists, and a big crowd following, was being led to the police station two blocks away.

"It's all a mistake," he persisted. "I'll have

the law on yer,—me, a peaceable citizen, what's jest come here to git my rights. Yer've got no license to 'rest me," he said to the policeman. But that functionary did not release his hold.

Tom Foley had been an interested spectator from the time his mother came into the church on the arm of Mr. Jebb, until the arrest of his father. He remained discreetly in the background and was careful not to express any opinion. At the hearing at the police station he stood at the back of the crowd, but listened attentively to all the proceedings. After the prisoner had given his name, the sergeant asked:

"What is the charge, officer?"

"Burglary and attempted murder."

"Who makes the charge?"

"Sandy Coggles, sir."

"Sandy Coggles, step forward."

Sandy came up to the desk.

"State in your own words, on what grounds you make this charge."

"It was this 'ere way, Sergeant," began Sandy. "I wuz a-stayin' at Colonel Franklin's with the little codger las' Thursday night, 'cause his folks had gone down to Grimes' Four Corners to a weddin'. 'Long 'bout twelve o'clock I wakes up, an' I hears Gil's little sister, Lillian, a-callin' fer Gil. I shakes him, an' then he hears her callin', 'Gil, somebody's in my room.' Both of us, me an' Gil, starts down as fast as we kin, an' Gil runs into his sister's room, while I keeps a-goin' down, follerin' somebody what was a-runnin' helter-skelter. When I gits to the bottom, I feels my way, 'cause it's dark as pitch, an' afore I knows it, this 'ere feller flashed a bull's-eye lantern in my face, an' when I jumps fer his throat, BIFF, he gives me one fer keeps, an' I didn't see nuthin' no more."

"But how do you know he is the man?" asked the sergeant.

"Why, because he's one finger shy on his right hand, an' a button short on his coat."

"Well, what o' that?" broke in Foley.

"What o' that?" Sandy replied, looking at the prisoner, "when yer raised yer blackjack ter bang me, I seen yer only had three fingers, an' when I came to, I had this button in my hand, which b'longs right there on yer coat," pointing to a spot where the button was missing, and the cloth torn.

"Why, I lost that button yesterday," snapped Foley.

"I s'pose yer lost that finger yesterday, too," sarcastically suggested the Jedge.

"The prisoner stands committed until ten o'clock to-morrow, when the justice can hear further testimony in the case," said the sergeant sharply, making his record very carefully on the docket.

Foley was led to the little lockup in the rear of the station, and left to his own meditations, while the crowd slowly dispersed, Sandy, Gilbert and the Jedge going away together.

"I know'd I'd know him, if I ever seen him ag'in, an' I felt it in my bones that he'd know I know'd him, an' I guess he does," said the wounded boy.

"I've got it in fer him any way he takes it," interposed the Jedge decidedly. "It wuz bad 'nuff fer him ter whack yer in the dark, but after all, that may be excused in the line of perfessiónal duty, as scientific men say, as burglars do that sort of thing, an' therefore that may be overlooked. But I'll never fergive the mean sucker fer breakin' up a nice weddin' like Mr. Jebb's an' the widder's. No way yer can see it, can yer make it out that that wuz in the line o' duty. It wuz jest pure cussedness, combined with total de-

pravity, an' he orter be kicked from Alpha to
Omaha, an' back ag'in; hangin's too good fer
him."

As Tom Foley heard the sergeant commit his
father to the lockup for the night, he slipped out
of the station and hurried home. With a show
of tears, he put his arms around his mother's
neck, and told her how sorry he was that his
father had brought disgrace on her. She was so
struck by his unusual show of sympathy, that she
kissed him again and again. His touching solicitude for her, in this most trying situation, moved
her deeply.

After he had eaten a hearty supper, Tom approached his mother and kissing her with an appearance of great affection, said, "Mum, I'll be
home soon," took his hat and went out.

As he walked slowly toward the jail an old
man, greatly bent and apparently feeble, brushed
against him.

"Look out where you're goin'," snarled the
boy, raising his foot as if to kick.

"It's me, Tom," whispered the old man, who
was Hildey in disguise. "As soon as yer can,
come down to the old Burnt Bridge an' don't lose
a minute."

"All right," returned the boy, "I'll be down 'fore yer kin git there."

He flew along the streets and was soon at the river, where he awaited Hildey's coming. The other appeared, and led the boy along the dark and dreary shore, and into the cave.

"I'm 'fraid," said Hildey, "yer father made a mess o' goin' into that church. I tol' him a lot o' times to let the ol' gal git hitched, an' then git even. But he wouldn't listen to me, because he wanted revenge on the hull outfit, an' he sed if he broke up the weddin' in church, it would be er great sensashun, an' he could make money out er it, a-showin' hisself in er circus or a dime musyum, an' mebbe he could coax yer mother to go 'long with him, a-givin' exhibishuns like them marble staturs yer see ev'ry now an' then, but it didn't work, an' now pore Dennis is jugged."

"Why didn't yer tell me the ol' man wuz alive?"

"I wanted to, but yer father thought it might git yer inter trouble, if anythin' happened jest like what's happened to-day."

"Did dad whack that feller?"

"He did, fer truth."

"Bully fer dad. I hate that big, blowin' Coggles.   He's never been no frien' of mine, an' I wish dad had er knocked him out fer good, when he whacked him."

"Yer dad thought at fust he did.   It's wonderful he didn't put his lights out, fer he sez he tried to make it a case o' 'Dead men tells no tales.' "

"I 'spose they'll make it as hard as they kin fer poor dad, won't they?"

"Won't be much trouble provin' it on him, if we let's 'em, an' that's where you comes in," said Hildey.

"How d'yer mean?"

"Yer dad's got ter get out er that 'ere lockup ter-night, an' yer've got to git him out."

"How'm I goin' to do it?" asked the boy anxiously.

"Easy as dirt.   I looked at that calaboose to-day after yer dad wuz run in.   'Tain't nuthin' to saw out er there, if it's worked right.   Have yer got nerve to help him?"

"Course I hev, if I swing fer it," said the boy.

"To-night's the only time it kin be done. When he comes up to-morrer, they'll jug him in the big jail, an' before yer can say Jack Robi'son, he'll be railroaded to the pen fer fifteen years at least. Think er the awful disgrace on yer, Tom!"

"I tell yer I'll do anythin' to save dad."

"That's the talk. Jest take these two little tools, an' find a way to git 'em to yer dad to-night."

Snarley took the small file and saw offered by Hildey, carefully put them in an inside pocket, and, rising to go, said, "Well, good-by, old man. I'm off fer ter help dad. I do hope nobody'll ketch me,"—this apprehensively.

"Nobody 'll ketch yer, Tom, if yer keep yer eye peeled."

"I'm a-shiverin' at the thought of it," whispered the younger with fear in his heart, "but I'll try ter free the old man, if I swing fer it."

"Bosh! Yer won't swing fer it one way or t'other, Tom. Put some sand in yer craw, an' don't fergit I'll be a-settin' up an' waitin' fer yer all night."

The lockup was a one-story frame building containing four cells. It was located on an open lot, at least a hundred feet in the rear of the police station, and was approached through an alley that ran along the side of the "hall." To engage a special watchman for this little prison had never been thought necessary, since, ordinarily, it was occupied only by common drunks and petty violators of the law. True, a police officer passed the place every two hours, but only as a matter of form and perfunctory detail.

When Foley was taken from the sergeant's court he was placed in a rear cell, where, through a grated window, he could see every one using the alley as a thoroughfare.

As the night wore on, and travel in the neighborhood ceased, he threw himself on his iron bed and soon was fast asleep. Shortly after midnight, he was awakened by tappings on the ledge of his window.

"Who's there?" he asked gruffly, and sprang to the grating.

"Hush!" came from a boy's voice.

Standing on tiptoe Foley peered down through the bars.

"Dad, it's me," were the words he heard.

"Who's yer dad?" he asked almost savagely.

"You're my dad. I'm Tom Foley, an' I've come to git yer out," was the answer.

"What's yer game?" whispered the father, now awake and fully alert.

"Here's a saw an' file," said the boy, as he handed the tools to him, "an' yer can easy cut yer way out. The p'liceman will be round soon an' yer can hear him comin', fer he always whacks

his night-stick at the corner up there. After he's
gone, I'll be waitin' fer yer at the end er the alley,
an' I'll hide till yer come."

Then Tom disappeared hurriedly, warned by
the blow of the policeman's club against the pavement. A moment later, the officer was inspect-
ing the bars and locks of the little prison, and
finding that all was well, he continued as usual
on his beat.

In half an hour Foley had sawed and filed his
way out. Creeping cautiously up the alley he
was joined by his son, and together they hastened
through back streets, over commons and vacant
lots until they reached the river. Crawling under
the wharf, they entered the cave, where Hildey
greeted them with: "Well, yer fooled 'em, didn't
yer?"

"I'd 'a' died afore I'd a-stopped gittin' dad
out," was Tom's bravado answer.

" 'Twould 'a' meant fifteen years, if it had
meant a minit," interrupted Hildey, "if yer
couldn't a-got out to-night."

"That's so," said Tom, "fer I heerd that galoot,
Franklin, say when I come out er the station
yest'day, that he wuz goin' to prosecute the case
an' send dad away fer the longest term he could.

It jest made my blood bile, an' I could a-killed him on the spot."

"Spoke like a true son!" said the father, and the delectable pair embraced.

"Don't yer think we'd better vamoose?" asked Hildey apprehensively.

"No, not yet. We'd be ketched if we did. I've got a better plan. Pard, yer put on my coat an' hat, an' go to the B. and O. station. It'll be open afore light, to sell tickets fer the early train to Philadelphy. Sneak up careful, an' when yer git there, if yer don't see any one yer know, show yerself to ev'rybody roun' the station so they kin git a good look at yer. Then buy yer ticket, an' do as much talkin' with the ticket agent as yer kin. When the train comes 'long it'll still be dark, then yer jest git aboard, but as soon as it starts, jump off on t'other side an' come right back here. Of course, they'll all think I've gone 'way, and 'll try to trace me, but all the time we'll be restin' here, snug as a bug in a rug, an' a-settlin' what we're goin' to do to git even."

"But, don't yer think they might nab me?" ventured Hildey nervously.

"What if they did?" retorted the other. "There's nuthin' ag'in yer on the police record, 'cept lyin' 'bout my bein' dead, an' that wouldn't count."

"All right, pard, gimme yer coat an' hat. See yer later!" and Hildey was off.

Father and son were now alone in the cave, and for some time neither spoke. Then the elder grew reminiscent, and began to bewail his misfortunes.

"Sence I left the ol' woman five years ago, Tom," he said in a tone intended to convey his sense of a profound grievance, "I ain't had nuthin' but hard luck an' it's 'bout time things changed. I've got one more trick I'm goin' to work round here, an' if it comes out right I'll retire."

"I hope yer'll win, whatever it is," replied the son with proper filial piety.

"Have yer got any sand in yer craw?" asked the father.

"I've got lots; what d'yer want with me?" replied the boy.

"I want to steal that Franklin kid," said Foley briefly.

"Bully! I'm with yer." Tom spoke with real enthusiasm. "I know her well, an' she'd never 'spicion harm from me. She comes by our house

"WHEN YER GET HER HERE, I'LL DO THE REST"

Page 331

lots o' times an' talks to the ol' woman, an' laughs an' plays round me jest as if I wuz her brother."

"Then it's dead easy fer yer to bring her down this way," declared his father as the details of the plot grew clear in his mind, "as soon as yer kin, an' when yer get her here, I'll do the rest."

Foley looked at his watch and said, "Better git back home 'fore daybreak, an' I'll be expectin' yer with the kid mighty soon, but don't blab the plan to nobody."

CHAPTER XX

POOR LILY

Day was breaking as young Foley entered his home. His mother had just come down stairs, and was starting a fire in the kitchen stove. She was surprised to see her son, and greeted him with:

"Tom, where have you been all night?"

"Don't say nuthin', mother, yer could 'a' knock'd me over with a feather yesterday, when dad made such a fool of hisself. I felt so bad 'bout it, that I've been walkin' round, an' round, an' round all night."

"It was simply awful," said the mother, sighing heavily.

"Orful ain't no name fer it, mum. To think he'd come right in there an' hurt yer feelin's, to say nuthin' 'bout poor Mr. Jebb. Ev'rybody's talkin' 'bout his shameful conduct."

"Don't say nuthin' more 'bout it, Tom," said the grief-stricken mother.

"I can't git it out er my head, mum, an' I'm

almos' glad he's a-layin' roun' there in the jug
fer hittin' my dear ol' frien' Sandy. I think he's
gittin' sized up right."

"It'll be very hard, Tom, for any one to be
sorry for him. If your father had had one spark
of pity, he wouldn't have waited until I got in
church to let us know he was alive. I was so
ashamed I could 'a' died right there, an' I'll never
be able to hold up my head again in this world."
She brushed the fast-coming tears from her eyes,
and went about her household duties in a most
listless manner.

Breakfast was now ready, but only Tom had
any appetite. Three or four times the mother
made efforts to eat something, but without success, and each time the food was left untasted.
With a heavy heart she arose from the table,
cleared away the dishes and put the room in order.

Then, placing her arms about Tom's neck, she
said in a voice choked with shame and emotion:

"It's bad enough that he deserted me, but I
could forgive that, because, maybe, I'm not the
kind to hold a man like Dennis to his promise.
But now he's gone from bad to worse, and is a
thief and a burglar, and has brought everlasting
disgrace on you, Tom, his own kith and kin, flesh

of his flesh, and bone of his bone." She was almost in hysterics, as she pressed the boy to her heart.

"I wouldn't bother a little bit if I wuz you," was the son's reply, as he squirmed from his mother's embrace. "I'll bet dad isn't botherin'. He orter ketch it, an' he's goin' to ketch it. Colonel Franklin sed yesterday he wuz down on him like a pile o' bricks, an' wuz goin' to soak it to him good an' hard, 'cause he believes he wuz in with Hildey to fool yer, an' tried to hold up Mr. Jebb fer money. Makes me laugh, though, how he got fooled,"—and the hypocrite chuckled almost too joyously.

Tom hung about the kitchen, waiting for the news of his father's escape, which he was sure would be brought as soon as the authorities had learned of it. He had not long to wait, for soon a loud rap was heard at the door, and in came Mr. Jebb, much excited and exceedingly nervous.

"Have you heard the latest, Mrs. Foley?" he asked, breathless.

"Lor' sakes, Mr. Jebb; what's up now?" exclaimed the widow, momentarily forgetting her troubles.

"Foley has escaped!"

"Escaped? When?" she asked, now all excitement and interest.

"It must have been after midnight. He has been tracked to the railroad station, and the police sergeant has telegraphed a full description of him to Philadelphia, where it is believed he has gone."

"Why should they think he's gone there?"

"Because the ticket-seller and station-master both say they talked with a man whose appearance tallies exactly with Foley's, even to the button off his coat. He bought a ticket to Philadelphia, and they saw him get on the train."

"Good riddance to bad rubbish, an' I guess he'll never come back no more; thank the Lord!" said the widow fervently.

"I can't agree with you, Mary," objected Jebb. "I'm sorry, for more reasons than one, that he got away. I hoped, after the terrible experience in church yesterday, you would feel that a divorce would now be proper."

"Proper or not, Mr. Jebb," she replied, "I'll not have no man a-sayin' that I belonged to him, while I wuz a-wearin' another man's name."

"Well, little woman, I don't think you are wise," resumed Jebb, "but I love you enough to wait until eternity for you."

"Did yer say the old man bought a ticket fer Philadelphy?" broke in Tom. "But s'pose he got off at some other station?"

"Yes," said Jebb, "but the station-master at Baltimore telegraphs that no one got off there, and as that train does not make another stop until it reaches Philadelphia, he must have gone through."

"It's orful, when yer've got a daddy like that," whimpered the young scalawag, pretending to wipe away the tears. "Yer'll scuse me, won't yer, mum, an' Mr. Jebb? I never felt so bad 'bout anythin' afore, an' I'd like to go off by myself an' have a good cry."

Melodramatically, and sighing heavily, Tom deliberately went up stairs to his room, where, throwing his arms out with wild exultation, he exclaimed, "Oh, dad, I'm proud of yer!"

Then, clenching his fists and shaking them at an imaginary foe, he threw himself on the bed, muttering:

"Fools, fools, dad is one too many fer yer! Now, if I kin work what the ol' man wants me to, we'll have a double-barreled laugh on the hull caboodle."

The torpedoes and fire-crackers exploding outside aroused and attracted him to the window, where he watched the children of the neighborhood playing with their gifts and toys, for it was Christmas morning.

"Durn yer!" he said, as if addressing the merry little ones, "how I hate yer all! Yer think ye're happy, but I'm happier than you are 'cause my dad fooled yer."

Then putting on his hat, he walked slowly down the stairs, and wandered about the streets until he met a group of boys, among whom were Sandy and Gilbert. To them, he put on a long face and lamented that "ev'rybody is happy today but me," and continued, "I feel so bad I 'most wish I wuz dead."

Gilbert tried to cheer up the miserable pretender and gave him a liberal supply of candies, nuts and fire-crackers, while Sandy also shared his gifts with him.

"If your mother doesn't mind," said Gilbert, "you might come over to our house and make yourself at home to-day. We have lots of everything, and will give you a good time. Besides, father has invited the members of our hunting and fishing club to dinner, and I'm sure he'll be glad to have you join us."

"I'll come, if yer think I won't be in the way, an' won't spile yer fun ev'ry time yer look at my glum face."

"Come right along," said Gilbert, determined to make Tom happy, if at all within his power.

Promptly at one o'clock the Franklin family, with their guests, the Jedge, Leander, Sandy, Dink and the morose young Foley, sat down to eat their Christmas dinner. The table's center-piece was a miniature *Lillian,* in candy.

The conversation concerned itself almost wholly with the exploits of the club's memorable hunting trip of Thanksgiving week.

"Ev'ry time I look at that 'ere candy boat," mused Sandy, "I thinks er the river. I wonder how the river is to-day. Golly, I'd like to see her."

"So would I," exclaimed Gilbert enthusiastically.

"I tell you what we will do," suggested Colonel Franklin. "After dinner, we'll walk to the river, sail up in the *Lillian,* and then, if it's not too cold we'll fish until sunset."

"That's a great idee," agreed the Jedge, and the boys cheerfully indorsed the proposition.

When the meal was over, the two men and the

boys started for the boat-house. They had gone perhaps half a mile, when Tom Foley said:

"Colonel, I hope yer'll 'scuse me, but I don't feel right to go a-fishin'. My daddy's actions has kind er upset me so that I jest wants to blubber all the time. So, if yer don't min', I'll go back an' keep mum comp'ny."

"Why, Tom," kindly spoke the Colonel, "I think it will do you good to go out on the river and get your mind off things. No one blames you for the conduct of your father, and I'm sure you have the sympathy of us all."

"Yes, I know, but I'm out er gear to-day, an' I don't want er spile yer party. So, good-by,"—and before Colonel Franklin could interpose further objections, the boy was retracing his steps in the direction of the Franklin homestead.

Arriving opposite the house, he took position in a near-by alley, where he could keep close watch on the front gate. At intervals, he walked around the square, avoiding, as nearly as possible, all passers-by, and ever returning to his first point of observation. After hours of nervous waiting on his part, little Lillian came out, and Snarley's heart gave a jump. She was alone, and once on the pavement, began to roll a hoop, which Sandy had given her that morning. Down the street she tripped, all smiles and happiness.

Tom watched her until she had turned a corner, then he rushed up the alley to intercept her. When he emerged into the street, he saw her resting on a rustic bench, and hastened to join her. As he came up, he was greeted with:

"Why, Tom, I thought you went fishing with Gil, and papa, and Sandy, and the rest."

"No, Lily. I felt so bad 'bout what happened to my dad yest'day I couldn't git up no courage to go," answered the boy with simulated contrition.

"I'm awful sorry, too. Maybe your father is sorry and won't do it any more," continued the little girl reassuringly, looking into his face.

"I hope he is," whined the young rascal.

"In Sunday-school, they say you should always forgive. I hope Sandy will forgive your father for striking him, and if he hasn't, I'm going to ask him to."

"That's very nice of yer, Lily. What d'yer say? let's s'prise Gil, and go down to the landin' an' meet him when he comes in from fishin'," suggested Foley, knowing the intense love she had for her brother.

"I'm afraid to go so far," answered the child, "although I'd like to surprise Gil."

"Oh, I'll go with yer, an' Gil'll be delighted to see yer. You jest roll yer hoop, an' I'll run alongside of yer all the way," said Snarley coaxingly.

"That'll be lovely, won't it? And Gil will be so glad if I come."

"Cert'nly he will, an' so'll yer father," assured the boy.

Lillian whipped the hoop rapidly, and Tom kept pace with her. After she had gone several blocks, she was out of breath, and said, "I guess we'd better rest a little bit, Tom."

"Yes, let's rest," agreed Foley. "Let me carry yer hoop, while we walk."

She gave him the hoop, then confidingly placing her little hand in his, she said joyously:

"Gil will be surprised, sure enough, when he sees me coming, won't he?"

"Yes, he'll be s'prised, you bet!" said the boy, taking a firmer hold of her hand, and accelerating his steps.

The night was fast approaching and Snarley was leading the child through unfrequented alleys and streets.

"I don't remember seeing these streets when I went to the landing, the day I christened the *Lillian*," said she, growing timid.

"Oh, it's all right; it's really a shorter way than t'other," reasoned Foley.

"But, Tom, don't you think Gil must be through fishing by this time?"

"If he is, we'll meet him."

"But maybe he won't come back this way, and it's getting awful dark."

"Oh, he'll come back this way, all right."

"Are you sure?" asked the child doubtingly.

"Dead sure," answered the other.

They walked along in silence again for five minutes.

"Tom, maybe we'd better go back," pleaded little Lillian. "Mama may be worried, for we didn't tell her we were going, and don't you think it is too late to go to the river now?" Then, shuddering, she added, "I'm afraid, Tom; I'm awful afraid."

"Come on," he said gruffly, grasping her hand viciously, as she drew closer to him, and almost pulling her off her feet.

"Tom, don't hurt my hand," she cried, and made a futile effort to pull away.

"I ain't a-hurtin' yer. If yer wants ter see yer brother, come on."

"But, Tom, I can see him at home. Please let's go back. I'm so tired, and we're walking so fast, and my hand pains me so, you're holding it so tight."

They were now on the shore of the river, dark and desolate in its winter dress. The restless splash of the water sent icy sprays over the child, and, clinging still closer to her treacherous companion, she stopped him for a second and begged him to return.

"Don't be afear'd, nuthin's goin' ter happen to yer," he said, jerking her savagely, and almost breaking into a run at the same time.

"Oh, Tom, please let's go back," supplicated the child.

They were now at the old wharf. He gave a low whistle, and, without waiting for an answer, pulled the helpless child through the entrance. Then, groping his way over the slimy stones and through the oozing mud, he dragged the affrighted little one after him, to the mouth of the cave, and called:

"Dad, I'm here."

"Come right in," answered a voice.

"I've got her, an' I got her easy as dirt," said the son, pushing the terrified child into the cave, and then roughly into the arms of his father.

"Don't yell, yer brat!" said the older, clasping his hand over her mouth, and drawing her brutally toward him. "Shut up, or I'll kill yer."

She stopped crying, and looked at him in amazement. She was trying to solve the meaning of it all.

Dennis Foley pulled out of his pocket a large knife, and keeping the child a prisoner with his knees, opened the blade and held it aloft in the faint gleam of a sputtering candle. Then he hissed into her face:

"D'yer know what that is? Answer me."

"It's a knife," said the trembling child.

"I'm glad yer know one when yer see it,"— and he clutched her beautiful hair. Pulling her head backward, he raised the long knife threateningly.

"Now hear me," he rasped, "if yer cry, or even speak, unless I sez yer kin, I'll cut yer throat an' throw yer inter the river fer the snakes ter eat. D'yer understan'?"

Frenzied with fear, she raised her arms, begging for mercy, and cried in terror:

"Please don't kill me."

"It depends on yerself. I won't kill yer, so long as yer obeys me. Don't cry, an' don't talk, an' I'll spare yer life, but if yer do,"—he glared at the little innocent, "I'll cut yer throat from ear to ear, an' chuck yer inter the river; d'yer understan'?"

She nodded, and covered her face with her hands.

Foley now called Hildey, who was asleep in the corner, and said, "Cul, we've got to git out er this place jest as quick as possible. It's a durn good place to hide in, but it's no good place fer to negotiate fer big money fer the kid. It's too near the city, an' if we're tracked here we'll stand no more chance than a snowball on Beelzebub's gridiron."

"What's yer lay, Dennis?" questioned Hildey.

"Move up the river," was the reply. "I knows jest the place where we wouldn't be found in a thousand years, an' where we kin git in and out from ev'ry p'int er the compass."

"When d'yer want to start?" asked Tom.

"Right away, afore the town hears the brat's lost. Take what grub yer've got stored away an' we'll make a break right off."

In ten minutes the abductors, with the stolen

child, were slowly winding their way along the deserted beach.

"As soon as we comes across a boat we'll take it an' skip 'long to the place I want ter stop at," broke in Foley.

It was now very dark. No stars were shining, and it had become bitterly cold. Suddenly voices were heard, and the abductors stopped to listen. They were in a ravine near the magazine landing, not more than fifty feet from the spot where the *Lillian* was launched. Foley, Tom and Hildey crouched low, and drew the little girl closer.

The steady dip of oars was heard up stream, and the voices grew plainer. Out of the mingled sounds was heard, "I agrees with Sandy, he's the dirtiest coward as ever went unhung."

Lillian started, for she recognized the voice of the Jedge, who with Colonel Franklin, Sandy, Dink, Leander and Gilbert, were returning from the sail up the river.

Foley became frightened, and bending over, hissed into the child's ear:

"Remember what I tol' yer: if yer utter a sound, I'll kill yer."

The sailing party meantime had reached the landing and stepped ashore. Sandy and the other three boys lowered the sail, rolled and carried it into the boat-house. The whole party then, marching three abreast, with steady step, went up the graveled walk of the old magazine road, singing in unison:

> "Hep— Hep—
>   Shoot that nigger if he don't keep step.
> Hep— Hep—
>   Shoot that nigger if he don't keep step."

While its cadence was continued by Colonel Franklin and the Jedge, the four boys, in marching rhythm, sang out cheerily into the crisp cold night:

> "When other lips and other hearts,
>   Their tales of love shall tell,
> In accents whose excess imparts,
>   The power they feel so well.
> There may, perhaps, in such a scene,
>   Some recollection be,
> Of days that have as happy been,
>   And you'll remember me."

The three scoundrels listened, as the voices rose and fell on the air. The child, with the fear of death before her, and in the clutches of her horrible captor, gave one convulsive sob and sank swooning at his feet.

Foley picked her up and, walking quickly, placed her in the very boat her father and friends had left but a moment before. He wrapped her in a ragged coat, loosened the hasp of the door on the boat-house, and took out the oars.

Quickly the captors pushed the craft into deep water, and with muffled stroke moved through the inky waves, a somber specter sneaking along the banks of the sleeping marshes.

When they neared the upper bridge, Foley ran the boat ashore and abandoned it. Picking up the exhausted and benumbed child, he led his two companions along the causeway and over the road leading to the bridge.

"That's to take 'em off the scent, when they find the boat's gone," he said.

Foley, Hildey and Snarley walked down the incline on the other side, and found a narrow path through the meadow.

"I saw a lot o' skiffs up here a few days ago, when I wuz lookin' roun' here to see how the land lays," Foley whispered, "an' we jest need one now."

It was soon found, and with Hildey sitting on the bottom of the boat and holding the child, Foley and his son using the paddles, they went up stream, past the Sycamores, under the Banks, and fairly abreast with the giant sentinels of oak and poplar.

The wind came out of the north, howling through the leafless boughs of the mighty monarchs of the forest. The last flickering light of the town was left far behind, and darkness, like a great shroud, enveloped river, valley and woods.

CHAPTER XXI

SANDY TO THE RESCUE

In due time Colonel Franklin and his party reached home, hungry after their fine sail on the river, and all in high spirits.

"Where are the women-folks, Delia?" was the Colonel's first question.

"Gran'ma Franklin, Mis' Nanny, an' Edith done gone to de church dis aft'noon, to help trim de Chris'mas tree fo' to-night," replied the servant, "an' dey sed dey would stay at de pahsonage fo' tea. Lily, I 'spects, rolled her hoop up dar an' is wif 'em."

"Oh, that's all right, if they're all together," said the Colonel. "Jedge, you and the boys sit right down, and we'll have supper in a jiffy."

The guests needed no second invitation, and thoroughly enjoyed the evening meal. The repast was about concluded when Edith, who had just returned from the parsonage, came in, and called cheerily:

"Hurry up, Lily, it's time to go to the festival.

They're going to light up the tree at half-past eight, and it's nearly that now."

"Why, chil', Lily ain't here. She's wif yo' folks," exclaimed Delia.

"With us? She hasn't been with us at all," responded Edith.

"Ain't ben wif you! She went out to roll her hoop jest befo' dark, an' sed she wuz gwine to de church to see yo' trim de tree an' Lor' sakes! she orter be dar."

"Well, we haven't seen her," spoke Edith, with positiveness.

"It's likely she's at one of the neighbors," ventured the Colonel. "At these glad Christmas times it's only natural that the child should be interested in the toys and gifts of her playmates, and no doubt, Delia, if you'll run around to some of the houses, you'll find Lily enjoying herself."

"I'll fin' her, Muster Franklin, an' I'se gwine to scol' her good an' hard fo' worryin' her ol' mammy." At this she put a shawl over her head and shoulders, and started in search of the absent one.

"Suppose I go, too," suggested Gilbert, rising.

"I don't think that's necessary," interposed the Colonel.

"It'll only take me a minute," assured the son, as he began to put on his overcoat.

"Go if you like then," consented the Colonel.

"An' if yer don't mind, Miss Deed," volunteered Sandy, "I'll go up to church with yer, an' then come back an' fetch Lily and Gil."

"That's a good idea," answered Edith, "bring her right over to the church, and I'll be waiting for you there."

"I guess I'll go up to my house an' look. Mebbe Lily is playin' with Zorah, an' if she is, I'll come right back an' tell yer," put in Dink.

Edith, Delia and the three boys departed, leaving the Colonel and the Jedge alone, smoking their pipes and discussing the sensational events of the week, in which Dennis Foley was the central figure. His attempted burglary in the Colonel's own house was reviewed in detail, as were also his interruption of the wedding and the dastardly attack upon Sandy.

"I can't git it through my noddle," broke in the Jedge, as he puffed at his pipe, "how that Foley had the monumental gall to show hisself round here after he had tried to burglarize yer home. I should think he'd a been afear'd he'd be pulled."

"My theory is," said the Colonel, "that his

lucky escape made him feel sure that neither Sandy nor any one else had seen his face, and, therefore, no one would now recognize him."

"What wuz his lay, I wonder, in breakin' up the weddin'?" queried the Jedge. "He might 'a' know'd that Mary Foley would never have nuthin' to do with him ag'in, if there wuzn't another man in the universe."

"He probably did know that, but no doubt he was aware that, as he had not been away from her quite the full five years, he was still alive in the eyes of the law, and could claim his rights as her husband. Perhaps, too, he had concocted some rogue's scheme to turn the situation to his own financial profit."

"Yes, I guess that's so," mused the Jedge, "fer I know Titcomb well 'nuff to say that he would 'a' given that feller his bottom dollar, ruther than have him a-hangin' round here, worryin' the widder, even if she wouldn't marry him. But his dirty trick was knock'd inter a cocked hat when Sandy seen him, an' I guess that's the last we'll hear o' Dennis Foley."

"It's hard on Jebb," sympathized the lawyer, "but it simply goes to show the charming inconsistency of the gentler sex, for, after all, Mary could have invoked the law, and obtained her release from the rascal, and thereby made happy the man she loves by marrying him."

"It's one thing more to be sorry fer, as the monkey sed when he kissed the baboon's sister," remarked the Jedge.

The conversation at this point was stopped by the appearance of Delia and Gilbert, who declared that not one of the neighbors had seen Lillian that afternoon.

"It seems almost incredible that she could be lost," said the father, "she must be somewhere about here. Perhaps she went to the church, and fell asleep in one of the pews."

The searching party set out once more, this time accompanied by the Colonel himself, and by the Jedge. At the church they heard from Sandy and Dink that no trace of the child had been found, so the father requested the minister to inquire of the congregation if the missing one had been seen anywhere. There was no response from those present, and the family and friends began to show grave concern.

Another effort at finding her was immediately made. The police sergeant was notified, and he sent out a general alarm.

All night long, and all the next day the hunt was continued. Wells were explored, basements, cellars and out-of-the-way places were ransacked, lumber yards and coal yards were gone through most carefully. In fact, not a foot of the town was left unsearched, but all to no avail, and the once happy home of the Franklins was steeped in sorrow and despair.

The morning after Lillian's disappearance, Mrs. Foley inquired of the boys in the neighborhood if they had seen anything of her son Tom, who, she declared, had been gone since the previous morning.

From Sandy she learned that Tom had taken dinner at Gilbert's the day before, but that when the party had started for the river he had dropped out, claiming he was too down-hearted to join in the pleasure.

"That's the way he acted at home," said the widow, "and it seemed to me it was almost un-nacheral for him to talk against his father, as he did. However, I'm not bothered about him, for he comes and goes just as he pleases, and when he gets good and ready he'll turn up, like a bad penny. I've stopped worryin' about him years an' years ago."

"If I see Tom," volunteered the boy, "I'll tell him yer want him,"—and he hurried away.

The next morning Sandy left home earlier than usual, and on his own account began a search for Lillian. A new theory had taken possession of him, and he started at once for the river. At the magazine gate he chatted with the sentry about the mysterious disappearance, and passed on. When he reached the shore half a mile beyond, he was surprised to find that the padlock on the door of the shed had been pried off, and that his boat was missing.

Opening the door he saw that his oars and blankets were gone, and he began to feel that his theory might lead him to important discoveries. For fully five minutes he stood motionless, and gazed into the river, buried deep in his own thoughts. Then he soliloquized: "I wonder if Lily's been stolen? S'pose, while we've been searchin' fer her high an' low, Snarley an' the galoot what whacked me jest took the little girl an' carried her off in my boat? That 'ere story 'bout Dennis Foley buyin' a ticket for Philadelphy struck me as fishy when I fust heerd it, an' now I don't believe it a t'all. They couldn't git through the magazine gate 'thout the guards

seein' them, an' whoever took my boat either
came up the shore or down the shore. 'Tain't
likely they came from up shore, 'cause they could
'a' found a hundred boats 'tween here an' the
upper bridge."

Turning around, Sandy started down the beach
toward the cemetery. He was studying carefully
the ground beyond the point of high tide, and
in a few moments reached the ravine where, two
nights before, the three abductors had stopped,
upon hearing Colonel Franklin and his sailing
party approach.

"Well, I'll be durned," he exclaimed, for in the
sand before his very eyes was the impress of four
pairs of shoes. Two were evidently those of men,
one small enough to be that of a boy, and one so
tiny as to convince him it was that of a child.

"This is the way they come," he continued,
"and there wuz three of 'em in the gang besides
the little one, an' I'm sure er that."

He followed the footprints until he reached the
old wharf. Peering through the rotten timbers,
he said:

"That's a rum ol' hole. I don't believe Satan
hisself would go in there, but I'm goin', an' see
what I kin see."

Sandy had no difficulty in entering the cave, which he found strewn with whisky bottles, pieces of bread and newly-picked bones, evidence enough that some one had been there but a short time before. Penetrating deeper in his search, he made a find of the utmost importance. Lying at one side, and near a bed of rags, was an envelop addressed to Dennis Foley, and, on a peg which had been driven into the wall, was hanging an old hat, which he had often seen on Hildey's head.

Elated at the results of his quest, he began to retrace his steps, and in eager haste he left the cave. Picking his way along the slimy stones under the wharf, he soon neared the outlet and there was startled by the most significant of all his discoveries. Right before him lay the identical hoop which he had given the lost child only Christmas Day, and which bore the inscription, "From Sandy Coggles to Lillian Franklin."

Every suspicion now was confirmed, and he was sure he knew the culprits. Taking the hoop, he returned to his boat-house with all possible speed, and leaping into his skiff, paddled up the river, his eyes scanning the marsh lines on either bank of the channel. Arriving at the bridge, he learned by inquiry from the tender stationed there that he had not seen the *Lillian* coming up stream within the past three days.

"But," explained the bridge-tender, "I'm only on from six to six during daylight, and of course if anything comes through at night I wouldn't know about it. I'm pretty sure, though, there's been nothing up this way for a month of Sundays, 'cept Buck Wesley, who creeped up 'bout two hours ago, following a gang of ducks that uses right over there above Mayhew's Meadows. And the way Buck's been shooting for the last hour, he must be having a time and no mistake."

"Well, so long," called Sandy. "I guess I'll go up the river a little further and have a look." And once more he took up his paddles. As he came abreast of the Meadows he saw Buck Wesley coming out of the creek in his gunning skiff.

"Is that you, Sandy?" shouted the gunner.

"That's me," was the boy's answer.

"Come over here, I want to talk to you," requested Buck.

When Sandy got alongside the hunter's boat, he asked:

"Well, Buck, what's the trouble?"

"No trouble, Sandy, but when I come up the

river this mornin'—I ain't been up for three weeks, it's been such pore weather for ducks—I seen a bunch of widgeon go down right over here, an' as I skims up by the collard patch t'other side of the bridge, I noticed a boat lyin' in the mud, and when I gits near to her, I knows by the cut of her jib that she's yer *Lillian*."

"My *Lillian?* Wher'd yer say yer seen her?" asked Sandy excitedly.

"Why, by the collard patch, not fifty yards from the Causeway. She looked like she'd drifted on the marsh. I calc'lated when I got through shootin' that I'd pick her up an' take her down to yer landin'. The oars wuz in, an' I guess she must 'a' strayed from the shore, through somebody fergittin' to tie her up."

"I'm much 'bliged, Buck," thanked Sandy, "but yer needn't bother. I'll bring her down, an' the next galoot that takes her an' lets her git away from him, is goin' to hear from me."

Sandy retraced the course he had come, and after turning on the other side of the bridge, had no trouble in finding his boat. She was lying on a sand-bar, but he soon succeeded in floating her and bringing her ashore.

Safely securing the skiff and the boat, he began

another search along the beach, and almost immediately was rewarded by finding a knot of blue ribbon, such as he had often seen Lillian wear in her hair. Farther along, he discovered tracks in the sand. These he followed, Indian fashion, up the embankment, lost trace of them for a moment on the hardened surface of the carriage way, but speedily picked them up again in the soft soil that ran downward on the other side.

Then, it was easy to pursue them along a pathway that led to a graveled beach where a dozen or more skiffs had been drawn up and tied to stakes for the winter. From here on, all further traces were obliterated.

Thoroughly familiar with all the river craft belonging there, even to the individual ownership, Sandy noticed at once that one of the boats was missing, and that its painter had only recently been cut.

"Why, it's Willie Bagner's boat they've got," he said to himself as he recognized which boat was missing, "an' I'll bet my life the scalawags are hidin' somewhere up the river."

Hurrying back, he rowed to the landing and started in haste for his home, with a plan of rescue fully developed in his mind. He sought out Leander, Dink and Gilbert, and asked them to call at his house without delay.

While Sandy's investigation had convinced him that Lillian was stolen, Colonel Franklin had been made to realize the same terrible fact in another and more brutal way. When he reached his office on the same afternoon, he found on his desk a letter that read as follows:

dere sur—if U meen bizness i can put U on to whar your dorter is but its goin to kost U sum muney if U evr want to see her agin theres a big gang got her hid where U woodnt find hur in a 100 yerze but if U will plank down 10000 dolers sheze yourze if U dont youll nevr see hur no moar if sheze wurth thet much to U U can git her by not blabin to nobudy that yer got this leter an plankin down the rino taint no use fer U to try an git the police on our trax fer one uv the gang is alwayz with the kid an we have sworn to kill her if enny of us is jugged if U meen bizness an will leeve a noat under the big stone in front of the ded tree by oyster shell landin up the river we will git it an rite U where to meet us to bring the muney and git the child member we dont stand fer no trechery an if U squeel we ll no it and we ll take it out on the kid   mums the word if yer want ter see the kid agin   c o d an fare deelin is our moto   a word to the wize is sufishent

yourze trooley   a frend

The Colonel was completely unnerved by the horrible knowledge that his little daughter was in the hands of desperate criminals. Without delay he wrote a note offering to pay the money demanded, agreeing to deliver it at any spot they might name, and vowing to share his secret with no one.

Sealing the missive, he placed it carefully in his pocket, and drove out along the river turnpike to a point about a quarter of a mile from the place designated by the annoymous writer. Tying his horse to a tree, he walked through the woods, and hid the note under the stone mentioned in the letter. It was after nightfall when he reached home, where he was met with the heartrending and oft-repeated question,

"Have you heard anything from Lily?"

Fearing to betray himself, even to his family, and thus perhaps endanger the life of his child, he was compelled to answer, "No, not a thing." With a heavy heart, he passed into his study.

Supper was announced shortly afterward, **and** as the family gathered about the table, the **father** noticed that his son was not present.

"Where is Gilbert?" he inquired nervously.

"Sandy was here and asked Gilbert to come over and spend the night with him," answered Mrs. Franklin. "I hadn't the heart to refuse him, for I don't believe any one has worked harder to find our lost darling than Sandy, and he seems to be the only one that can give Gilbert any consolation."

"I think it's better that the boys stop searching," said the father. "They might get themselves into trouble; it's too dangerous."

"I don't believe you could stop those boys from hunting for Lillian, if they had to go into the very jaws of death," interposed the grandmother.

"Oh, well," spoke the father; "they must not wear themselves out, and to-morrow, I will tell Gilbert and Sandy to leave the investigation to the police."

"They'll never do it," objected the grandmother, "they love Lillian too much. You mark my words."

At this very moment, Sandy, Leander, Gilbert and Dink were together, in Sandy's little **garret** room. Sandy closed the door carefully, locked it, and called his companions about him in the middle of the room.

"Boys," he whispered, "afore I sez anythin', I wants yer to gimme yer word, honor bright, an' cross yer heart three times, that yer won't spout a syllable of what I tells yer to a soul."

All were agreed, and the boy began:

"Now, it's this 'ere way. My boat wuz stolen an' left, right below the upper bridge, an' I foun' footprints an' this 'ere piece of ribbon, which Gil knows b'longed to his sister, fer she wore it round her hair. Willie Bagner's skiff's bin stolen, an' I believe the party that took it hez got little Lily, because I foun' the hoop I give her, an' this en-vellup in the same place, an' it seems to me the galoot whose name's on it is hid somewhere up the river, an' I'm goin' after him if I has to go alone."

"But you won't go alone, while I'm alive," insisted Leander, intensely excited.

"An' I'm goin', too, even if I never come back," added Dink, taking it for granted that he was needed.

"And you must take me," said Gilbert imploringly.

The four boys grasped one another's hands, and Sandy declared in a solemn tone:

"We'll stick together to the bitter end."

"What's your plan?" asked Leander, with great interest.

"Without breathin' a word to a soul, to-night about nine o'clock we wants to leave the boat-house, you an' Dink in one skiff, an' me an' Gil in t'other, an' sneak up the river, an' try so nobody won't see us. When we gits to the upper bridge, paddle in as close to the Causeway on the right, as we kin, huggin' the marsh all the way. Jest before we git to Beaver Dam, there's a deep gut that runs 'longside of it fer a hundred yards, or more. Foller me in there, Leander, an' stay hid till I sez move. Don't speak a word, from the time we push off till I sez so. Beaver Dam is the lonesomest creek in the world, an' mebbe Gil's little sister is kept in one of them ol' shacks what muskrat hunters live in, in the spring an' summer. If them galoots is in there, they're mighty apt ter come out late at night, when they don't expec' nobody's roun'. Of course, nacherelly they have some plan about gettin' paid fer little Lily, an' they ain't a-goin' to stay in hidin' without tryin' to find out the lay er the land, an' jest how hot the police is on their trail. My idee is to go an' lay in ambush fer 'em all night. If they don't come out, we'll explore in the mornin', an' if we don't find 'em hidin' roun' Beaver Dam, then we'll lay low all day, an' push up the river to-morrer night. But somehow, I think that's the place they would pick out to hide in. 'Tain't one person out er a million that would know how to git through Beaver Dam without gittin' lost, an' I'm a recollectin' I took Tom Foley through there onct an' that's why I'm goin' there to-night. I knows it so well, I could go through with my eyes shet.

"Each of us wants his pistol loaded fer keeps, a knife, an' about three yards er rope he can tie round his waist. Let's have a bite o' supper right here in my house, an' then we'll start fer the river, but each feller goin' alone, an' in a different way. Now, remember, no talkin' to nobody, an' let's all say honor bright, an' cross our hearts three times ag'in."

CHAPTER XXII

ON THE RIVER

Sandy was the first to arrive at the boat-house. Securing the paddles, he put them into the skiffs and watched for his companions. He had not long to wait. Gilbert came in a few moments, then Leander, and shortly afterward, Dink. Not a word was spoken. Sandy motioned Gilbert to sit in the center seat of the *Dolly,* while he took his accustomed place at the stern. Noiselessly they pushed into the stream, followed by Leander and Dink.

The tide was going out, and had, perhaps, two hours to ebb. The boys hugged the channel bank on the right, passed under the bridge unnoticed, and kept on their silent and anxious way, mile after mile. Finally, Sandy steered into a creek and glided softly against the mud bank, holding his skiff firmly by driving a paddle into the soft soil. Leander and Dink followed suit. That they might be screened from any one coming out of Beaver Dam, which was separated by a narrow strip of marsh-land, they lay flat on the bottom of their boats.

The night was not especially dark, for the moon was looking through a mist of hazy clouds. It was bitingly cold, and though the boys became numb from the many minutes of inactivity, not one of them moved. For fully an hour they had remained motionless, when faintly over the water was heard the splash, splash, splash, of paddles, far away.

The searching party were all alert in an instant, and with raised heads, peered cautiously over the top of the marsh line in the direction of the sounds. Hardly a minute had passed, when out of the shadows that hid the entrance to Beaver Dam, there came slowly a skiff into the clear water. It approached to within fifteen feet of the hidden boys, when they recognized a voice, distinctly saying:

"I hope that guy Franklin's ben up to the landin' an' left the note where I tol' him to, an' don't try no shenanigan."

"He ain't goin' to try no flapdoodles with us," was the quick answer.

"Well, if he knows when he's well off," the first voice resumed, "he'll come round with the rhino mighty quick, an' give us no more trouble."

"I kin see us livin' like gent'men, a'ready."

"Gent'men born an'—" the other began, but the last of his sentence was lost as the boat turned up the river, and the cadence of the paddles died in the distance.

Sandy waited until the rascals had disappeared around the bend, then shoving his skiff quickly alongside Leander's, he whispered into the latter's ear:

"Me an' Gil is goin' in to Beaver Dam. Yer knows them two fellers, an' so do I. One of 'em is the feller what whacked me, an' the t'other is that bum Hildey. If they gits here afore I come back, you an' Dink'll have to do somethin' desp'ret."

"All right," said Leander, clutching his pistol, "you can trust me."

Sandy rounded the point that divided the two creeks, and in a short time had paddled past the trees and vines that hung over and partly covered the entrance to Beaver Dam. The boat was managed with consummate skill, now left, now right, through the sinuous waterway, and the two boys had gone fully half a mile, when, without warning, they were rudely jolted as the skiff grated harshly on a bar. Ordinarily, such an incident would have been without effect upon them, but now their nerves were so highly strung, that the noise of the boat rubbing against the gravel seemed as loud as the report of a cannon.

Using all possible force, Sandy and Gilbert succeeded in shoving their craft back into the water. Then they pressed forward into the shadow of an embankment on the left, and not a moment too soon did they reach cover, for the door of a hut was thrown open, and the voice of Tom Foley was heard, asking:

"Is that you, dad?"

An instant later Snarley was seen standing in the dim light of the doorway, shading his eyes and peering into the darkness.

"I say, dad, is that you?" came again. "I'll be doggoned if I didn't think I heerd somebody comin'. I guess 'tain't nuthin'," —looking anxiously to the right and left. "I cert'nly does git scared out er my boots aroun' here, though, when I'm left alone. I'm goin' to wake up the brat an' make her keep me comp'ny,"—and the door closed with a bang.

He had hardly gone inside when the piteous

cry of a child was heard, "Please don't beat me, Tom."

"I ain't beatin' yer; go ahead, dance fer me."

Sandy and Gilbert were fairly crazed, and in their anger rushed up toward the hut.

Again came the cry, "Please don't hit me, Tom."

"Dance, I say,"—and the sharp swish of a whip was heard.

It took but a second for Sandy to bound into the room. Surprised and terrified, Foley made a dart for the door, but was met by Gilbert, who, pistol in hand, held him stock still. In desperation Snarley reached for a club and ran back of the frightened child in the hope that she might serve as guard against his assailant. Like a flash, Sandy followed, and knocked the cowardly brute senseless with the barrel of his pistol.

Gilbert ran to his sister, and, taking her up, showered loving kisses upon her. With her arms clasped about his neck and her head nestling on his shoulder, she cried:

"Oh, Gil, I'm so glad you've come. I've been waiting all this time for you. I knew Sandy would come, because he ain't afraid of robbers, or anybody else, even if he had his hands tied behind him. I've been praying for you every minute, and here you are." Again Gilbert pressed his sister to his heart, and kissed her.

Young Foley was still lying unconscious, as the result of the blow he had received, and Sandy was clutching him tightly by the throat.

"Take yer sister, little codger," said Sandy, "wrap her up, git in the skiff, an' I'll be with yer as soon as I tie this chuckle-headed idiot fast and tight."

Gilbert left the hut with Lillian, while the other boy remained behind long enough to loosen the rope around his waist, and bind the young ruffian securely. Then he placed him in a corner of the room. Locking the door behind him, Sandy joined Gilbert in the skiff, and together they paddled furiously out of the creek into the river.

The moon was up in all her splendor, and objects on the water were plainly visible for some distance. Lillian was seated in the bow, facing the two boys at the paddles. Leander and Dink fell in the wake of Sandy's skiff, about ten yards in the rear.

As the party reached the middle of the channel, a skiff came into view from the bend, a short way above, and steered directly toward them. With a cry, Lillian stood up:

"Oh, Gil, here come those two bad men that took me away."

The boys turned, and they, too, recognized Dennis Foley and Hildey as the occupants of the approaching boat.

"Lie flat, little one," whispered Sandy, "an' don't move till I tells yer."

The child obeyed, but already Foley and his partner had espied her, and it was evident they were using all their efforts to catch up. Leander now called:

"It's the same gang, Sandy, that came out of the creek. What shall we do?"

"Paddle fer all ye're worth," was shouted back.

"Hold up, or we'll shoot," yelled Dennis Foley.

With that a pistol-shot was heard coming from the direction of the pursuers, but the bullet went wide of its mark, and the boys sped on.

"Don't waste yer load unless yer have to," cautioned Sandy, " 'cause yer won't have time to put in 'nother, an' I don't want er draw their fire, fer fear they might hit Lily."

The race had become one of life and death. The boys strained to the utmost their strong young muscles, and, with paddles bent almost double, drove their little craft like the wind before them. Down past Turtle Creek they flew; Licking Banks were soon left behind, and shortly, they were alongside the Sycamores. Dink looked back over his shoulder, and whispered:

"We ain't gained on 'em a bit, an' they seem to be goin' strong."

When the Meadows were reached, Dink said again:

"They're comin' like everythin'."

"Don't weaken," urged Leander; "as long as we're between them and Sandy's skiff, they'll have to kill us before they can get to Lillian."

The moon was casting its light on the waters like a great silvery path, and the splashing of the paddles was the only sound that awakened the echoes. Again came the sharp report of a pistol, and Dink dodged, as if by instinct. He wheeled in his seat and shot point-blank at Foley, but the ball imbedded itself in the side of the skiff behind and did no further damage.

"That's tit for tat," said Dink, "but it wuz a mighty close call fer me. When the bullet whizzed past my ear I thought I was plugged, sure."

There were now not more than fifteen yards between the boys and their pursuers. Turning about, Leander saw Hildey raise his pistol and take careful aim at him. Quick as thought, the boy fired first, and Hildey uttered a sharp cry of pain, as his right arm fell helpless, and his pistol dropped into the water.

"Curse the luck!" muttered Foley. "Don't give up, pard; we'll ketch 'em afore they git much further."

Though Hildey's right arm was useless, he plied the paddle with his left, and the men continued to gain. As the boys passed through under the bridge, Leander's boat was abreast of Sandy, who whispered:

"I'll take the swash on the right that goes through the big marsh and comes out at the Devil's Elbow. You hug the channel bank, an' mebbe we'll fool 'em."

Sandy knew that, after the river left the bridge, it went almost southerly for half a mile, then made an abrupt turn at right angles, pursued its way westward for another quarter of a mile, and then met the swash channel, which cut diagonally through the big marsh. At this junction of the two streams a whirlpool called the Devil's Elbow had been formed, a treacherous spot for small craft, and requiring rare skill to pass in safety.

When Sandy told Leander to take the main channel, it was with a desperate hope that Foley and Hildey would be in doubt, for the moment, which skiff to follow as they came out under the bridge. Within himself, he reasoned that this hesitation, on their part, would consume sufficient time to permit the boys to gain a lead and reach in safety the landing, two miles below.

"The chances are jest even-Stephen," he said to Gilbert, "though it separates us from Leander, till we reach the Devil's Elbow."

But alas! Sandy's reasoning failed him for once this time.

As Foley and Hildey came through under the bridge, the former cried:

"Steer to the right channel an' foller that boat; that's the one the kid's in."

"They're after us, darn 'em," said Sandy, "but we're gittin' ahead bully. Keep it up, Gil, an' we'll come out all right, see if we don't."

Dripping with perspiration, and with hands burned and blistered, Sandy and Gilbert were forging ahead and gaining on their pursuers, straining every nerve to increase their lead. As they rounded a bend in the channel, Hildey shouted:

"There's yer chance to plug 'em, pard. Shoot!"

Foley obeyed, and the boys' skiff, which was a metallic one, was bored through by the pistol ball. The water poured through the hole, and Sandy shouted to Gilbert:

"Drop yer paddle; take yer hat an' put it over the leak, tight as yer kin; bale out with the other hand, or we'll sink in a minit. Lily, sit up, so yer won't get wet; but don't show yer head," and with a courage born of despair, Sandy renewed his efforts.

Foley was gaining rapidly, and it seemed that only a miracle could prevent the boys' capture before they reached the Devil's Elbow.

Three minutes passed with only the sound of the lightning-like dip of the paddles. Another short bend in the channel, and a hundred yards ahead was the confluence of the two currents, which were ever at war.

"Keep on bailing, Gil," cried Sandy, "an' when we git past the Elbow, if they're too close to us, I'm goin' to use my pistol on 'em, but I don't want ter shoot till I can make the shot tell fer all it's worth. Steady, Lily; hold tight, Gil; don't

move, I'll git yer through without swampin',
'cause I knows every current in the Elbow."

Through the mad swirl of waters the boy held
his boat, and steered her into the quiet tide beyond.

Leander and Dink were just turning the bend
of the main channel an eighth of a mile away,
and the skiff containing Foley and Hildey had
reached the outer current of the eddy.

"Now you've got 'em," yelled Hildey, as
Sandy's skiff veered to the left, not twenty yards
from the other.

"Not if I knows it," cried Sandy as he shot
square at Foley, the ball going through the sleeve
of his coat, but leaving him unharmed.

"Curse yer fer a fool!" came from Foley, dropping his paddle and standing up in the skiff, which
now had nothing to guide it but Hildey's exhausted arm. The skiff was rocking violently.
Foley attempted to balance himself as he raised
his pistol to shoot. In a flash the frail craft was
caught in the conflicting currents, it careened and
capsized, and the two men were battling for life
in the whirlpool.

Sandy was so intent on escape that he had gone
some distance down stream before realizing he

was no longer pursued.   Suddenly an agonizing cry was borne on the midnight air:

"Help! Help! I'm drownin'!"

The boy rested on his paddle, and scanned the river in the direction of the voice.

"Don't let's let 'em drown like rats in a hole," said Sandy, and he started his boat back toward the bend.

"Gil, gimme yer pistol. They may be tryin' to play some trick on us, an' if they are, we'll be ready for 'em."

The precaution was unnecessary, for when they came near, they saw the upturned skiff circling around in the eddy, its paddles bobbing with the waves, and the hats of Foley and Hildey slowly drifting toward the bank.

Leander and Dink, meanwhile, had come up, and with the other two boys remained for fully half an hour waiting for some sign of the two robbers, but in vain; for far beneath the surface of the water in the maddening current, the ill-spent lives of Foley and Hildey were ended. They were dead in the cruel embrace of the Devil's Elbow.

"HELP! HELP! I'M DROWNIN'!"   *Page 380*

CHAPTER XXIII

GOOD-BY

It is not difficult to imagine that there was a sensation when Pipetown awoke the next morning and learned that Lillian had been rescued, and was safe in her father's house.

Over and over, the four boys were compelled by admiring listeners to relate their adventures, and the minutest detail was seized upon with avidity.

Sandy, of course, was the center of interest, because it was he who had conceived the daring expedition. When asked at Jebb's store, the night after the rescue, how he came to hit upon the river as offering a possible solution of the mysterious disappearance, he replied:

"It's this 'ere way. I wouldn't 'a' thought so much 'bout it, if Dennis Foley hadn't sawed his way out er jail, an' Snarley hadn't turned up missin', jest 'bout the time Gil's little sister couldn't be found. I jest put two an' twice tergether, an' after a while I makes up my mind she wuz up there, an' up there she wuz."

"That 'ere act o' Sandy's," remarked the Jedge, "in goin' right to the bull's-eye of a thing without knowin' where it is, is what scientific men calls 'sagaciousness an' particular conclusion,' which words is too whoopin' big fer plain folks, so we calls it common-sense, which reminds me that, when it comes to lookin' through a grindstone as fur as the next feller, combined with grit, mentality an' hang-on, them four boys rolled together seem more like me when I wuz their age, than anybody I ever seen." The Jedge lighted his pipe, and smoked away in silence.

When the June roses bloomed again, Mr. Jebb and Widow Foley were quietly married, for, in the words of the Jedge, the widow was a widow and no mistake this time.

Colonel Franklin persuaded Mrs. Coggles and Dink's parents to accept a scholarship for their two boys in the preparatory school selected for his son Gilbert.

It was the first of September. Four boys, surrounded by relatives and friends, were in the railroad station; one on his way to Annapolis to become a middy; the other three starting to attend a school in the North.

As the train slowly steamed away, amid the

waving of handkerchiefs and cries of "Good-by," a group stood on the platform of the last car, arm in arm, shoulder to shoulder,—Leander and Dink, Gilbert and

PIPETOWN SANDY.

THE END